POWER TO EXCEL THROUGH PRAYER

DALE A. ROGERS

POWER TO EXCEL THROUGH PRAYER

TATE PUBLISHING
AND ENTERPRISES, LLC

Published by Tate Publishing & Enterprises, LLC
127 E. Trade Center Terrace | Mustang, Oklahoma 73064 USA
1.888.361.9473 | www.tatepublishing.com

Tate Publishing is committed to excellence in the publishing industry. The company reflects the philosophy established by the founders, based on Psalm 68:11,
"The Lord gave the word and great was the company of those who published it."

Cover design by Gian Philipp Rufin
Interior design by Gram Telen

Published in the United States of America

ISBN: 978-1-63367-503-2
1. Religion / Christian Life / Prayer
2. Religion / Prayerbooks / Christian
14.10.03

Acknowledgments

I give all the praise, glory, and honor to my Lord Jesus Christ for all he has done. Without him, nothing would be possible (John 15:5). Jesus has brought me to places in my life that I never considered to be possible. I would like to thank my wife, Jarmila, for her unceasing love, support, and encouragement.

Contents

Preface 3
Introduction 9

1. The Importance of Relationship 19
2. The Need for Repentance Today 33
3. A Precursor to Repentance 45
4. Hindrances to Prayer 67
5. God's Judgment 99
6. Who You Are in Jesus Christ 119
7. Power of the Spoken Word 131
8. An Effective Style of Prayer 135
9. Prayers to Start With 171
10. Morning Prayers 181
11. Evening Prayers 189
12. Prayers for Spiritual Growth 193
13. Prayers for Cleansing the Mind 201
14. Prayers for the Home 207
15. Health 213
16. Salvation for Others 227
17. Finances and Employment 231
18. Family Relations 243
19. Ungodly Influences 249
20. Anger 255
21. Anxiety, Fear, and Worry 259
22. Depression and Suicide 265

23. Failure at the Edge of Breakthroughs 273
24. Deliverance from Generational Problems 277
25. Power to Excel and Prosper 285
26. Sexual Sins.. 289
27. Finding the Right Spouse... 297
28. Prayers against Marriage Destroyers 301

Final Thoughts.. 307

Preface

The Plan of Salvation

If you don't already know Jesus as Lord and Savior, I urge you to ask him into your life. Being a Christian is not a religion. It is a relationship. In order to have a relationship, all parties must be real. A relationship must be tangible. It must have substance. You can't have a relationship with a fantasy. God is real. He is alive. God loves you more than you can imagine regardless of what you may think or know.

Learn about God. Give him a chance. If you take a few minutes and read these pages, you will discover God's greatest gift and miracle for mankind. It doesn't matter who you are or what you have done. God will always love you and receive you with open arms.

Step 1

Understand that God's desire for you is life, abundant, and eternal. The Bible declares: "The thief comes only to steal and kill and destroy; I came that they may have life, and have it abundantly" (John 10:10).

Giving you abundant life required the supreme sacrifice: "For God so loved the world, that He gave His only begotten Son, that whoever believes in Him shall not perish, but have eternal life" (John 3:16).

God desires fellowship and companionship with you. What a wonderful gift the Father has given, yet if God gave his own Son to provide an abundant and everlasting life, why don't more people have what he has designed for us to receive? It is a question answered by this sobering realization.

Step 2

Realize that you are separated from God.

There is a gap between God and mankind. He has provided a way for us to receive an abundant and eternal life, but people throughout the ages have made selfish choices to disobey God Almighty. These choices continue to cause separation from the Father.

God's word shows us that the result of sin is death. He says in his word: "There is a way which seems right to a man, But its end is the way of death" (Proverbs 14:12).

And God also said, "But your iniquities have made a separation between you and your God, And your sins have hidden His face from you so that He does not hear" (Isaiah 59:2).

Paul the apostle states in Romans 3:23, "For all have sinned and fall short of the glory of God."

And in Romans 6:23, we read, "For the wages of sin is death, but the free gift of God is eternal life in Christ Jesus our Lord."

Every human was created with the ability and need to know God and fellowship with him. Augustine, a minister who lived during the fourth and fifth centuries, called this longing in each of us "that God-shaped vacuum."

Every day, we hear of all kinds of people who are self-righteous, who are always good to others. Many think that all they achieved in their lives was with their own wisdom and strength. They don't realize that God was there with them, helping them. Many people don't realize that there is a creator who created all and he is holding all things together. If not for him, there would be no order in the universe. Many scientists today realize the way so much has been put together, from individual pieces of a single-celled creature to the galaxy, it can only be done through intelligent design.

Many people have achieved a great deal in their lives and have risen to prominent positions in society, yet they try to fill that empty void in their lives with "things." They even try good works, morality, and religion. Yet they remain empty, for only God, through his Son, can fill that emptiness.

Step 3

Accept the fact that God has provided only one solution to sin and separation from himself. Jesus Christ, his Son, is the only way to God. Only he can reconcile us to God the Father. Mankind may seek other solutions and worship other gods, but Jesus Christ, alone, died on the cross for our sins and rose in triumph over the grave and eternal death. He paid the penalty for our sin and bridged the gap between God and mankind.

The Bible explains, "But God demonstrates His own love toward us, in that while we were yet sinners, Christ died for us" (Romans 5:8). We are also told, "For Christ also died for sins once for all, the just for the unjust, so that He might bring us to God, having been put to death in the flesh, but made alive in the spirit" (1 Peter 3:18).

There is only one way provided: "For there is one God, and one mediator also between God and men, the man Christ Jesus" (1 Timothy 2:5). For in John 14:6, we read, "Jesus said to him, 'I am the way, and the truth, and the life; no one comes to the Father but through Me.'"

God Almighty has provided the only way. Jesus Christ paid the penalty for our sin and rebellion against God by dying on the cross, shedding his blood, and rising from the dead to justify and reconcile you back to God the Father.

Step 4

Pray to receive Jesus Christ into your life. You can be brought back to God, and your relationship with him can be restored by trusting in Christ alone to save your life from destruction. What an incredible exchange: Your worst for God's best! This step happens by asking Jesus Christ to take away your sin and to come into your heart to be your Lord and Savior.

God's word is very clear: "Behold, I stand at the door and knock; if anyone hears My voice and opens the door, I will come in to him and will dine with him, and he with Me" (Revelation 3:20).

And the Bible tells us "that if you confess with your mouth Jesus as Lord, and believe in your heart that God raised Him from the dead, you will be saved" (Romans 10:9).

- Are you willing to let go of your burdens and sins?
- Are you willing to turn away and repent from your sins?
- Are you willing to receive Jesus Christ as your Lord and Savior now?

Step 5

Pray to receive Jesus Christ into your life. At this moment, you can pray the most important prayer of your life by simply saying:

> Lord Jesus,
>
> I believe you are the Son of God. I believe you came to earth two thousand years ago. I believe you died for me on the cross and shed your blood for my salvation. I believe you rose from the dead and ascended on high. I believe you are coming back again to earth. Dear Jesus, I am a sinner. Forgive my sins. Cleanse me now with your precious blood. Come into my heart. Save my soul right now. I am giving you my life. I am receiving you now as my Savior, my Lord, and my God. I am yours forever, and I will serve

> you and follow you the rest of my days. From this moment on, I belong to you only. I no longer belong to this world, nor to the enemy of my soul. I belong to you, and I am born again.
> Amen!

By praying this prayer and meaning it with all your heart, confessing your sins, and receiving Jesus Christ into your heart, God has given you the right to become his forgiven child. The Bible gives you this assurance: "But as many as received Him, to them He gave the right to become children of God, even to those who believe in His name" (John 1:12).

Introduction

This book introduces an uncompromising approach to prayer. The effectiveness of prayer is dependent upon a variety of factors, the greatest of which is one's relationship with Jesus. This relationship is stressed throughout this book as the primary goal for all Christians. Prayer and one's relationship with Jesus are inseparably linked. It is through this relationship and through prayer that we are able to fulfill the responsibilities we have as Christians. When reading the Bible, you will find that from cover to cover, it is about the relationship between God and man. Prayer is the key to building this relationship. Throughout this book, many issues are addressed repeatedly. Repetition is one of the mechanisms by which people learn a subject. The purpose is not to beat an issue to death but to help the message stay in your mind.

Because of the repetition of a number of points, many of the sections and chapters in this book may also be used as separate lessons.

The subject of sin is also addressed extensively. There is a great need for the church to face sin today since most churches fail to adequately deal with it. A culture with such a cavalier attitude toward sin is dangerous. Sin is an issue, however unpleasant, that we must all face and deal with. The church in general is so compromised with the world that people don't even recognize the sins they commit. In order for people to repent of their sins, they first need to know what they are.

The trend today for many churches is to only preach and teach feelgood messages rather than to preach and teach the truth in its proper balance. Paul writes about this in 2 Timothy 4:3–4:

> [3]For the time will come when they will not endure sound doctrine; but wanting to have their ears tickled, they will accumulate for themselves teachers in accordance to their own desires, [4]and will turn away their ears from the truth and will turn aside to myths.

The benefits of walking with Jesus in a holy and righteous manner are immeasurable. Maintaining a lifestyle of holiness and righteousness does take work, but the results are so sweet and glorious it is more than worth the effort. Prayer is the key to success.

There are a multitude of churches, denominations, and ministries throughout the world today. Many of them have a mechanism in place for people to submit prayer requests. This presents an unfortunate situation. People become conditioned to rely on others whom they view as being closer to God, more anointed, more faithful, and so on, rather than relying on their own prayers and relationship with Jesus. The outcome of this is that people seldom mature to the point that their own faith grows and their own prayers are effective. They forever remain in their spiritual diapers. Of course, people do need help and prayer support from time to time regardless of their spiritual level. However, that need will diminish as one becomes more mature. Remember the saying that says if you give a man a fish you feed him for a day but if you teach a man to fish you feed him for a lifetime. This analogy is true for prayer too.

This book teaches you how to rely on Jesus and to build faith by building your relationship with him through prayer. It will take work and it isn't always easy. Another analogy of this is going through basic training for the military. It is there a prospective soldier learns the discipline and ways of warfare. So, too, we as Christians must be educated in our relationship with Jesus and the ensuing responsibilities we have. We must discipline ourselves to accomplish these things. Spiritual warfare is a part of this. This education and application is a process.

The church today is much different than it was during the time the book of Acts writes about, or even sixty years ago. Today, the church for the most part is apostate and sound asleep. It is amazing that many people, even though realizing the apostate state of the church and what Scripture has to say about it, choose to remain asleep thinking they are okay.

> "Be dressed in readiness, and keep your lamps lit. "Be like men who are waiting for their master when he returns from the wedding feast, so that they may immediately open the door to him when he comes and knocks. "Blessed are those slaves whom the master will find on the alert when he comes; truly I say to you, that he will gird himself to serve, and have them recline at the table, and will come up and wait on them. "Whether he comes in the second watch, or even in the third, and finds them so, blessed are those slaves. "But be sure of this, that if the head of the house had known at what hour the thief was coming, he would not have allowed his house to be broken into. "You too, be ready; for the Son of Man is coming at an hour that you do not expect." Peter said, "Lord, are You addressing this parable to us, or to everyone else as well? " And the Lord said, "Who then is the faithful and sensible steward, whom his master will put in charge of his servants, to give them their rations at the proper time? "Blessed is that slave whom his master finds so doing when he comes. "Truly I say to you that he will put him in charge of all his possessions. "But if that slave says in his heart, 'My master will be a long time in coming,' and begins to beat the slaves, both men and women, and to eat and drink and get drunk; the master of that slave will come on a day when he does not expect him and at an hour he does not know, and will cut him in pieces, and assign him a place with the unbelievers.
>
> —Luke 12:35-46

Today is the day of salvation. Now is the time to prepare for Jesus's return.

In so many of today's churches, we are told what we need to do without being told how, and then often in vague terms. We are often told that we should accept the attacks of the devil (defeat) without complaining or doing anything about it. We are sometimes expected to treat spiritual defeat as a measure of spirituality. This is heresy! You can have an overwhelming victory through Jesus, if only you go after it.

> But in all these things we overwhelmingly conquer through Him who loved us.
>
> —Romans 8:37

> But thanks be to God, who gives us the victory through our Lord Jesus Christ
>
> —1 Corinthians 15:57

It is time for all of us to wake up and accept our God-ordained responsibilities to make disciples of all the nations. The primary tool we as Christians have at our disposal to make this happen is prayer.

One's relationship with Jesus transcends everything else in life and must be the top priority and focus. Virtually everything else is secondary.

The church has a job description and it is summarized in Matthew 28:19–20 and is known as The Great Commission:

> [19]Go therefore and make disciples of all the nations, baptizing them in the name of the Father and the Son and the Holy Spirit, [20]teaching them to observe all that I commanded you; and lo, I am with you always, even to the end of the age.

This is a top-level description of our responsibilities. Underneath this heading, there are many jobs and functions within the church that need to be accomplished to realize this goal. This is no different than a corporation where the president has a high-level job description that may be as simple as "lead this company and make it profitable." Underneath the president will be many people working many different positions in order to realize this highest goal.

The Apostle Paul outlined the various positions and gifts provided by the Holy Spirit throughout his letters so the church will be able to fulfill its mission here on this earth.

Jesus started this ministry and expects us to follow in his footsteps, using himself as our example, and by relying on the empowering of the Holy Spirit. We are expected to do the things he did, and more.

> Truly, truly, I say to you, he who believes in Me, the works that I do, he will do also; and greater works than these he will do; because I go to the Father.
>
> —John 14:12

The details of how we are to fulfill the duties and responsibilities of this job are presented throughout the entire Bible.

We can see primarily in the book of Acts how this commission was fulfilled and learn some important lessons from this and the other letters Paul wrote. Remember that at this time in the history of the church, the Bible as we know it today did not exist. These early Christians only had what we call the Old Testament (the Law and the Prophets, or the Tanakh) today. Given what our Lord was able to accomplish through them should serve as sufficient evidence of the value of the Old Testament.

In Acts 6:2–4, we see a hierarchical structure of responsibilities emerge in the early church.

> [2]So the twelve summoned the congregation of the disciples and said, "It is not desirable for us to neglect the word of God in order to serve tables. [3]Therefore, brethren, select from among you seven men of good reputation, full of the Spirit and of wisdom, whom we may put in charge of this task. [4]But we will devote ourselves to prayer and to the ministry of the word.

The apostles were few in number and by definition of their position were expected to live at the highest spiritual level, and have the closest relationship with Jesus. This certainly doesn't preclude others from having a close relationship but it is a requirement for this office. At this level, it is expected that their level of faith will bring solid answers to their prayers and provide a covering for the church. As apostles of the church, they facilitate the health and growth of the church. This is a high level of responsibility and much is required of this position.

For us today, there are several things that need to happen first in order for the church to be prepared to a sufficient degree to fulfill its responsibilities. Repentance of sin is the most important followed by education of what these responsibilities entail and how to accomplish them.

Many will argue they live a holy life and are not involved in the many vices of the world today. This is all good. However, when you read God's word, you will find there are many things that the church fails to do. *Webster* (*Webster's Dictionary of American English*, published 1828, public domain) defines *sin* as:

> The voluntary departure of a moral agent from a known rule of rectitude or duty, prescribed by God; any voluntary transgression of the divine law, or violation of a divine command; a wicked act; iniquity. Sin is either a positive act in which a known divine law is violated, or it is the voluntary neglect to obey a positive divine command, or a rule of duty clearly implied in such command. Sin comprehends not action only, but neglect of known duty, all evil thoughts purposes, words and desires, whatever is contrary to God's commands or law.

The omission of fulfilling God-ordained responsibilities is just as much a sin as the commission of any number of evil acts. It is this failure to do his will that we, both individually and collectively as a church, need to repent of. We need to open our eyes to the vision and resources God has provided in his word.

Prayer is the most powerful and effective tool we have at our disposal to accomplish all of these goals. The church has largely lost sight of its vision and, to an even greater degree, how to fulfill it.

> Where there is no vision, the people perish: but he that keepeth the law, happy is he.
>
> —Proverbs 29:18 (KJV)

It is time for this situation to change. It is only through prayer and revelation that we will be able to build our relationship with Jesus and fulfill our God-ordained responsibilities.

- Prayer is man's communication with God.
- Revelation is God's communication with man.

Prayer is the most power tool we as Christians have at our disposal. One only needs to read the book of Acts to see the results of fervent prayer on the part of the early Christians. Notice that throughout the book of Acts, prayer was an important part of the lives of the apostles, church leadership, and the entire body of Christ. It was through prayer that God worked many miracles and that the church grew and prospered despite the obstacles they faced. It is imperative to effectively learn the lessons from their example and put them into practice in our lives and churches today.

Prayer is the primary mechanism by which we communicate and build our relationship with the Holy Spirit; overcome obstacles, trials, and tribulations; and spread the Gospel throughout the world.

The effectiveness of prayer is based on faith, and faith is based on one's relationship with Jesus. In order to be effective in prayer, we first must know Jesus, know who we are in him and understand what that relationship means, what our roles and responsibilities are, and how to fulfill them. This relationship must be our primary focus for virtually everything else is secondary to this. We must understand the power and authority that we possess and be willing and able to exercise it at any time, so long as it is within the bounds of God's word and will. We are to be ready in season and out of season.

> [1]I solemnly charge you in the presence of God and of Christ Jesus, who is to judge the living and the dead, and by His appearing and His kingdom: [2]preach the word; be ready in season and out of season; reprove, rebuke, exhort, with great patience and instruction.
>
> 2 Timothy 4:1–2

> Therefore, confess your sins to one another, and pray for one another so that you may be healed. The effective prayer of a righteous man can accomplish much.
>
> —James 5:16

The key words in James 5:16 are *effective* and *righteous*. In order for one's prayers to accomplish much, the individual must be righteous and they must understand what it takes to be effective.

In the book of Acts and throughout Paul's letters, we read about the many miracles, signs, and wonders worked through the Christians of the day. James 1:17 makes it clear that God doesn't change. Therefore, there is no reason or excuse for these miracles, and more, to not be worked today. The only difference between the church then and now is the dismal state we are in today. It is time to repent and get to work for our Lord Jesus Christ.

In 2 Chronicles 7:13–14, we read:

> [13]If I shut up the heavens so that there is no rain, or if I command the locust to devour the land, or if I send pestilence among My people, [14]and My people who are called by My name humble themselves and pray and seek My face and turn from their wicked ways, then I will hear from heaven, will forgive our sin and will heal our land.

Notice that this is a promise with a condition. If and only if the repentance is real and sincere will God hear from heaven, forgive their sins, and heal their land. Revival must begin with the church.

The spiritual health of this (or any) nation is the responsibility of the church. And it is the responsibility of the church, individually and collectively, to repent of their sins, to maintain a high moral standard, and to be a priestly nation. There are countless examples of this throughout history. There are countless examples of what happens when a people fails to repent as well, much of it at our fingertips in the Bible.

Intercession is a priestly responsibility that cannot be given to anyone who is not a Christian. What we are witnessing today is an epic failure of the church to fulfill its responsibilities. There is no excuse for this. Fifty plus years ago, this nation was much different and spiritually better than it is today. The church was the focal point of the community and a significant force in maintaining the moral character of the nation. When I look around, listen to testimonies in church, listen to prayers, etc., there is one common factor throughout—a selfish attitude. It is almost always something to do with what God did for them rather than how God worked through them to advance the church. Many are trying to get what they want from God rather than focusing on what they can do for him. This is unacceptable. This attitude is indicative of a lack of maturity and all too often is founded on humanism, which is of the devil.

> My people are destroyed for lack of knowledge. Because you have rejected knowledge, I also will reject you from being My priest. Since you have forgotten the law of your God, I also will forget your children.
>
> —Hosea 4:6

The word *Torah* refers to the first five books of the Bible. The word Torah does not mean "law." It is Hebrew for "instruction" or "teaching." The Torah is the foundation for the rest of the Bible and is just as valid and applicable to our lives today as it was when it was written. God has provided us all the information necessary to accomplish all he has destined his people to do through his word, the Bible, and through the Holy Spirit. Knowledge of the Bible is sorely lacking today. Many things, particularly in the Old Testament (or Tanakh), have been dismissed as being archaic and dated; not applicable today. Much of these philosophies are based on church or denominational doctrines, as well as evil influences by the world. Things ought not to be this way.

The Importance of Relationship

Your relationship with the Holy Spirit is the most important part of your life. It is from this relationship that we are able to fulfill our God-ordained responsibilities. Many churches focus on all the benefits of salvation rather than the responsibilities that come with that relationship. This is wrong. It is humanism and this is sin. Others chase after miracles and some people will even travel around the country following a particular ministry. This is idolatry. In Matthew 12:39 and 16:4, Jesus made it clear that those who seek after signs are evil and adulterous. This is because we are to seek him. If you seek him and grow in him, then those miracles, signs, and wonders will be a natural outflow of that relationship.

The Apostle Paul made his position on this clear in Philippians 3:7–14,

> [7]But whatever things were gain to me, those things I have counted as loss for the sake of Christ. [8]More than that, I count all things to be loss in view of the surpassing value of knowing Christ Jesus my Lord, for whom I have suffered the loss of all things, and count them but rubbish so that I may gain Christ, [9]and may be found in Him, not having a righteousness of my own derived from the Law, but that which is through faith in Christ, the righteousness which comes from God on the basis of faith, [10]that I may know Him and the power of His resurrection and the fellowship of His sufferings, being conformed to His death; [11]in order

> that I may attain to the resurrection from the dead. [12]Not that I have already obtained it or have already become perfect, but I press on so that I may lay hold of that for which also I was laid hold of by Christ Jesus. [13]Brethren, I do not regard myself as having laid hold of it yet; but one thing I do: forgetting what lies behind and reaching forward to what lies ahead, [14]I press on toward the goal for the prize of the upward call of God in Christ Jesus.

2.1 The Holy Spirit

The Holy Spirit is the most misunderstood, neglected, and ignored person of the trinity. More often than not, people treat him like a thing rather than a person. This attitude not only grieves him, but it is insulting and sinful.

- The key to an anointed life is intimacy with the Holy Spirit.
- The key to realizing the four points of spiritual growth presented in Section 2.4 is intimacy with the Holy Spirit.
- The key to accomplishing the things Jesus did, and more, is intimacy with the Holy Spirit.
- The key to accomplishing our mission (the Great Commission) in the way Jesus intended is intimacy with the Holy Spirit.

This intimate relationship with the Holy Spirit must be closer than with anyone else, regardless of who they may be.

> How precious also are Your thoughts to me, O God! How vast is the sum of them!
>
> —Psalms 139:17

> Draw near to God and He will draw near to you. Cleanse your hands, you sinners; and purify your hearts, you double-minded.
>
> —James 4:8

> [16]Rejoice always; [17]pray without ceasing; [18]in everything give thanks; for this is God's will for you in Christ Jesus. [19]Do not quench the Spirit.
>
> —1 Thessalonians 5:16–19

In James 4:8, we see that it is up to us to first draw near to God. When you do this then he will draw near to you. The Holy Spirit is more passionate about having an intimate relationship with you than you can possibly understand. It is up to you to make this happen. The Holy Spirit is a perfect gentleman and will not force himself on you so it is up to you to initiate the relationship.

> [4]You adulteresses, do you not know that friendship with the world is hostility toward God? Therefore whoever wishes to be a friend of the world makes himself an enemy of God. [5]Or do you think that the Scripture speaks to no purpose: "He jealously desires the Spirit which He has made to dwell in us"?
>
> —James 4:4–5

In 1 Thessalonians 5:17, we are instructed to pray without ceasing. We are to engage with communication with the Holy Spirit. This is a two-way communication and not a monologue. In verse 19, we are instructed to not quench the Spirit. How do people quench the Holy Spirit? Although the lack of prayer is a significant part of this, refusing to die to self is the greater reason for quenching the Spirit.

Going back to James 4:8, that drawing near is accomplished through communication.

> [4]Gathering them together, He commanded them not to leave Jerusalem, but to wait for what the Father had promised, "Which," He said, "you heard of from Me; [5]for John baptized with water, but you will be baptized with the Holy Spirit not many days from now."
>
> —Acts 1:4–5

We see here in Acts that Jesus commanded his disciples to not do anything until they were empowered by the Holy Spirit. Of the five hundred who witnessed Jesus ascending into heaven and the many more who were by now His disciples, only 120 were obedient. Those 120 were the ones that were filled with and empowered by the Holy Spirit. It should be clear that our Lord takes obedience very seriously.

> And we are witnesses of these things; and so is the Holy Spirit, whom God has given to **those who obey Him**.
>
> —Acts 5:32

> If you love Me, you will keep My commandments.
>
> —John 14:15

It is interesting to note that in the very next verse of John, Jesus tells his disciples that they will be given the Holy Spirit. Obedience and the receiving of the Holy Spirit are clearly linked.

> I will ask the Father, and He will give you another Helper, that He may be with you forever.
>
> —John 14:16

How many people today attempt to fulfill the Great Commission without the power of the Holy Spirit operating in their lives? The Holy Spirit should have the freedom to operate as he did through Jesus, the disciples, and the early church.

You will never experience the power and intimacy of the Holy Spirit to any appreciable degree as long as you maintain control of your life. You must die to self and put self on the cross. The only life you can live is a surrendered life. There is no other way.

Back in the 1960s, the buzz word that went around and became a fad was *commitment*. Although this happened decades ago, we are still feeling the effects of it today. Commitment isn't enough. Commitment indicates only a superficial attachment.

Surrender indicates one's will, emotions, intellect, and virtually their entire being is given fully up to Jesus Christ.

You must surrender yourself and all that you are to your Lord Jesus Christ. This surrender is the top level of obedience written about in Acts 5:32. It is only then that the Holy Spirit will have the freedom to provide that anointing he so desires to give you. It is only then that you will experience an intimacy with the Holy Spirit that is precious beyond description.

> The grace of the Lord Jesus Christ, and the love of God, and the **fellowship of the Holy Spirit**, be with you all.
>
> —2 Corinthians 13:14

2.2 Spiritual Gifts

The subject of miracles, signs, and wonders is brought up repeatedly throughout this book. Miracles, signs, and wonders are the signature of the church. Just preaching the Gospel is not enough. Those words need to be backed up with power and demonstration of the Spirit (2 Corinthians 2:4). The unsaved have an almost instinctive knowledge of this so it is understandable why they laugh and mock Christians for their lack of power.

> 27Now you are Christ's body, and individually members of
> it. 28And God has appointed in the church, first apostles,
> second prophets, third teachers, then miracles, then gifts of
> healings, helps, administrations, various kinds of tongues.
> 29All are not apostles, are they? All are not prophets, are
> they? All are not teachers, are they? All are not workers of
> miracles, are they? 30All do not have gifts of healings, do
> they? All do not speak with tongues, do they? All do not
> interpret, do they? 31But earnestly desire the greater gifts.
> And I show you a still more excellent way.
>
> —1 Corinthians 12:27–31

It is important to provide some clarification concerning the various gifts. The gifts Paul is talking about here are for *public ministry*. Not everyone has a gift for public service. Just because you may not have a gift in a certain area doesn't mean you don't have the power and authority through Jesus Christ to fill that capacity outside of the public ministry.

God never removes your power and authority because he has not given you an anointing (gift) in a particular area. All Christians have access to power and authority through Jesus Christ to bring about any miracle the Holy Spirit desires.

For example, my public gift is to teach. This is an anointing the Holy Spirit has given me and so it is easy and natural to flow in it, and to stand in front of a church or even one person and teach. I don't have the same kind of anointing for healing and so I don't feel comfortable exercising this. Nevertheless, I still possess the power and authority through Jesus Christ to command healing. I have seen this happen. I just spoke the words and God did the rest. I've had similar experiences with prophecy and words of knowledge.

You don't need to be a spiritual giant for the Holy Spirit to work through you. It's just a matter of a little faith and trust in him—a childlike faith. As you grow in your relationship with the Holy Spirit, you can expect these things to become more commonplace. Trust him! It's that simple. It is the devil who deceives people into thinking this is complicated or that you need to be at some spiritual level that is well beyond your reach.

Another example concerns a friend I worked with some years ago. He wanted the gift of healing. He would take advantage of the ministries in his church as well as any opportunity that arose to pray for someone to be healed. He also kept a log of all the successes and failures so he could monitor his progress. In a very typical scenario, my wife and I were in a restaurant with him and his family after church. He told the waiter that he likes to pray for people and asked if he had any medical problems he would like to be prayed for. The waiter said he had a bad elbow so my friend prayed a simple prayer of healing and asked if anything had changed. Nothing happened. He did this two more times before the waiter's elbow was healed. In the course of a year of praying for people, his success rate increased. Today, he has some absolutely incredible testimonies.

My friend was willing to step out of his comfort zone to pray for people. He never made a big scene out of it either. When we were in the restaurant, the conversation and prayer were all done quietly and without fanfare. It was all tastefully and diplomatically done. No one was put on the spot, embarrassed, or made to feel uncomfortable. I doubt anyone in the adjacent tables were even aware of what was going on. God was glorified that day.

An important issue to deal with is the fear of failure. This is especially important with healing since this is a matter that touches people deeply. As my friend did, he simply stated that he liked to pray for people. He never made any promises. This had the effect of minimizing negative reactions on the part of the people he prayed for if they didn't get healed. Even though he grieved over the failures where people he prayed for were not healed, he persisted and this persistence paid off. In time, his success rate improved. In my case of teaching, I remember a particular situation when I taught something that was incorrect. It turned someone away from the study I was conducting. Although it bothered me a lot when I realized my error, the only thing I can do is learn from my mistakes, correct the problem, and go on. None of us is perfect, so we must learn from our mistakes and be persistent to grow and learn.

Another principle that is easy to miss is that my friend never pursued this gift to glorify himself. He always made it clear to those who were healed that it was Jesus who healed them. Healing is a powerful witnessing point and opens the door to spreading the Gospel in a way that gets peoples' attention like no other.

All of this points to some important biblical principles. Faith without works is dead (James 2:20, 26) being the foremost. You have to work it to build it, just like building your physical muscles and strength. If you want something, go after it (Matthew 7:7–8). God is true to his word. I don't know what my friend's primary spiritual gift is, but he wanted the gift of healing so he went after it and God honored his efforts.

Don't let church or denominational doctrines (the traditions of man) prevent you from exercising the simplicity of the Gospel!

People who say that some or all of these gifts are not for today or they have passed away call God a liar and his word a lie. These are people who quench the Holy Spirit, stuff God into a tiny box, and refuse to be obedient to his word. Their religion consists of a social club rather than an intimate relationship with the Holy Spirit.

> They profess to know God, but by their deeds they deny Him, being detestable and disobedient and worthless for any good deed.
>
> —Titus 1:16

> [16]Do not be deceived, my beloved brethren. [17]Every good thing given and every perfect gift is from above, coming down from the Father of lights, with whom there is no variation or shifting shadow.
>
> —James 1:16–17

2.3 The Fear of the Lord

The fear of the Lord is a subject that is largely misunderstood today. There are two primary types of fear—the fear of the Lord and a worldly fear. The word *fear* occurs 400 times in the King James version of the Bible and 313 times in the New American Standard. With this high a number, it is well worth the effort to investigate and study the subject. Here are but a few of the hundreds of verses.

The fear of the LORD is clean, enduring forever; The judgments of the LORD are true; they are righteous altogether.

—Psalms 19:9

Behold, the eye of the LORD is on those who fear Him, On those who hope for His lovingkindness.

—Psalms 33:18

And to man He said, "Behold, the fear of the Lord, that is wisdom; And to depart from evil is understanding."

—Job 28:28

The fear of the LORD is the beginning of wisdom; A good understanding have all those who do His commandments; His praise endures forever.

—Psalms 111:10

So the church throughout all Judea and Galilee and Samaria enjoyed peace, being built up; and going on in the fear of the Lord and in the comfort of the Holy Spirit, it continued to increase.

—Acts 9:31

There is no fear in love; but perfect love casts out fear, because fear involves punishment, and the one who fears is not perfected in love.

—1 John 4:18

Only do not rebel against the LORD; and do not fear the people of the land, for they will be our prey. Their protection has been removed from them, and the LORD is with us; do not fear them.

—Numbers 14:9

A worldly fear leads one into rebellion against God (Numbers 14:9, 1 Samuel 12:14). Worldly fear is also an indicator of the lack of faith and hence a lack of relationship with the Holy Spirit.

Webster defines *worldly fear* as:

> A painful emotion or passion excited by an expectation of evil, or the apprehension of impending danger. Fear expresses less apprehension than dread, and dread less than terror and fright. The force of this passion, beginning with the most moderate degree, may be thus expressed, fear, dread, terror, fright. Fear is accompanied with a desire to avoid or ward off the expected evil. Fear is an uneasiness of mind, upon the thought of future evil likely to befall us.

Webster defines *Godly fear* as:

> In scripture, fear is used to express a filial or a slavish passion. In good men, the fear of God is a holy awe or reverence of God and his laws, which springs from a just view and real love of the divine character, leading the subjects of it to hate and shun every thing that can offend such a holy being, and inclining them to aim at perfect obedience. This is filial fear.

Rewording this a bit, a holy awe and reverence are the *products* of a Godly fear. Fear is fear, but the distinguishing characteristic is the motivating factor behind it. One way to further understand this better is to review the characteristics of Godly fear.

1. Godly fear recognizes one's humble and sinful state in comparison to a holy and righteous God.
2. Godly fear realizes one's total dependence upon God for his provision, forgiveness, and mercies.
3. Godly fear is clean and endures forever.
4. Godly fear brings humility.
5. Godly fear brings a holy awe and reverence of God to the believer.

6. Godly fear hopes for his lovingkindness.
7. Godly fear is the beginning of wisdom.
8. Godly fear brings the comfort of the Holy Spirit.
9. Godly fear provides motivation to live a righteous and holy life.
10. Godly fear provides motivation to be obedient to God's commandments.
11. Godly fear coexists with love. From 1 John 4:18, we see that worldly fear cannot coexist with love.

A Godly fear comes from the realization of these characteristics, especially the first two.

In view of the general condition of the church today, this Godly fear is sorely lacking. When Godly fear is lacking, the desire and motivation to live a holy and righteous life is also lacking. This opens the door for sin to enter the church and sets the stage for the church to go to sleep.

2.4 A Growing Relationship

As you develop your relationship with the Holy Spirit, Paul's words will become more of a reality. It is one thing to understand these scriptures with the mind. It is another to know and live it from the depths of your soul. The following is evidence of a relationship that is continually growing in Jesus. Each point demonstrates a general progression of this spiritual growth.

1. When you grow in your relationship with your Lord Jesus, his word will come alive. When you speak, you will speak his word. It will flow out of you like rivers of living water (John 7:38). It will be a priceless joy to you. The things of this world and your attachment to them will fade away and the glory of God will shine into and through you.

2. When you grow in your relationship with your Lord Jesus, you will know what it means to be righteous and holy. Sin will be abhorrent to you. Righteousness and holiness are sweet and precious beyond description, as well as are the freedom, blessings, and fellowship with the Holy Spirit.
3. When you grow in your relationship with your Lord Jesus, your life will be blessed and you will be a blessing. The trials you experience will pass because you will learn the lessons much more easily. Your faith will grow and you will not be concerned about the things of the world, just as Jesus spoke of in Matthew 6:27–34. The calamities that those in the world tremble over will not concern you because you know your Lord and his word. Others will see an anointing on you and will want what you have.
4. When you grow in your relationship with your Lord Jesus, the Holy Spirit will work through you in miraculous ways. Miracles, signs, and wonders will manifest through you. As a result, people will get saved, healed, delivered, and raised from the dead. You will not accept glory or credit for these things because you will be keenly aware of your humble state, and because you will know without a doubt that these miracles are from the Holy Spirit. This will be a lifestyle and a normal experience, not a rare occurrence. You will consider the miracles, signs, and wonders worked through you to be of little consequence compared to the surpassing value of your relationship with Jesus. Knowing who you are as sons and daughters of the Most High through Jesus Christ will be cause to give him praise and worship from the depths of your soul and every fiber of your being to a degree that others cannot comprehend. The glory you experience and live in will be beyond words. The words of 1 Corinthians 2:9–10 and 2 Corinthians 1:20 will come alive for you.

Although the above points seem ideal or perhaps even fantastic, remember that from the book of Joshua, Israel never fully occupied the land God had promised them. This is true with Christians today. We have a long way to go to occupy all that God has prepared for us. We must endeavor to enter that promised land to the greatest extent possible (Philippians 3:8–14). Compare the last point with Jesus who demonstrated what his people can do when in right standing with God.

Prayer is the most effective and fundamental tool we have available to develop this relationship. It is therefore imperative to learn an effective method of prayer and to apply it on a continual basis. It should also be easy to see that knowledge of God's word is without exception an essential ingredient for building your relationship with Jesus.

The importance of prayer in the church is evidenced throughout the early church in the book of Acts of the Apostles. The advancement of the Gospel and the numerous miracles performed are clear evidence of answered prayer. If only the church would grab hold of this truth today and apply it!

The Need for Repentance Today

Much of the church today exists in a false sense of security. People are simply unaware of the sin that is present in their lives and churches. Much is excused through church or denominational doctrine. The little box so many Christians live in today and attempt to stuff God into is labeled *Ignorance is Bliss*. Things ought not to be this way.

> [1]Then the LORD spoke to Moses, saying: [2]"Speak to all the congregation of the sons of Israel and say to them, 'You shall be holy, for I the LORD your God am holy.'"
>
> —Leviticus 19:1–2

Notice that what God said to his people is not just a decree, it is a command. As a command, it means people have certain things they must accomplish in order to be holy. God provided us with all the instruction necessary to accomplish this in his word. At this period of time, this can only point to the Mosaic laws, or Torah. Jesus never abolished the law (Matthew 5:17). By this simple logic alone, we can see the validity of the Old Testament and the Torah in particular today. We would do well to be obedient to our Lord.

Someone will inevitably ask the question if animal sacrifices are then required. In my opinion, the answer to this is no. This is only a picture of the price Jesus paid on the cross. Nevertheless, and believe it or not, there is merit to this, even if you just picture it in your mind. Take a lamb that you have raised from birth. This lamb is more than a pet. It is part of your family. Picture yourself slicing this lamb's throat and watching it bleed to death right in front of you, with the full understanding of what this represents. I know a messianic rabbi who sacrifices a lamb for every Passover and it is never a pleasant experience. It is a vivid and painful picture of the gravity and cost of sin. How much more diligent to avoid sin should we be then, knowing that Jesus, the Son of God, paid such a horrible price in full for us. The movie *The Passion of the Christ*[1] provides the most vivid and most accurate depiction of Jesus's last hours and crucifixion ever produced in the entertainment industry. It is a horrible way to die and yet he did this for us. We should *never* have a cavalier attitude toward sin.

Because of the flesh and the fact we must all deal with sin, fulfilling this command from our Lord to be holy takes work. In order to be holy, one must be free from sin as much as possible. Taking a passive attitude toward this Scripture, thinking this is just a decree from God that doesn't require any effort on your part, is inconsistent with all of scripture. Throughout both the Old and New Testaments, we are instructed what we must do to be holy and righteous.

Because of these issues, it is therefore critical to examine God's word to see what and where those failures are and to be diligent to repent and go forward. Indeed, the greatest failure is the failure to develop your relationship with the Holy Spirit to the point that your life will be as Jesus described in John 14:12, "Truly, truly, I say to you, he who believes in Me, the works that I do, he will do also; and greater works than these he will do; because I go to the Father," and what Paul described in 1 Corinthians 2:4–5, "[4]and my message and my preaching were not in persuasive words of wisdom, but in demonstration of the Spirit and of power, [5]so that your faith would not rest on the wisdom of men, but on the power of God."

Paul did not have the Bible as we know it today. After all, he wrote much of what we know of as the New Testament. In his day, all they had was the Tanakh, or Old Testament. It is this that was taught and practiced. It was only later that pagan teachings polluted the church. These teachings are still with us today. For example, why do we still observe holidays and customs that are of a pagan and sordid origin rather than observe the holidays and customs we are commanded to in the Bible?

> If you love Me, you will keep My commandments.
>
> —John 14:15

Are the traditions of man more important to you than being obedient to your Creator and Lord Jesus Christ?

It is more often the omission of good works, or, more accurately, the lack of relationship with Jesus, rather than the commission of evil acts that need to be repented of by the church today.

God has destined his people, the church, to be a priestly nation. As such, we as Christians have the responsibilities of a priest. A priest must provide intercession, guidance to salvation, and spiritual leadership in the community and nation in which they live. The church should be the primary moral foundation for the nation. This is a civil responsibility. As such, the church should have a majority vote in public policy and ensure the nation maintains a moral foundation.

This failure in civic responsibilities is but one clear example of the spiritual decay within the church.

The so-called separation of church and state is a legal doctrine based in part on a private letter Thomas Jefferson sent to the Danbury Baptists in 1832. The phrase was taken grossly out of context. Thomas Jefferson was writing about the importance of Christians being involved in the civil affairs of this nation. In addition, this statement is not found in any of the founding documents or the Constitution of this nation.

America was originally a British colony. As such, many of the British customs, both social and civil, became prevalent. One was a legal requirement to belong to the established Anglican church. People were taxed in order to support the church. People who were part of another denomination (e.g.. Baptists and others) and refused to be party to this were persecuted and some thrown into prison. This situation was eventually dealt with through the 1st Amendment to the Constitution which was enacted in 1791:

> Congress shall make no law respecting an establishment of religion, or prohibiting the free exercise thereof; or abridging the freedom of speech, or of the press; or the right of the people peaceably to assemble, and to petition the government for a redress of grievances.

It is the government that is bound from either instituting, giving favor to, or prohibiting the free exercise of one's religion. Nothing whatsoever is stated that prevents or discourages Christians from being involved in civil affairs.

If you read historical documents, you will find that it was important and even required by some state constitutions that a political office be held by a true (in word and in deed) Christian. If you read the writings of the Founding Fathers, as well as many other prominent people of the day, you will find that they considered it very important that Christians be involved in the civil and governing affairs of the nation. George Washington even stated, "It is impossible to rightly govern a nation without God and the Bible."

Charles Finney (1792–1875) started his professional life with the desire to be an attorney. He became a Christian and was a leader and revivalist in what is known as the Second Great Awakening which occurred during 1825–1835. One of his famous quotes (circa 1832) is:

> The time has come that Christians must vote for honest men and take consistent ground in politics, or the Lord

> will curse them... God cannot sustain this free and blessed country, which we love and pray for, unless the Church will take right ground. Politics are part of religion in such a country as this, and Christians must do their duty to the country as part of their duty to God.

All too many Christians today have accepted today's interpretation of the "separation of church and state" as fact and have withdrawn from their civil responsibilities. Worse yet, few have put forth any effort to maintain their God-given and lawful rights.

As a result of this and many other issues, the church has withdrawn from society and now represents an epic failure as a nation of priests.

> Our constitution was made only for a moral and religious people. It is wholly inadequate to the government of any other.
>
> —John Adams

It is time for this to change. It is time for the church to take its right stand in society.

Apathy on part of the people breeds corruption and tyranny on part of the government.

If Christians fail to be involved in the civil affairs of this nation, that power vacuum will by definition be filled by the wicked. This is a fact that is so readily apparent today.

> They profess to know God, but by their deeds they deny Him, being detestable and disobedient and worthless for any good deed.
>
> —Titus 1:16

Sadly, many peoples' Christianity is displayed only within the walls of a church.

> [13]If I shut up the heavens so that there is no rain, or if I command the locust to devour the land, or if I send pestilence among My people, [14]and My people who are called by My name humble themselves and pray and seek My face and turn from their wicked ways, then I will hear from heaven, will forgive their sin and will heal their land.
>
> —2 Chronicles 7:13–14

2 Chronicles 7:13–14 is a promise with a condition. God will forgive our sin and heal our nation *if and only if* we, his people, repent.

Revival starts with the church.
Repentance is a decision and it starts with you.

We must build our relationship with our Lord Jesus Christ so he will fulfill his part of Scripture and bring revival first to the Church, then to the rest of the nation and world. It must be emphasized that we as Christians will be held accountable before our Lord Jesus on judgment day for what we do, both the good *and the bad.*

> For we must all appear before the judgment seat of Christ, so that each one may be recompensed for his deeds in the body, according to what he has done, **whether good or bad**.
>
> —2 Corinthians 5:10

With the compromising behavior of such a large percentage of the church, it is no surprise that God's blessings and anointing are so rare today. Matthew 12:29–30 says,

> [29]Or how can anyone enter the strong man's house and carry off his property, unless he first binds the strong man? And then he will plunder his house. [30]He who is not with Me is against Me; and he who does not gather with Me scatters.

It is through compromise with the world that we, as Christians, allow the devil to plunder our churches and our nation.

Such an epic failure is inexcusable, especially when we have the Holy Spirit, the Bible, and such easy access to resources to a far greater capacity than at any time in the history of the human species.

> *Surely we will be judged for our failures, especially when those failures result in the downfall of an entire nation, and the multitude of souls who die without Christ in the process.*

> [1]For this reason we must pay much closer attention to what we have heard, so that we do not drift away from it.
> [2]For if the word spoken through angels proved unalterable, and every transgression and disobedience received a just penalty, [3]**how will we escape if we neglect so great a salvation?** After it was at the first spoken through the Lord, it was confirmed to us by those who heard, [4]God also testifying with them, both by signs and wonders and by various miracles and by gifts of the Holy Spirit according to His own will.
>
> —Hebrews 2:1–4

In Deuteronomy 28, God tells how he will bless obedience and curse disobedience. Verses 1 to 14 outline the blessings for being obedient. Verses 16 to 68 outline the curses for disobedience. Clearly, much more is said concerning the consequences of disobedience than for obedience. This shouldn't be hard to understand why. We are far more inclined to sin than we are to be righteous. This is true, even for Christians.

Since God doesn't change, Deuteronomy 28 is still just as valid today as when it was written. It is time for the church to take God's word and its relationship with him seriously. The following statement has its foundation in Matthew 12:30 and Luke 11:23:

> *If you reject the truth, you will by definition embrace a lie. In the end truth will become an offense and object of hatred to you.*

This fact is all too abundantly clear in our society today. So much so that we are witnessing what Paul wrote in Romans and in 2 Thessalonians:

> [28]And just as they did not see fit to acknowledge God any longer, God gave them over to a depraved mind, to do those things which are not proper, [29]being filled with all unrighteousness, wickedness, greed, evil; full of envy, murder, strife, deceit, malice; they are gossips, [30]slanderers, haters of God, insolent, arrogant, boastful, inventors of evil, disobedient to parents, [31]without understanding, untrustworthy, unloving, unmerciful; [32]and although they know the ordinance of God, that those who practice such things are worthy of death, they not only do the same, but also give hearty approval to those who practice them.
>
> —Romans 1:28–32

> [8]Then that lawless one will be revealed whom the Lord will slay with the breath of His mouth and bring to an end by the appearance of His coming; [9]that is, the one whose coming is in accord with the activity of Satan, with all power and signs and false wonders, [10]and with all the deception of wickedness for those who perish, because they did not receive the love of the truth so as to be saved. [11]**For this reason God will send upon them a deluding influence so that they will believe what is false,** [12]in order that they all may be judged who did not believe the truth, but took pleasure in wickedness.
>
> —2 Thessalonians 2:8–12

All of this points to the dire need for prayer on behalf of the church—first for repentance and receiving forgiveness for sins, and secondly for intercession on behalf of our communities, our nation, and the rest of the world.

> Be diligent to present yourself approved to God as a workman who does not need to be ashamed, accurately handling the word of truth.
>
> —2 Timothy 2:15

There are those who will absolve themselves of any responsibilities by stating that God is in control so there are no worries, and that they are in right standing with God because they pray and ask forgiveness regularly. Asking for forgiveness and true repentance are not the same thing. That true repentance will come when sin is revealed by the light of the knowledge of God's word in view of his holiness, and what he expects of us.

Although it is true that God has a plan, it is presumptuous to think you know all about it and have everything figured out. A presumptuous mindset such as this is based on pride rather than humility. It is not God's will that this nation fail and fall from its place of blessing and prosperity in the world. Scripture makes it clear that we as Christians have a duty to ourselves and to our nation to be priests. As priests, the church should be doing the things (miracles, etc.) that Jesus and the early apostles and church did. Clearly this is not happening today to anywhere near the degree that it should.

It is amazing to observe how so many Christians are

- so willing to expend energy and resources rationalizing away their responsibilities,
- criticize and judge others who speak outside their small box of understanding, and
- analyze how to cope with the present state of the world through social programs and psychological means such as counseling rather than doing the very thing that will bring the greatest and best solution—to *repent*!

Those who would take offense to these statements are those who are living in a spirit of pride (likely without realizing it) and as such will not take an honest look at themselves in view of the entire Bible. Humility is not an emotion. It is a choice.

This phenomenon is clear evidence that people love their sins more than they love God, and would rather adhere to man's traditions and methods of solving problems rather than God's. This is not God's way.

> And do not be conformed to this world, but be transformed by the renewing of your mind, so that you may prove what the will of God is, that which is good and acceptable and perfect.
>
> —Romans 12:2

> Now we have received, not the spirit of the world, but the Spirit who is from God, so that we may know the things freely given to us by God.
>
> —1 Corinthians 2:12

> Do not love the world nor the things in the world. If anyone loves the world, the love of the Father is not in him.
>
> —1 John 2:15

Compromising with the world is not an option. It is sin. Many churches attempt to make themselves acceptable to the world through a variety of church programs, entertainment, etc., that compromise with the world to some degree. Although many of these things have their place, it is the wrong approach.

> You adulteresses, do you not know that friendship with the world is hostility toward God? Therefore whoever wishes to be a friend of the world makes himself an enemy of God.
>
> —James 4:4

No church will become successful in God's eyes if they compromise with the world. All too many pastors today view church membership and finances as a measure of success. This worldly view of success will not float on judgment day. Fulfilling the Great Commission according to God's plan as laid out in his word is the only way to bring true success. If a church will do this and not compromise with the world, then and only then will the membership and financial prosperity increase as God has promised and in the way he has promised. The measure of success for any church should be in the fulfillment of the Great Commission in Matthew 28:19–20 and Ephesians 4:11–12. The preparation spoken of in Ephesians involves education and that education involves practical application for faith without works is dead.

The blessings of obedience cannot be overstated.

The way to become more acceptable to the world, to fulfill the Great Commission, is to use Jesus as the prime example and do what he did.

Actions speak louder than words.

When people are healed, delivered, raised from the dead, and so on, then multitudes will flock to the church. Evidence of this is clear throughout Jesus's ministry, the rest of the New Testament, and the book of Acts in particular.

> [18]"Come now, and let us reason together," Says the LORD, "Though your sins are as scarlet, They will be as white as snow; Though they are red like crimson, They will be like wool. [19]"If you consent and obey, You will eat the best of the land; [20]"But if you refuse and rebel, You will be devoured by the sword." Truly, the mouth of the LORD has spoken.
>
> —Isaiah 1:18–20

Notes

1. *The Passion of the Christ*, Icon Productions, directed by Mel Gibson (2004).

A Precursor to Repentance

Humility and brokenness are the primary precursors to repentance. As mentioned earlier, repentance is the first step to a successful prayer life and relationship with the Holy Spirit. In order for true repentance to take place, we must first humble ourselves before our Lord and experience the brokenness that leads to repentance. This humility and brokenness is a decision but may also come as a result of the revelation of one's sins and how horrible and insane sin is.

The nature of pride is to hide and deny sin.
The nature of humility is to reveal and acknowledge sin.

There are many Scriptures that speak of the dangers of pride. As Christians, it is essential for us to maintain a humble state of mind throughout our lives. Today, the term *brokenness* has the connotation of being crushed, fractured, forcible subdued. Brokenness is viewed as a state more often brought about by an act or situation external to the individual. It is a state of mind that is a choice; an act of one's will.

> The sacrifices of God are a broken spirit; A broken and a contrite heart, O God, You will not despise.
>
> —Psalms 51:17

Many years ago, brokenness had a different meaning to Christians. Charles H. Spurgeon (1834–1892) put it well in his commentary[1] on Psalms 51:17:

> "*The sacrifices of God are a broken spirit.*" All sacrifices are presented to thee in one, by the man whose broken heart presents the Saviour's merit to thee. When the heart mourns for sin, thou art better pleased than when the bullock bleeds beneath the axe. "A broken heart" is an expression implying deep sorrow, embittering the very life; it carries in it the idea of all but killing anguish in that region which is so vital as to be the very source of life. So excellent is a spirit humbled and mourning for sin, that it is not only a sacrifice, but it has a plurality of excellencies, and is pre-eminently God's "sacrifices." "A broken and a contrite heart, O God, thou wilt not despise." A heart crushed is a fragrant heart. Men condemn those who are contemptible in their own eyes, but the Lord seeth not as man seeth. He despises what men esteem, and values that which they despise. Never yet has God spurned a lowly, weeping penitent, and never will he while God is love, and while Jesus is called the man who receiveth sinners. Bullocks and rams he desires not, but contrite hearts he seeks after; yea, but one of them is better to him than all the varied offerings of the old Jewish sanctuary.

It is unfortunate that brokenness has lost much of its original meaning. This original meaning would likely be revived again if spiritual revivals of the magnitude that occurred in previous centuries would come to us again. It is most unfortunate and irresponsible that we Christians don't take sin as seriously as we should. Such a cavalier attitude is not only unacceptable, it is sin and it is dangerous. As long as this cavalier attitude persists, revival will not come.

4.1 Humility

Humility is a state of mind that is required for those who desire to have a relationship with the Holy Spirit. Humility is what allows the operation of the Holy Spirit in the lives of Christians. One who does not maintain a humble state of mind is living in the flesh, and the flesh is at enmity with God. In other words, if you are not humble, you are living in the flesh and that is sin. Humility is a lesson that we should all have learned as part of our basic introduction to the Christian life and our relationship with our Lord Jesus Christ. Humility provides a degree of insulation between yourself and sin (pride in particular) and allows the Holy Spirit to reveal sins to you that would otherwise go unnoticed.

Humility comes before exaltation.
Pride comes before destruction.

Humility is a state of mind that is a decision. It is not a feeling that just happens to come on you. It is a decision. In James 4:10, we are instructed to humble ourselves before God and he will lift us up. "Humble yourselves in the presence of the Lord, and He will exalt you."

Humility before God is to know his righteousness, his holiness, his justice, his grace, his judgments, and indeed, his whole nature in view of our sinful nature and the nature of the flesh. This knowledge and experience will not be realized without humility.

Humility is the foundation upon which our relationship with the Holy Spirit is constructed. This concept cannot be emphasized enough. Without humility, we will not grow.

Without humility:

- You will resist the lessons needed to learn.
- You will refuse to yield to the lordship of Jesus Christ.

Humility is something that should be taught as part of the most fundamental traits of our relationship with him. It is important to understand that humility does *not* translate into being a doormat!

The nature of humility is to surrender one's will to the Holy Spirit. This act will make the lessons to be learned in life much easier. How often do we resist and complain about the trials and tribulations we go through? The resisting and complaining have their roots in an unsurrendered life. An unsurrendered life is a life founded on pride. Pride will always resist the will of God. This is why our Lord needs to put people through the same lesson over and over. Either this or they are continually stuck in the same lesson because they don't learn. How much better would it be to be humble and surrendered to him so that a trial would only need to be endured and learned once? In much of our life experience, humility is not the only ingredient we need. We need to learn and apply the word of God to every situation in which we find ourselves.

When people cry out and pray for the wealth of this world, they do so, more often than not, with an attitude of selfishness. Selfishness desires to exalt one's self. To seek these things before seeking God is idolatry. To see God as a means rather than an end is to make him your servant. To make him your servant is to elevate yourself above God. This can never be. This is sin. God will not answer such a prayer. This is the spirit of humanism and it has no place in the life of a Christian. How many people operate in this manner without realizing it?

When one is truly humble, they will come to understand what Paul wrote in Philippians:

> [8]More than that, I count all things to be loss in view of the surpassing value of knowing Christ Jesus my Lord, for whom I have suffered the loss of all things, and count them but rubbish so that I may gain Christ, [9]and may be found in Him, not having a righteousness of my own

> derived from the Law, but that which is through faith in Christ, the righteousness which comes from God on the basis of faith, [10] that I may know Him and the power of His resurrection and the fellowship of His sufferings, being conformed to His death; [11]in order that I may attain to the resurrection from the dead.
>
> —Philippians 3:8–11

Please don't misunderstand this. There is nothing wrong with wealth and enjoying the good things this world has to offer. There are many Scriptures that attest to this. It is a problem when these material things or the desires for them become an idol. Jesus comes first. When we grow to the point that our greatest delight is in our Lord, he will give us the desires of our heart (Psalm 37:4, Matthew 6:33). This doesn't necessarily mean it will all come at once. He will give us our desires in accordance to our ability to receive, and in accordance with his will. Don't forget, all things may be lawful, but not all things are expedient (1 Corinthians 6:12). We must not lose focus of what we are on this earth to accomplish. Once at this level of maturity, the surpassing value of knowing Jesus will overshadow everything of this world. Although, at this point we may enjoy the good things of this world, they will never take precedence over our relationship with Jesus and become an idol.

Humility is the avenue by which all the blessings of God flow. It is the avenue by which the Holy Spirit is able to operate through the his people.

If only we would all endeavor to humble ourselves and let Jesus reign in our lives. If we would do this then we would experience what Paul wrote in Philippians 4:13, "I can do all things through Him who strengthens me." This is not just a statement concerning the endurance of trials and tribulations. It is a statement of an overwhelming conqueror (Romans 8:37). All things. Not some, but *all.*

It is clear throughout Scripture that God gives favor to the humble of heart. Jesus proclaimed that we are holy because he is holy (Deuteronomy 7:6, 14:2, 28:9; Isaiah 62:12). In order to receive the holiness he has proclaimed for us, we must open the door of brokenness and obedience. Pride and holiness cannot coexist. We need to see our sins as our Heavenly Father sees them. We need to experience repentance. What is repentance?

From *Easton's Bible Dictionary*[2] on the word *repentance*, we read:

> There are three Greek words used in the New Testament to denote repentance.

1. The verb *metamelomai* is used of a change of mind, such as to produce regret or even remorse on account of sin, but not necessarily a change of heart. This word is used with reference to the repentance of Judas (Matt. 27:3).
2. *Metanoeo*, meaning to change one's mind and purpose, as the result of after knowledge.
3. This verb, with the cognate noun *metanoia*, is used of true repentance, a change of mind and purpose and life, to which remission of sin is promised.

Evangelical repentance consists of:

1. A true sense of one's own guilt and sinfulness.
2. The apprehension of God's mercy through Christ.
3. A hatred of sin (Psalms 119:128; Job 42:5–6; 2 Corinthians 7:10) and turning from it to God.
4. A persistent endeavor to live a holy life and to walk with God and keep his commandments.

The true penitent is conscious of:

- Guilt (Psalms 51:4, 51:9)
- The pollution of sin (Psalms 51:5, 51:7, 51:10).
- Helplessness without Christ (Psalms 51:11, 109:21–22).

> Thus he apprehends himself to be just what God has always seen him to be and declares him to be. But repentance comprehends not only such a sense of sin, but also an apprehension of mercy, without which there can be no true repentance (Psalms 51:1, 130:4).

When one sees himself in the light of God's holiness and man's sinful nature, it becomes apparent how hopeless they are, how much they need God's grace, and how dependent upon him they truly are.

> Be gracious to me, O God, according to Your loving-kindness; According to the greatness of Your compassion blot out my transgressions.
>
> —Psalms 51:1

> But there is forgiveness with You, That You may be feared.
>
> —Psalms 130:4

As Psalms 130:4 says, God's forgiveness brings a healthy fear to the forgiven. It comes from a realization of one's guilt and sin, and God's mercy, love, and willingness to forgive when there is no compulsion to do so because of their guilt, and in view of God's holiness. It is important to grasp the gravity of sin and the price Jesus paid for it.

> How much severer punishment do you think he will deserve who has trampled under foot the Son of God, and has regarded as unclean the blood of the covenant by which he was sanctified, and has insulted the Spirit of grace?
>
> —Hebrews 10:29

Perhaps the most important factor in repentance is that we need to be willing to face sin for what it is.

- We must be willing to allow the Holy Spirit to reveal our sins to us.

- We must be willing to experience that killing anguish and remorse that comes with the realization and revelation of the true nature of sin.
- We must be willing to see the cost of sin and the unfathomable price that Jesus paid for us.
- We must be willing to see the insanity that sin is, and how God's mercy toward us keeps us from experiencing the immediate effects of it (Matthew 7:7).

This is not a pleasant experience. Neither was dying on a cross. It is not something the flesh will easily submit to. It is nevertheless an experience we all must go through repeatedly and willingly. This is not an option for the Christian. When you experience this, you will be amazed at the subtleties of sin. The Holy Spirit will reveal things to you that never noticed before.

We all sin and we all need to maintain a lifestyle and attitude of brokenness. If Jesus as 100 percent man and 100 percent God willingly endured the suffering of the cross, how much more so should we whom he redeemed be willing to allow the Holy Spirit to bring us to a state of brokenness and repentance!

Without brokenness, there can be no repentance.

By allowing the Holy Spirit to accomplish this and by experiencing these things on a regular basis, it will become much easier and more natural to seek his righteousness and holiness and rid ourselves of a sinful lifestyle. The flesh must be put in subjection to our spirit and to the will of our Father in heaven. All of these things require a conscious effort and work on our part. This is all part of the "pressing forward" that Paul spoke of in Philippians 3:12.

There is an prophet by the name of Matt Sorger. Matt calls himself a prophetic revivalist. On a New Year's Eve several years ago, just past midnight, God gave him this prophetic word:[3]

I call you sons. I call you daughters, for you have longed to know My ways and you've longed to know My heart. This is the place where you learn My ways. This is the place where you know My heart (Sitting at His feet in His presence).

There's a washing that happens in this place (sitting at His feet in His presence). It's a washing off of things that keep you from Me, that hold you back. I draw you close to Me. My plan is greater than the plan the enemy has for you. My work in you is a glorious work and I'll bring it to completion.

I call you My own. You don't belong to the world, you belong to Me. My ways are higher, My thoughts are higher. You've been distracted by many things. Lay it all at My feet tonight.

Return to the secret place. I will crown you with My glory. This is where I want you to live—close to My heart, close to My heart, close to My heart!

You were created to live close to My heart. There's freedom in My presence.

The Holy Spirit says I am fighting for all of you tonight. For the enemy has sought to take you out. Know that this very night I am raising up a standard for you. I'm fighting for all of you. There's a new day ahead for you. Old things need to be let go of, released, and walked away from. (When saying "fighting for all of you" the Lord was saying that He was fighting for everything within us to be His.)

There's a new day I'm bringing you to—a day of great release, power and surrender. But you need to let go of things. Will you let go? As you let go you'll find that I have more for you. You have not reached the highest place yet. Will you let go of the things I want you to? If you release them, there's more for you. I'm waiting for your obedience. I'm waiting for your full surrender. There's more that I have for you. There's a walk I've called you to walk. It's a different walk. It's not a path that a lot of people go on—few will go on it.

> Tonight I call you to go up higher—but the higher you go, the narrower the path becomes. There are few who desire to walk on this path. But I have a higher path for you. There's more that I want to show you and give you. The narrower the path, the tighter the restrictions, but I have placed them there for a reason. The narrower the path, the firmer the foundation will be for your feet. The more secure footing you'll have. There are some that have desired to come close to Me, but they have drawn back because they thought the price was too great. Some came close, but have drawn back.
>
> I've shown you this mountain before. The higher you go, the less you can take with you. The higher you go, the less you can take with you. Are you willing to surrender? Are you willing to obey Me even when it's hard. Obedience is not easy. There's a wrestling that goes on inside of you—a wrestling of your will with My will. There's a place where you can go—it's called surrender. It's called obedience.
>
> Within your hands I will place a great anointing—greater than you've ever experienced up 'till now. For you will be My surrendered vessels, My obedient vessels, My instruments.

This prophecy is a promise with a condition. How does this fit in with brokenness? It fits because brokenness is a necessary condition to put the flesh in subjection and to surrender ourselves to our Lord. In so doing there is great reward, not only in this life but in the one to come. Through our surrender, we will do the works of God and thus store up treasures in heaven and great reward on the Day of Judgment.

Some important things to keep in mind are:

1. Repentance and the surrender of oneself to God must be done consciously and constantly. We must resist the devil and persevere in trials and tribulations. In so doing, we will grow closer to God and become more Christlike. The flesh does not surrender easily. James 4:7–10 says,

> [7]Submit therefore to God. Resist the devil and he will flee from you. [8]Draw near to God and He will draw near to you. Cleanse your hands, you sinners; and purify your hearts, you double-minded. [9]Be miserable and mourn and weep; let your laughter be turned into mourning, and your joy to gloom. [10]Humble yourselves in the presence of the Lord, and He will exalt you.

2. Bearing the fruit of and walking in the Holy Spirit are evidence of a humble life.
3. To live a broken life, one must avoid the ways of the world, counsel of the ungodly, and hate the way of sinners. Far too many churches today have compromised with the world thinking they will gain the acceptance of the world. It doesn't work this way. We must delight in the law of God and must meditate on it always and obey it (Psalm 1:1–2). The world would be far more willing to accept and respect the church if the church would learn the power of God and exercise it throughout their communities. Revival will come and the Gospel will spread like wildfire.
4. It needs to be emphasized that the love of this world must die in the life of a broken Christian. The mad rush for wealth, position, fame, and power is not the will of God. Willful disobedience to the word of God is also very dangerous for the believer. In 1 John 2:15–17, it says,

> [15]Do not love the world, nor the things in the world. If anyone loves the world, the love of the Father is not in him. [16]For all that is in the world, the lust of the flesh and the lust of the eyes and the boastful pride of life, is not from the Father, but is from the world. [17]And the world is passing away, and also its lusts; but the one who does the will of God abides forever.

In verse 16, John identifies the three root sins—the lust of the flesh, the lust of the eyes, and the boastful pride of life. It is from these three root sins that all other sins are categorized.[4] Let's look at this more closely:

a. The "lust of the flesh" is the motivation for sensual self-gratification. It could be called moral impurity, sexual lust, or in the broadest term, sensuality.

b. The "lust of the eyes" is the materialistic motivation in human nature. This lust could be called temporal values or idolatry. It is evidenced by a greater emphasis on material things than spiritual things. It is an ungodly concern for temporal or worldly possessions.

c. The "boastful pride of life" is simply stated as pride. It is an ungodly evaluation of one's importance or merit. This motivation is the most emotionally devastating of the three because an individual with a pride problem always has problems with bitterness and rejection.

5. Whether Jesus comes back in our lifetimes or not, we must prepare ourselves to meet him. This includes purifying ourselves from all unrighteousness and doing his work so we are ready to go with him when he comes (I John 3:2–3).

Once we allow the Holy Spirit to bring us to a genuine state of brokenness, what must be done to maintain it? How do you remain humble? We will find that the things we do to maintain a humble and broken state of mind are applicable to every aspect of our Christian life.

4.2 Maintaining Humility

Maintaining a state of humility and brokenness is not the nature of the flesh. It is so easy to allow self back on the throne. This is a conflict we all deal with.

In a nutshell, we are to use focus and discipline to maintain a humble mindset. Of course, the key ingredient here is prayer. Living in a state of brokenness and humility does not equate to feeling miserable as some attempt to portray. Rather, this mindset is the door through which the Holy Spirit will operate and we will experience the fruit of the Spirit in its fullness.

> [22]But the fruit of the Spirit is love, joy, peace, patience, kindness, goodness, faithfulness, [23]gentleness, self-control; against such things there is no law.
>
> —Galatians 5:22–23

Jesus was our perfect example and is our perfect help.

> These things I have spoken to you, so that in Me you may have peace. In the world you have tribulation, but take courage; I have overcome the world.
>
> —John 16:33

Some denominations and movies that depict the life of Jesus overemphasize his humility to the point that it is nauseating. He is unfortunately portrayed to be humble to the point of defeat, humble to the point of being a doormat. He was neither. There is also the tendency to equate humility with passivity. Jesus was certainly not passive, and so neither should we be.

Humility and a warrior mindset go hand in hand. This fact is clear, even among those who don't know Jesus. Observe the characteristics of the professional warriors, such as the Navy Seals, the Army Rangers, and various other Special Forces teams. Most of these people remain remarkably humble despite the fact that they are the most highly trained and capable warriors in the world. Pride and arrogance will get you killed in battle. Pride and arrogance try to make a hero out of a fool. Look at the men who were given the Congressional Medal of Honor. Most of these medals are given posthumously. Those who survived will tell you they were just doing their jobs, that they were not heroes and were not deserving of such a great honor.

It is important to keep in mind that the warrior mindset and the mental training and discipline that people go through in the military are directly applicable to the Christian life. You don't need to go into the military to accomplish this though. All of what we need to do is written in the Bible. All of what we need to get is from the Holy Spirit. Nevertheless, we can also learn from the experiences of those around us who have served in the military and law enforcement.

More is discussed on the warrior mindset in Section 9.2.

In the first chapter of Joshua, God proclaims courage and strength to Joshua. This is done so that he may lead Israel into the promised land. We recognize today that everything Israel went through is an example to us in our Christian walk. Likewise, God proclaims strength and courage to us today so that we might enter into that promised land that flows with milk and honey. It is up to us to appropriate this strength and courage through obedience to him.

> Have I not commanded you? Be strong and courageous! Do not tremble or be dismayed, for the LORD your God is with you wherever you go.
>
> —Joshua 1:9

> The LORD is the one who goes ahead of you; He will be with you. He will not fail you or forsake you. Do not fear or be dismayed.
>
> —Deuteronomy 31:8

All of these things may seem like a daunting task. However, if you start with the basics, the Holy Spirit will guide and provide. A tree doesn't come down with one swing of the ax. Although we can read about what needs to be done, the doing of it often seems beyond our capabilities. This is not so.

God made our job simple. It is the devil that deceives people into thinking it is so complex and difficult that it is unattainable.

Remember it is the Holy Spirit who is your helper!

> I am the vine, you are the branches; he who abides in Me and I in him, he bears much fruit, for apart from Me you can do nothing.
>
> —John 15:5

All too often, teachings and sermons instruct us *what* we need to do without telling us *how*. This unfortunate fact is what keeps so many in bondage (Hosea 4:6). The solution is education.

The most basic but important step of "how" is summed up in 2 Corinthians 10:5, which says,

> We are destroying speculations and every lofty thing raised up against the knowledge of God, and we are taking every thought captive to the obedience of Christ.

We are to take every thought captive to the obedience of Christ. In order to do so, we need to judge every thought, word, image, feeling, and emotion—that is, everything we receive through our senses as well as everything that goes on in our minds. This judgment is based on the word of God and the Holy Spirit. This is why we need to read and study the Bible, learn it from cover to cover, and learn it well. Everything that is not of God must be rejected. It is through entertaining evil things that we get into trouble. The practice and discipline of doing this is critical for spiritual warfare since it is the mind that the devil attacks more often than through external circumstances. This can take a lot of work and willpower, especially when dealing with emotions.

Of course, the devil uses external means and attacks to bring us down as well. In reality, those external circumstances are also meant to degrade our mind as well.

Defeat is in the mind. Victory is in Jesus.

If you want to gain victory over the devil, this is where it begins—the mind. Of course, prayer is the primary tool we have to gain this victory. In the chapters that follow, there are many warfare prayers to use for this purpose.

As we reject the bad, we must also dwell on the good. Paul wrote in Philippians 4:8–9,

> [8]Finally, brethren, whatever is true, whatever is honorable, whatever is right, whatever is pure, whatever is lovely, whatever is of good repute, if there is any excellence and if anything worthy of praise, let your mind dwell on these things. [9]The things you have learned and received and heard and seen in me, practice these things; and the God of peace shall be with you.

Although the task is simple, it takes mental discipline and effort to accomplish on a moment-by-moment and day-by-day basis.

In the course of growing in Jesus, we must always keep his word in mind. Paul makes this clear in his letter to the Colossians.

> [1]If then you have been raised up with Christ, keep seeking the things above, where Christ is, seated at the right hand of God. [2]Set your mind on the things above, not on the things that are on earth. [3]For you have died and your life is hidden with Christ in God. [4]When Christ, who is our life, is revealed, then you also will be revealed with Him in glory. [5]Therefore consider the members of your earthly body as dead to immorality, impurity, passion, evil desire, and greed, which amounts to idolatry. [6]For it is on account of these things that the wrath of God will come, [7]and in them you also once walked, when you were living in them. [8]But now you also, put them all aside: anger, wrath, malice, slander, and abusive speech from your mouth. [9]Do not lie to one another, since you laid aside the old self with its evil practices, [10]and have

> put on the new self who is being renewed to a true knowledge according to the image of the One who created him.
>
> —Colossians 3:1–10

As God told Joshua as he was about to lead Israel into the promised land,

> [7]Only be strong and very courageous; be careful to do according to all the law which Moses My servant commanded you; do not turn from it to the right or to the left, so that you may have success wherever you go. [8]This book of the law shall not depart from your mouth, but you shall meditate on it day and night, so that you may be careful to do according to all that is written in it; for then you will make your way prosperous, and then you will have success.
>
> —Joshua 1:7–8

So too we must put his word into practice in our lives if we are to enter into the land (relationship with Jesus) that he has promised us.

In all that has been said on the subject of brokenness, the most important aspect is the renewing of the mind. Indeed, the renewing of the mind is essential for us to experience and live a normal Christian life.

> And do not be conformed to this world, but be transformed by the renewing of your mind, that you may prove what the will of God is, that which is good and acceptable and perfect.
>
> —Romans 12:2

The renewing of the mind comes through this mental discipline and prayer with the result that the Holy Spirit will help bring about changes. The result is holiness and righteousness and a closer relationship with Jesus. The process of mental discipline also means making changes in how you do things. Priorities are likely going to need changing. There are things that you do now that may need to be placed lower on your priority list. Righteousness and holiness must become a higher priority.

In pursuing righteousness and holiness, we need to keep things in their proper perspective. Many Christians today place a higher priority on experiencing the supernatural than they do on their relationship with Jesus. Although we as Christians ought to experience the supernatural on a daily basis, we should not feel the need to chase miracles. Miracles, signs, and wonders are a natural product of one's relationship with the Holy Spirit. Scripture tells us in Matthew 12:39 and 16:4 that those who seek after signs are adulterous. Seeking these things before Jesus is idolatry and this is sin. We are to seek a relationship with him first and foremost. Everything else is secondary. Working to be righteous and holy is part of the process of building your relationship with Jesus.

You can't get there by warming a pew. You can't get there by sitting in front of the TV. You can't get there by being passive about your relationship with the Holy Spirit. You must go forward and not look back as Lot's wife did. Living in a comfort zone is a zone of defeat. If you think you are okay where you are, you are not and are deceived by the devil. You are right where he wants you. Don't forget you are here on this earth for only a very short time. What are you doing with the time God has given you?

People who go to college invest a lot of resources (money, time, effort) to learn and get a degree so they can be productive and provide their families with a decent income and financial security. Although there is obvious benefit to this, it is temporal. Realizing this, how much more important is it to devote even more resources to our relationship with Jesus knowing the consequences are eternal?

Where are your priorities?

Church is not a place for religious entertainment. First and foremost, it is a house of prayer.

> For My house will be called a house of prayer for all the peoples.
>
> —Isaiah 56:7

Secondly, it is a place of education.

> [11]And He gave some as apostles, and some as prophets, and some as evangelists, and some as **pastors and teachers,** [12]**for the equipping of the saints for the work of service, to the building up of the body of Christ**; [13]until we all attain to the unity of the faith, and of the knowledge of the Son of God, to a mature man, to the measure of the stature which belongs to the fullness of Christ.
>
> —Ephesians 4:11–13

> Let not many of you become teachers, my brethren, knowing that as such we will incur a stricter judgment.
>
> —James 3:1

Pastors and teachers have the God-ordained responsibility to prepare the saints for the work of service and to the building up of the body of Christ. The saints have the responsibility to apply their teachings. These verses in Ephesians are a high-level description that covers a wide range of responsibilities on the part of the congregation. Those responsibilities include doing the things that Jesus did, such as laying hands on the sick so they are healed, delivering those in bondage (deliverance from demons), and proclaiming the Gospel, to name a few. From James 3:1, we also see that pastors and teachers carry a significant responsibility in the church and are held to a higher standard. To emphasize again, we cannot afford to take these things lightly. All we say and do in this life has eternal consequences.

> [4]And my speech and my preaching was not with enticing words of man's wisdom, but in **demonstration of the**

> **Spirit and of power**: [5]That your faith should not stand in the wisdom of men, but in the power of God.
>
> —1 Corinthians 2:4–5

The church is a place for many other things as well. These include a place of worship, a focal point of the community and all the ministries that fall out of this, and so on. It is these two key tasks (prayer and education) that are so easily ignored, yet are the most important. Without them, the rest will never succeed to any significant degree.

In these verses from 1 Corinthians, Paul makes it clear that he used "demonstration of the Spirit and of power" to build up the body of Christ, and as a means to educate the people in the things they need to be doing.

A point that needs to be clear is that the performance of the power of God, which include performing various miracles, signs, and wonders, and proclaiming the Gospel, all go together. To go out and proclaim the Gospel without the power of God to back up the words looks foolish and empty. Many of the people who don't know Jesus have an inherent understanding of this and understandably laugh at the church.

> For God hath not given us the spirit of fear; but of power, and of love, and of a sound mind.
>
> —2 Timothy 1:7, KJV

> For the kingdom of God does not consist in words but in power.
>
> —1 Corinthians 4:20

> And He has said to me, "My grace is sufficient for you, for power is perfected in weakness." Most gladly, therefore, I will rather boast about my weaknesses, so that the power of Christ may dwell in me.
>
> —2 Corinthians 12:9

From a worldly viewpoint this seems daunting. It is the Holy Spirit who is our helper and who performs these miracles. No amount of piety on the part of the Christian will ever bring about even the smallest miracle. It is all about Jesus and our relationship with him. It is prayer that is the moving force for growing in Christ to the point that these things become a lifestyle.

It should be clear that we have a responsibility to our Lord Jesus to build our relationship with him so he is able to work miracles through us such that the Gospel is demonstrated with power, love, and a sound mind. This should not be viewed as obligation but a natural and free-will choice and a joy. No one will ever get there without prayer.

Getting where you need to be in your relationship with Jesus so that all these things will come to pass is *simple*. There is nothing complicated about this, but it does take work.

Growing in Jesus has its risks. There are dangers, trials, tribulations, spiritual warfare, and so on, and more importantly, rewards. The last thing the devil wants is a Christian who knows who they are in Christ and exercises that power and authority. This is a power and authority that he has no means to conquer. Are you willing to take that step of faith on a daily basis and develop your relationship with the Lord of lords and King of kings? You will never get there by existing in a comfort zone. Indeed there are plenty of dire warnings in Scripture concerning this attitude. Remember, everything you say and do in this life has eternal consequences.

Notes

1. *The Treasury of David*, commentary on Psalms 51:17, C. H. Spurgeon, (1869–1885), public domain.
2. *Easton's Bible Dictionary*, generally refers to the *Illustrated Bible Dictionary, Third Edition*, by Matthew George Easton, MA, DD (1823–1894) (published 1897), public domain.

3. *Matt Sorger Ministries*, from Matt's website http://www.mattsorger.com.
4. *Revelational Ministry*, George W. Seevers, Jr., possibly a seminary paper.

Hindrances to Prayer

Sin is the hindrance to prayer. Sin is a subject that is seldom heard from the pulpit today. Dealing with sin is never a pleasant issue.

> Every man's way is right in his own eyes, But the LORD weighs the hearts.
>
> —Proverbs 21:2

Sin is something we must all face, sooner or later. It is far better to deal with it now and work to live a holy and righteous life than to wait until one is standing before the Lord Jesus Christ to give an account of all they did in this life. By then, it will be too late.

There are those who teach that it is okay to sin because "it is all covered by the blood of Jesus" or "it is all paid for on the cross." Such a philosophy is clearly heresy.

> [12]Therefore do not let sin reign in your mortal body so that you obey its lusts, [13]and do not go on presenting the members of your body to sin as instruments of unrighteousness; but present yourselves to God as those alive from the dead, and your members as instruments of righteousness to God. [14]For sin shall not be master over you, for you are not under law but under grace. [15]What then? Shall we sin because we are not under law but under grace? May it never be! [16]Do you not know that when you present yourselves to someone as slaves for obedience, you

> are slaves of the one whom you obey, either of sin resulting in death, or of obedience resulting in righteousness?
>
> —Romans 6:12–16

> 26For if we go on sinning willfully after receiving the knowledge of the truth, there no longer remains a sacrifice for sins, 27but a terrifying expectation of judgment and THE FURY OF A FIRE WHICH WILL CONSUME THE ADVERSARIES. 28Anyone who has set aside the Law of Moses dies without mercy on the testimony of two or three witnesses. 29How much severer punishment do you think he will deserve who has trampled under foot the Son of God, and has regarded as unclean the blood of the covenant by which he was sanctified, and has insulted the Spirit of grace? 30For we know Him who said, "VENGEANCE IS MINE, I WILL REPAY." And again, "THE LORD WILL JUDGE HIS PEOPLE." 31It is a terrifying thing to fall into the hands of the living God.
>
> —Hebrews 10:26–31

Remember that Paul is writing this to Christians. From these and many other passages throughout scripture it is clear that sin is an issue that must be dealt with and not taken with a cavalier attitude.

It will invariably be more difficult and take more work and effort to recover from sin than it would to resist temptation in the first place.

Hindrances to prayer may be external or internal, but are always the result of sin. Some of the more common hindrances are wrong motives (James 4:3), pride, lack of faith, and so on. This chapter will address some of those that have been the most damaging to the church as a whole in recent years.

One only needs to look at the recent history of this nation, particularly since World War II. Back then the church was a significant force at all levels of society. Today it is little more than a religious social club. The church has over the years withdrawn from their moral and civic duties. This leaves a power vacuum that the devil most eagerly tries to fill. This fact is all too evident today. The church has compromised with the world, and hence the devil, and allowed a myriad of evil influences to gain a foothold in the church.

Seldom is holiness, righteousness, repentance, and the fear of God preached or taught today. Even if these subjects are taught, they are likely watered down to the point of no effect.

There are many Scriptures throughout the Bible that address God's judgment of the wicked. It is clear in Scripture that we as Christians will also be judged. The entire chapter of Deuteronomy 28 is devoted to the consequences of sin and righteousness.

> For we must all appear before the judgment seat of Christ, that each one may be recompensed for his deeds in the body, according to what he has done, whether good or bad.
>
> —2 Corinthians 5:10

> For the Son of Man is going to come in the glory of His Father with His angels, and WILL THEN REPAY EVERY MAN ACCORDING TO HIS DEEDS.
>
> —Matthew 16:27

> So then each one of us will give an account of himself to God.
>
> —Romans 14:12

If only we would grasp the importance of these verses! If only we would be diligent about our walk with Jesus!

Omission of good works, failure to fulfill the great commission. This is every bit a sin as committing a myriad of other crimes and sins. Where is your heart? Do you go to church to experience the presence of the Holy Spirit thinking this is enough. Do you rely on the anointing that is on the pastor thinking this is enough. Do you just go to church to get your spiritual batteries charged so you can get through the week only to repeat the process next week and the week after? Do you go to church, put some pocket change in the plate when it goes by thinking you are okay because you have paid your fire insurance? This behavior is irresponsible and unacceptable for the Christian. Church is not a social club. It is not a place to get an emotional high. Church is a place of prayer. It is a hospital for sinners. It is a place for Christians to grow, learn the word of God, live it, and put it into practice.

It is often said that salvation is a free gift from God. Salvation itself is since only Jesus himself is qualified to be the redemption for our sins. The Christian life is another matter. Scripture is clear that we have responsibilities to fulfill.

> [11]And He gave some as apostles, and some as prophets, and some as evangelists, and some as pastors and teachers, [12]for the equipping of the saints for the work of service, to the building up of the body of Christ; [13]until we all attain to the unity of the faith, and of the knowledge of the Son of God, to a mature man, to the measure of the stature which belongs to the fullness of Christ.
>
> —Ephesians 4:11–13

The focus in this passage in Ephesians is the "equipping of the saints for the work of service." It is the church leadership that is responsible for making this happen, and it is the congregation's responsibility to put it into action to build up the body of Christ, which also means to fulfill the Great Commission.

Scripture is clear that we are in for a struggle if we choose to grow in Jesus. That struggle will be minimized *if* we are obedient to his word. The beginning of our obedience is given in John 6:29, which says, "Jesus answered and said to them, 'This is the work of God, that you believe in Him whom He has sent.'" Building faith takes work, which also means building your relationship with Jesus takes work. The Gospel hymn "Trust And Obey"[1] says it well:

When we walk with the Lord
in the light of His word,
what a glory He sheds on our way!
While we do His good will,
He abides with us still,
and with all who will trust and obey.

Refrain:
Trust and obey, for there's no other way
to be happy in Jesus, but to trust and obey.

Not a burden we bear,
not a sorrow we share,
but our toil he doth richly repay;
not a grief or a loss,
not a frown or a cross,
but is blest if we trust and obey.

(Refrain)

But we never can prove
the delights of His love
until all on the altar we lay;
for the favor He shows,
for the joy He bestows,
are for them who will trust and obey.

(Refrain)

Then in fellowship sweet
we will sit at His feet,
or we'll walk by His side in the way;
what He says we will do,
where He sends we will go;
never fear, only trust and obey.

(Refrain)

You can't change the past but you can change the course of your life through the decisions you make. You can change the future. Now is the time to pursue Jesus and work on your relationship with him with all of your being! Now is the time to repent!

5.1 The Spirit of Entertainment

For several generations now, the spirit of entertainment has had a detrimental effect on the church. This has come primarily through television. How easy it has become to be complacent about spiritual matters in our own lives and push so many responsibilities on the pastor!

The spirit of entertainment has the effect of feeding information with no effort on the part of the recipient. Many churches today have used resources to develop the best drama club, the best choir, the best worship team, and so on. These things should be secondary to prayer. People sit in church, listen to a sermon, and forget a majority of what was spoken even before they get out the door. Lessons and sermons seldom get written down and put into practice.

> [12]And Jesus entered the temple and drove out all those who were buying and selling in the temple, and overturned the tables of the money changers and the seats of those who were selling doves. [13]And He said to them, "It is written, 'MY HOUSE SHALL BE CALLED A HOUSE OF PRAYER'; but you are making it a ROBBERS' DEN."
>
> —Matthew 21:12–13

Although culture is different today, human nature has not changed. How have we made the church into a robbers' den? By catering to the spirit of entertainment, we succumb to an emotional feeling we call worship rather than making our relationship with the Holy Spirit the top priority. We are robbing our Lord of the relationship he desires to have with us and replacing it with an emotional high. Many will no doubt argue this point, but all one needs to do is to observe any of the majority of church services.

Where is repentance and serious prayer found in the church today? Where is the weeping and remorse for sins? It is only *after* true repentance and fervent prayer that praise and worship will be experienced in its fullness as intended by our Lord Jesus.

It is all too easy to fall into the trap of wanting all the benefits of salvation and none of the responsibilities.

There is a time and a place for everything. The church should first and foremost be a place of prayer. Entertainment, however necessary and pleasing it may seem, should never take precedence over your relationship with the Holy Spirit and the mission the church has to fulfill. Entertainment has unfortunately become an idol in the churches. This sin is polluting the church and quenching the Holy Spirit (1 Thessalonians 5:19). God will never be able to work in his people as he desires until these sins are dealt with. Although the motive for providing entertainment (concerts and such) in the church may be to attract people for the purpose of evangelizing, it is seldom backed up with enough prayer to make this effort effective to the degree it should be. In reality, people have greater concerns than being entertained. There are many health problems, family problems, financial problems, and so on that need to be dealt with. Our nation is sick and dying. The church needs to provide the solution, which is to use the power of God to give substance to the words.

> 4And my message and my preaching were not in persuasive words of wisdom, **but in demonstration of the Spirit and of power,** 5so that your faith would not rest on the wisdom of men, but on the power of God.
>
> —1 Corinthians 2:4–5

In the above scripture, the "persuasive words of wisdom" can also take the form of entertainment or any other means of communication other than demonstration of the Spirit and of power. Until the church repents of its sins, it will never be able to back up the Gospel with the demonstration of the Spirit and of power.

5.2 Spiritual Laziness

The spirit of entertainment is perhaps the greatest, but not the only, contributor to laziness. It is all too easy to become a couch potato and park one's self in front of the TV. This has the effect of being fed information with no effort on the part of the recipient. This spirit of laziness has had a significant negative effect on the church. It has become too easy to think it is okay to ride on the pastor's coattails (after all, that's what we pay him for). Too many pastors teach that being a Christian requires no effort at all. This attitude won't go anywhere on judgment day. Laziness is a sign of spiritual decay.

One example of the results of spiritual laziness is the suicide rate today. It is all too high. Man's solutions to this problem can never make up for the vacuum felt by the absence of the Holy Spirit. One of the primary results of this vacuum is hopelessness. It is the church's responsibilities as a nation of priests to make sure this problem is minimized. This takes prayer as well as accepting our personal, spiritual, and civil responsibilities. All too many Christians absolve themselves of their God-ordained responsibilities by saying something to the effect, "I don't need to do anything because God is in control." This is spiritual laziness.

People inevitably attempt to solve the near unfathomable complexities of the problems of society today with complex solutions. Man's solutions are doomed to failure. God's solution is remarkably simple and workable and is found in 2 Chronicles 7:13–14.

> [13]If I shut up the heavens so that there is no rain, or if I command the locust to devour the land, or if I send pestilence among My people, [14]and My people who are called by My name humble themselves and pray and seek

> My face and turn from their wicked ways, then I will hear from heaven, will forgive their sin and will heal their land.

In verse 13, we see that God causes the weather and environment to change in order to get his people's attention. It is sad that a lot of Christians see what is happening, know what Scripture has to say about it, but do nothing. This is a failure of epic proportions on the part of the church. This is founded on spiritual laziness and is completely inexcusable.

In verse 14, the solution is remarkably simple—humble one's self, seek God (that is, to work on your relationship with Jesus), pray, and *repent*! Once the church does this, God will do the rest.

> 26For if we go on sinning willfully after receiving the knowledge of the truth, there no longer remains a sacrifice for sins, 27but a terrifying expectation of judgment and THE FURY OF A FIRE WHICH WILL CONSUME THE ADVERSARIES. 28Anyone who has set aside the Law of Moses dies without mercy on the testimony of two or three witnesses. 29How much severer punishment do you think he will deserve who has trampled under foot the Son of God, and has regarded as unclean the blood of the covenant by which he was sanctified, and has insulted the Spirit of grace? 30For we know Him who said, "VENGEANCE IS MINE, I WILL REPAY." And again, "THE LORD WILL JUDGE HIS PEOPLE." 31It is a terrifying thing to fall into the hands of the living God.
>
> —Hebrews 10:26–31

We would all do well to take God's word seriously. No one has the luxury to be lazy, especially when such decisions have dire consequences that will be felt for all eternity. Look at the parable of the talents from Matthew 25. In particular, we need to examine the demise of the third and lazy slave who failed to multiply the talents given him.

> [26]But his master answered and said to him, 'You wicked,
> lazy slave, you knew that I reap where I did not sow and
> gather where I scattered no seed. [27]'Then you ought to have
> put my money in the bank, and on my arrival I would have
> received my money back with interest. [28]'Therefore take
> away the talent from him, and give it to the one who has
> the ten talents.' [29]"For to everyone who has, more shall be
> given, and he will have an abundance; but from the one who
> does not have, even what he does have shall be taken away.
> [30]"Throw out the worthless slave into the outer darkness;
> in that place there will be weeping and gnashing of teeth.
>
> —Matthew 25:26–30

Keep in mind that the two parables in Matthew 25 refer to Christians as stated twice in verse 1. When Scripture states something twice like this, it is intended to leave absolutely no doubt concerning the subject. The one who is lazy is worthless and will be thrown into the outer darkness, which is hell (see also Matthew 13:42, 50). It is a terrifying thing to fall into the hands of the living God! This parable is discussed in greater detail later in Chapter 6.

Although the ills of society will never be completely eliminated, the church has the responsibility to minimize these problems as much as possible. The consequences of spiritual laziness are grave. We will all be judged for what we have done and failed to do in this life.

> [9]How long will you lie down, O sluggard? When will you
> arise from your sleep? [10]"A little sleep, a little slumber, A
> little folding of the hands to rest"— [11]Your poverty will
> come in like a vagabond And your need like an armed man.
>
> —Proverbs 6:9–11

> The soul of the sluggard craves and gets nothing, But the soul of the diligent is made fat.
>
> —Proverbs 13:4

He also who isz slack in his work Is brother to him who destroys.

—Proverbs 18:9

[30]I passed by the field of the sluggard And by the vineyard of the man lacking sense, [31]And behold, it was completely overgrown with thistles; Its surface was covered with nettles, And its stone wall was broken down. [32]When I saw, I reflected upon it; I looked, and received instruction. [33]"A little sleep, a little slumber, A little folding of the hands to rest," [34]Then your poverty will come as a robber And your want like an armed man.

—Proverbs 24:30–34

[13]The sluggard says, "There is a lion in the road! A lion is in the open square! " [14]As the door turns on its hinges, So does the sluggard on his bed. [15]The sluggard buries his hand in the dish; He is weary of bringing it to his mouth again. [16]The sluggard is wiser in his own eyes Than seven men who can give a discreet answer.

—Proverbs 26:13–16

By much slothfulness the building decayeth; and through idleness of the hands the house droppeth through.

—Ecclesiastes 10:18, KJV

Spiritual laziness is a wasting and destructive spirit. Others can see one who is lazy and become lazy themselves. The result is that lives are wasted in a multitude of ways. This waste is the cause of destruction for many.

God calls people when they are busy.
Satan calls people when they are lazy.

God will not use someone who is lazy. Note that all the great men of God written about in Scripture were busy doing something when God called them. They weren't sitting around waiting for some great anointing or revival to drop out of heaven. Daniel, Joshua, Gideon, and David are among many who were busy and diligent when God called them.

Laziness is the greatest hindrance to spiritual growth in the church today. If nothing is done to reverse this trend, persecution will become the norm. Persecution is already happening throughout the nation today, and more so in other countries. There are many people who are not inherently lazy but have been taught that this behavior is acceptable in the church. Such teaching is most often based on church culture and doctrines that foster this behavior, often without anyone realizing what is happening. Laziness is a tool and deception of the devil used to render the church ineffective so he can go about his evil deeds with as few hindrances as possible.

It is really quite amazing to observe some people. They may be diligent, successful, and prosperous people in their careers but that good mental attitude they employ every day is left at the door when they walk in the church. It is a horrible tragedy that church culture fosters this attitude.

> So then, my beloved, just as you have always obeyed, not as in my presence only, but now much more in my absence, work out your salvation with fear and trembling.
>
> —Philippians 2:12

The following are some of the characteristics of one who is spiritually lazy:

1. One who is lazy will always be the servant of others. The people of this nation are more and more becoming the servants of the wicked.
2. One who is lazy lacks discipline.
3. One who is lazy brings others into laziness.

4. One who is lazy will be defeated by the enemy. One who is stagnant in their growth is in a state of defeat.
5. One who is lazy will live in spiritual poverty. Spiritual poverty can also bring about physical poverty.
6. One who is lazy turns on their bed but doesn't get out of it. This is to say they are full of words but lack action.
7. One who is lazy is subject to fear. Faith is the opposite of fear and requires work to build.
8. One who is lazy is afraid to take any risk. Spiritual growth requires taking risk and stepping out in faith.
9. One who is lazy is wise in their own eyes without realizing just how foolish they really are.
10. One who is lazy will resist work. Building a relationship with Jesus takes work so one who is lazy will never grow out of their spiritual diapers.
11. One who is lazy will resist growing because this requires sacrificing self on the cross.
12. One who is lazy is a procrastinator. They will fail to do what needs to be done when it needs to be done.
13. One who is lazy prides himself in it.
14. One who is lazy doesn't want to struggle for any spiritual gain. They won't read and study the Bible by themselves. They won't go through spiritual exercises (such as fasting and prayer) that will help them to grow. They are not willing to go through the trials and tribulations necessary for growth.
15. One who is lazy thinks they are entitled to every spiritual blessing without having to do any work to earn them. This problem is compounded by the entitlement mentality so prevalent in society today.

16. One who is lazy doesn't want (or perhaps even believes or cares) to be held accountable for their sins.
17. One who is lazy will leave before the work begins.
18. One who is lazy has a distaste for the things of God. This is to say that the things of God are not worth pursuing because they think they are okay in their present state (Revelation 3:17).
19. One who is lazy will never experience the power of God.
20. One who is lazy is full of excuses (Luke 14:16–24).
21. One who is lazy fails to finish a task.
22. One who is lazy doesn't contribute anything positive.
23. One who is lazy is unteachable as they think they know everything or that they know enough. This is also the spirit of pride.
24. One who is lazy will cry out to others for help if tragedy strikes, hoping others will do all the prayer and work necessary to change their situation.
25. One who is lazy is a spiritual parasite instead of a contributor to the edification of the church. Such a person is always being fed the word but never puts it into action.
26. One who is lazy will fail to do anything about a problem until after it is too late.

I recently saw a church that was looking for a senior pastor. They published the job description on the church website. The roles and responsibilities for the pastor were very typical of the average church today. The job description listed three pages of responsibilities expected of a prospective pastor. Three pages! Rather than heaping a significant number of responsibilities on the pastor (Well, that's what we pay him for!), the church elders should pick much of this up. Being an elder in the church carries with it a lot more than holding a title. The pastor should devote much more of his time to prayer and pursuing means of preparing the saints, and should not need to be concerned about such details. The delegation of authority written about in chapter 6 of Acts makes this clear. This is a condition of laziness on the part of the congregation and is all too pervasive throughout the modern church today.

Many Christians desire to advance spiritually but are unwilling to go through the work to get there. You can't climb a mountain by looking at it.[†] It takes effort and work. The way has its cost, risks, and dangers but the Lord will always be there. In the end, there is great reward. Running the race that Paul discussed throughout his letters requires discipline and work.

Scripture is filled with wonderful promises. Many are conditional—that is, if we fulfill our condition, then Jesus will bring blessings beyond our imagination (1 Corinthians 2:9).

> 14"To the angel of the church in Laodicea write: The Amen, the faithful and true Witness, the Beginning of the creation of God, says this: 15'I know your deeds, that you are neither cold nor hot; I wish that you were cold or hot. 16'So because you are lukewarm, and neither hot nor cold, I will spit you out of My mouth. 17'Because you say, "I am rich, and have become wealthy, and have need of nothing," and you do not know that you are wretched and miserable and poor and blind and naked, 18I advise you to buy from Me gold refined by fire so that you may become rich, and white garments so that you may clothe yourself, and that the shame of your nakedness will not be revealed; and eye salve to anoint your eyes so that you may see. 19'Those whom I love, I reprove and discipline; therefore be zealous

† The book *Hinds Feet on High Places* by Hannah Hurnard is a beautiful allegory dramatizing the spiritual walk with Jesus we all need to pursue.

> and repent. [20]'Behold, I stand at the door and knock; if anyone hears My voice and opens the door, I will come in to him and will dine with him, and he with Me. [21]'He who overcomes, I will grant to him to sit down with Me on My throne, as I also overcame and sat down with My Father on His throne. [22]'He who has an ear, let him hear what the Spirit says to the churches.'"
>
> —Revelation 3:14–22

It can be inferred from the letter to the church in Laodicea that spiritual laziness is the most likely cause of their dismal state. This message comes with a stern warning to those who refuse to repent. They will be utterly rejected by Jesus (v. 16). It has been recognized by many scholars that the church of Laodicea is representative of the present-day church. Whether it does or not is not the issue. It is the spiritual condition of the church that is the issue. The spiritual condition of the present-day church fits the description of the church in Laodicea all too well.

> He who overcomes will thus be clothed in white garments; and I will not erase his name from the book of life, and I will confess his name before My Father and before His angels.
>
> —Revelation 3:5

> My Father, who has given them to Me, is greater than all; and no one is able to snatch them out of the Father's hand.
>
> —John 10:29

> [38]For I am convinced that neither death, nor life, nor angels, nor principalities, nor things present, nor things to come, nor powers, [39]nor height, nor depth, nor any other created thing, will be able to separate us from the love of God, which is in Christ Jesus our Lord.
>
> —Romans 8:38–39

In Revelation 3:5, Jesus makes it clear that he and he alone has the authority to erase or not to erase someone's name from the Book of Life. The verses listed after this make it clear that no *created thing* can separate us from God.

This is a fearful state with consequences that are eternal! None of us can take this lightly. Don't forget that everything we do in this life will determine our condition for all eternity!

Of all the seven churches addressed in Revelation, the church of Laodicea is the only one that did not receive a commendation from Jesus.

Realize there are only two possibilities here.

- If you are accepted by Jesus you go to heaven and live in His presence for all eternity.
- If you are rejected by Jesus you go to hell and eventually the lake of fire for all eternity.

If you try to rationalize away the word of God in an effort to avoid this accountability, you are lazy and you love your sins more than you love God. It is far, far better to repent of your sins and build your relationship with the Holy Spirit than to risk the alternative. The choice is up to you.

Laziness is combated with vision, focus, aggression, and discipline. This requires you to be hard on yourself and to work on it now. Procrastination is not an option. Time is short.

A good start is to get up early enough in the morning to spend time in prayer and Bible reading before taking on other daily responsibilities. Stay away from activities that contribute to laziness. Watching TV is one of the greatest contributors to laziness. Although in moderation watching TV is okay, it should not be allowed to interfere with one's spiritual growth.

Laziness is one of the greatest sins the church needs to repent of today. Observe how many take notes during a sermon or teaching. After a service, ask anyone what the pastor's sermon was about. Most people forget the message before they even get out of the sanctuary. The church leadership is not without blame either. It is their responsibility to effectively teach the church. A boring sermon or one that fails to provide sufficient teaching for the people to grow only exacerbates the problem of laziness.

Apostles, prophets, evangelists, pastors, and teachers are responsible for the preparation of the saints (Ephesians 4:11–12). That preparation involves teaching people to do the things Jesus did so the Great Commission will be fulfilled. The words of the Gospel need to be backed up with power and demonstration of the Holy Spirit. Given the lack of knowledge of these things today, it is absolutely necessary for church leaders to learn to listen to the Holy Spirit—to allow the Holy Spirit to provide revelation into his word and how to put it into action. Relying on the current level of knowledge is not enough to get the job done. Failing to pursue the greater things of God is evidence of laziness.

> [4]And my message and my preaching were not in persuasive words of wisdom, **but in demonstration of the Spirit and of power,** [5]so that your faith would not rest on the wisdom of men, but on the power of God.
>
> —1 Corinthians 2:4–5

Preparation also means assisting those being taught what their spiritual gifts are and helping and guiding them to grow in those areas until they are mature.

Remember what James had to say concerning this responsibility: “Let not many of you become teachers, my brethren, knowing that as such we will incur a stricter judgment” (James 3:1).

In Romans 12:11, we are instructed to be diligent in spirit, serving the Lord, “Not lagging behind in diligence, fervent in spirit, serving the Lord.”

It is only through this attitude and its application that the church, collectively and individually, will grow. *Webster's* defines *diligence* as:

> Steady application in business of any kind; constant effort to accomplish what is undertaken; exertion of body or mind without unnecessary delay or sloth; due attention; industry; assiduity.

In 2 Peter 1:5–11, we see the progression that starts with diligence:

> [5]Now for this very reason also, applying all diligence, in your faith supply moral excellence, and in your moral excellence, knowledge, [6]and in your knowledge, self-control, and in your self-control, perseverance, and in your perseverance, godliness, [7]and in your godliness, brotherly kindness, and in your brotherly kindness, love. [8]For if these qualities are yours and are increasing, they render you neither useless nor unfruitful in the true knowledge of our Lord Jesus Christ. [9]For he who lacks these qualities is blind or short-sighted, having forgotten his purification from his former sins. [10]Therefore, brethren, be all the more diligent to make certain about His calling and choosing you; for as long as you practice these things, you will never stumble; [11]for in this way the entrance into the eternal kingdom of our Lord and Savior Jesus Christ will be abundantly supplied to you.

The results of diligence are a number of invaluable Godly qualities that not only benefit the individual but all those around. Diligence clearly has its eternal benefits as well.

To apply diligence, faith must also be applied. From 2 Peter 1:5–11 above, these qualities are built in the following order:

1. Moral excellence
2. Knowledge

3. Self-control
4. Perseverance
5. Godliness
6. Brotherly kindness
7. Love

And finally, in verse 11, Paul states that accomplishing this work will ensure the entrance into the eternal kingdom of our Lord and Savior Jesus Christ will be abundantly supplied. If you fail to be diligent and fail to work at these qualities, then the only alternative is that the eternal kingdom will either not be supplied or not be supplied abundantly. It is a fearful thing to fall into the hands of the living God!

> [1]For this reason we must pay much closer attention to what we have heard, so that we do not drift away from it. [2]For if the word spoken through angels proved unalterable, and every transgression and disobedience received a just penalty, [3]**how will we escape if we neglect so great a salvation?** After it was at the first spoken through the Lord, it was confirmed to us by those who heard, [4]God also testifying with them, both by signs and wonders and by various miracles and by gifts of the Holy Spirit according to His own will.
>
> —Hebrews 2:1–4

Repentance is not just a feeling. It is a decision followed by an action. Are you willing to let the Holy Spirit bring you to the state of repentance as was defined by Spurgeon?

5.3 The Traditions of Man

There is a great deal of culture and doctrine embedded in the church that has worldly and demonic origins. If the church is to succeed in its God-ordained responsibilities, this worldly culture must be replaced with the culture provided in his word and through a relationship with him. This present-day culture can be called the traditions of man.

One of the most subtle and damaging sins in the church as a whole concerns the traditions of man. Because the traditions of man have the effect of invalidating the power and meaning of God's word, many other sins are tolerated and allowed into the church.

The traditions of man invalidate the word of God. In Matthew 15:2–9, we read:

> 2"Why do Your disciples break the tradition of the elders? For they do not wash their hands when they eat bread." 3And He answered and said to them, "Why do you yourselves transgress the commandment of God for the sake of your tradition? 4For God said, 'HONOR YOUR FATHER AND MOTHER,' and, 'HE WHO SPEAKS EVIL OF FATHER OR MOTHER IS TO BE PUT TO DEATH.' 5"But you say, 'Whoever says to his father or mother, "Whatever I have that would help you has been given to God," 6he is not to honor his father or his mother.' **And by this you invalidated the word of God for the sake of your tradition.** 7"You hypocrites, rightly did Isaiah prophesy of you: 8'THIS PEOPLE HONORS ME WITH THEIR LIPS, BUT THEIR HEART IS FAR AWAY FROM ME. 9BUT IN VAIN DO THEY WORSHIP ME, TEACHING AS DOCTRINES THE PRECEPTS OF MEN.'"

Although circumstances and culture have changed since Jesus spoke these words, human nature has not. If you look around at the church today, there is far more tradition ingrained in the church culture than most realize. Jesus's words are still just as valid today as they were when he spoke them!

We can call the traditions of man in the church denominational and church doctrines. How easy it is to adhere to these doctrines rather than the word of God and at the same time thinking it is all biblical. We are no different than the Pharisees of Jesus's day. In reality, we are worse off today since we have the Holy Spirit and the Pharisees did not. We are more guilty of this sin than the Pharisees!

Many churches and denominations simply rationalize away miracles and various spiritual gifts in general. This doctrine is heresy. It is completely inconsistent with Scripture and serves only to invalidate God's word and excuse their sin and lack of faith. Adhering to such doctrines is to call God a liar and his word, the Bible, a lie. Because these people have refused to believe the Bible, God has largely withdrawn his presence from these churches. The result is there is no power and anointing, and the church is nothing more than a religious social club.

In another example, there are many churches that advertise themselves as "New Testament" churches. To adhere only to the teachings of the New Testament and ignore the Old Testament is heresy. You can't have the New without the Old as the New is founded and builds upon the Old. The New cannot be understood without the knowledge, wisdom, and instruction the Old provides.

A simple case in point is the early church we read about primarily in the book of Acts. At this point in history, what we know as the New Testament today didn't exist. These early Christians only had the Law and the Prophets, or Tanakh. In addition, the early church culture was founded upon Judaism because it was the natural progression of it since Jesus fulfilled the redemption plan. It was several hundred years later that a cultural divide occurred that resulted in the present-day church culture. Look at the early church and you will see how God moved in his people to heal the sick, deliver those in bondage, work myriads of miracles, and advance the church. There is nothing but our sins to prevent the church from making this happening today.

When discussing God's "law," it must be understood that this does not just include the New Testament. All Scripture in the

New Testament is written with the understanding that the reader has a solid understanding of the Old Testament, or Tanakh, and the Mosaic Laws, or Torah, in particular. Those churches who proclaim they are "New Testament" churches are only deceiving themselves into thinking they are more righteous and attractive to the world than those who don't adhere to this false doctrine.

The view that the teaching of the Torah is a collection of burdensome laws is a stand that is born out of ignorance and the spirit of rebellion. Virtually all of the Torah points to Jesus and is for our benefit. It defines the boundaries of behavior we should keep. Many will argue that, as Christians, we have the Holy Spirit and don't need to follow the teachings of the Torah. If this were not so, then God would not have ordained the Torah to be part of the Bible today. Others will quote Matthew 5:17–19:

> 17Do not think that I came to abolish the Law or the Prophets; I did not come to abolish but to fulfill. 18For truly I say to you, until heaven and earth pass away, **not the smallest letter or stroke shall pass from the Law until all is accomplished.** 19Whoever then annuls one of the least of these commandments, and teaches others to do the same, shall be called least in the kingdom of heaven; but whoever keeps and teaches them, he shall be called great in the kingdom of heaven.

Jesus *fulfilled* the Law and the Prophets (Old Testament, or Tanakh), and that is the plan of redemption that was initiated in Genesis 3:15. He *did not* abolish the Law and the Prophets. Therefore, the Law and the Prophets still stand today just as much as it did thousands of years ago. In this passage, Jesus said nothing concerning what it meant by fulfilling the Law and the Prophets. Rather, he focused on the fact that nothing in the Law and the Prophets has been abolished. He also provides a stern warning to those who would teach otherwise. Sadly, there are many today who teach doctrines that are quite contrary to Scripture.

Having said this, much could be written concerning the extent of what we should practice today. This has been debated for generations and the subject is beyond the intent of this book. Suffice it to say, there is a lot more we should be doing when it pertains to keeping his commandments. At a minimum, the holidays and festivals written of in the Torah should be practiced. These are not just empty religious practices. They have the purpose of a continual reminder and education of who Jesus is and of the plan of redemption. Putting this head knowledge into physical action helps to solidify these things in our hearts and minds as well as to build faith (Romans 10:17). Keeping his commandments should be a joy to the believer and not considered burdensome. God's word, in its entirety, is the best source for learning about our Lord and Savior.

The Christian church started as a natural progression of Judaism. It was early in this era that pagan doctrines were allowed to take hold, resulting in a cultural divide that we have with us today. Constantine (272–337) and others during this era are the primary cause of this rift. It is time for the church to take note and return to its roots.

The danger in the false interpretation of Matthew 5:17 is this: Many say that in fulfilling the Law, Jesus did everything so all we need to do is sit back and enjoy the ride to heaven. The extent of this view of fulfillment is such that nothing in the Old Testament is relevant today, and in one sentence of misinterpretation, the Old Testament and the the Torah in particular is abolished from church vocabulary. This, of course, is directly contrary to what Jesus stated in Matthew 5:17. This interpretation is one of the most dangerous, and there are many Scriptures that warn against this.

> You shall not add to the word which I am commanding you, nor take away from it, that you may keep the commandments of the Lord your God which I command you.
>
> —Deuteronomy 4:2

> These are the statutes and the judgments which you shall carefully observe in the land which the LORD, the God of your fathers, has given you to possess as long as you live on the earth.
>
> —Deuteronomy 12:1

> Be careful to listen to all these words which I command you, so that it may be well with you and your sons after you forever, for you will be doing what is good and right in the sight of the LORD your God.
>
> —Deuteronomy 12:28

> Whatever I command you, you shall be careful to do; you shall not add to nor take away from it.
>
> —Deuteronomy 12:32

> [18]For truly I say to you, until heaven and earth pass away, not the smallest letter or stroke shall pass from the Law until all is accomplished. [19]Whoever then annuls one of the least of these commandments, and teaches others to do the same, shall be called least in the kingdom of heaven; but whoever keeps and teaches them, he shall be called great in the kingdom of heaven.
>
> —Matthew 5:18–19

> [18]I testify to everyone who hears the words of the prophecy of this book: if anyone adds to them, God will add to him the plagues which are written in this book; [19]and if anyone takes away from the words of the book of this prophecy, God will take away his part from the tree of life and from the holy city, which are written in this book.
>
> —Revelation 22:18–19

Along with this false doctrine, there are others who refuse to accept their responsibilities because they expect Jesus to return at any moment. They do little more than sit back and wait for his return, thinking there is no sense in wasting effort to accomplish anything. This attitude is indicative of the worthless slave Jesus spoke of in the parable of the talents (Matthew 25:14–30).

Those who teach doctrines that fail to teach the substance of faith or excuse lack of faith ignore priestly responsibilities and many other things of this nature. Such teachers come under the judgment described in the Scriptures above. It is a fearful thing to fall into the hands of the living God (Hebrews 10:31). We must all be careful to take God at his word and obey it with all diligence. Christianity is not a hobby.

> [44]For this reason you also must be ready; for the Son of Man is coming at an hour when you do not think He will. [45]Who then is the faithful and sensible slave whom his master put in charge of his household to give them their food at the proper time? [46]Blessed is that slave whom his master finds so doing when he comes.
>
> —Matthew 24:44–46

Biblical prophecies are being fulfilled around the world at an unprecedented rate, but we simply do not know when he will return. There is a clear benefit in knowing the signs of the times, but our primary focus should be on being ready. Until that hour, we need to be busy fulfilling our mission.

> Be diligent to present yourself approved to God as a workman who does not need to be ashamed, accurately handling the word of truth.
>
> —2 Timothy 2:15

It is indicated in 2 Timothy 2:15 this work takes education and application. This, along with many other Scriptures, indicates that we as Christians have responsibilities to fulfill. As was said earlier, most churches today amount to nothing more than religious social clubs. The church is asleep and the world around them is going to hell, but no one seems to notice or care enough to take their God-given responsibilities seriously enough to do something about it.

> [16]**All** Scripture is inspired by God and profitable for teaching, for reproof, for correction, for training in righteousness; [17]so that the man of God may be adequate, equipped for every good work.
>
> —2 Timothy 3:16–17

Notice that the first word states *all*, not *some*, Scripture. At the time Paul wrote this, there was no New Testament as we know it today. Paul was referring to the the Old Testament. It is therefore imperative that we put our primary focus on the Old Testament, and the Torah in particular, and to do so without ignoring the New Testament. Scripture must be studied and kept *in its entirety*, not just portions taken out of context to suit someone's or some church's doctrine (tradition).

People by nature enjoy traditions. Traditions are a familiar pattern of behavior that are generally enjoyable. Traditions will eventually become an integral part of a culture. It makes much more sense to enjoy the traditions and practices God has provided in his word because they have a distinct purpose and are, by definition, of Godly origin. They not only edify but educate. They are designed to keep one focused on their relationship with him. Man's traditions will inevitably have the effect of invalidating Scripture.

It is imperative that all of us be diligent about our relationship with Jesus. Because of sin, repentance and the daily pursuit of holiness and righteousness is a requirement, not an option.

The importance of the following steps cannot be emphasized enough. In a nutshell, they describe the process of how to get to the level where all of us need to be so God's will is fulfilled in the church. These steps are not a one-time process. They need to be repeated as often as necessary because of our sinful nature.

1. Repentance removes the wall between you and God (Isaiah 59:2).
2. Humility opens the door to the Holy Spirit and to answered prayer.
3. Prayer builds your relationship with Jesus.
4. Building your relationship with Jesus builds faith.
5. Faith comes by hearing and hearing by the word of God (Romans 10:17, Galatians 3:5). Faith comes through the education and knowledge of his word.
6. Faith is built with prayer, prayer, prayer, and practice, practice, practice (James 2:17).
7. Faith brings the anointing and empowerment from the Holy Spirit to go out and make disciple of all the nations (Matthew 28:18–20). Miracles will be worked through you wherever you go. The glory of God will rest on you to a degree beyond your comprehension.

It must be made clear here that although prayer is a powerful mechanism through which we accomplish many things, it does not nor is it intended to supersede one's relationship with Jesus. That relationship with him must transcend everything else. Your relationship with Jesus should be the primary focus of your life. Although this statement has been made multiple times already, its importance cannot be understated. It is important to state this repeatedly.

> [11]"For I know the plans that I have for you," declares the Lord, "plans for welfare and not for calamity to give you a future and a hope. [12]Then you will call upon Me and come and pray to Me, and I will listen to you. [13]You will seek Me and find Me when you search for Me with all your heart."
>
> —Jeremiah 29:11–13

5.4 The Deceptive Nature of Wealth

Once people discover the wonderful things God has for them, there is a tendency to use prayer for selfish gain and consequently lose sight of their mission. This is a trap. The "prosperity doctrine" preached in a number of churches is clear evidence that many have fallen into this trap. The subject of money is a stumbling block to many people. Wealth can be deceptive and can lead one to take their eyes off their Lord and Savior.

There is nothing wrong with wealth and possessions. It is the love of these things that gets people in trouble. It is God's desire to bless his people and he often does so in miraculous ways. However, there is so much more he wants to give us. I have personally known people whom God blessed with wealth but, unfortunately, they were not able to deal with it properly and eventually fell into great ruin. On the other hand, those who were prepared to receive wealth did well and continued to prosper once it came their way. This also points to the need for wisdom.

We all need to have an income to provide for our families and to meet the obligations we have. Scripture is clear that our Lord will take care of us. Perhaps the most notable passage is found in the Sermon on the Mount in Matthew 6:24–34:

> [24]No one can serve two masters; for either he will hate the
> one and love the other, or he will be devoted to one and
> despise the other. You cannot serve God and wealth. [25]For
> this reason I say to you, do not be worried about your life,
> as to what you will eat or what you will drink; nor for your
> body, as to what you will put on. Is not life more than food,
> and the body more than clothing? [26]Look at the birds of
> the air, that they do not sow, nor reap nor gather into barns,
> and yet your heavenly Father feeds them. Are you not
> worth much more than they? [27]And who of you by being
> worried can add a single hour to his life? [28]And why are
> you worried about clothing? Observe how the lilies of the
> field grow; they do not toil nor do they spin, [29]yet I say to

> you that not even Solomon in all his glory clothed himself like one of these. 30But if God so clothes the grass of the field, which is alive today and tomorrow is thrown into the furnace, will He not much more clothe you? You of little faith! 31Do not worry then, saying, 'What will we eat? ' or 'What will we drink? ' or 'What will we wear for clothing? ' 32For the Gentiles eagerly seek all these things; for your heavenly Father knows that you need all these things. 33**But seek first His kingdom and His righteousness, and all these things will be added to you.** 34So do not worry about tomorrow; for tomorrow will care for itself. Each day has enough trouble of its own.
>
> —Matthew 6:24–34

> 3Trust in the LORD and do good; Dwell in the land and cultivate faithfulness. 4Delight yourself in the LORD; And He will give you the desires of your heart. 5Commit your way to the LORD, Trust also in Him, and He will do it. 6He will bring forth your righteousness as the light And your judgment as the noonday. 7Rest in the LORD and wait patiently for Him; Do not fret because of him who prospers in his way, Because of the man who carries out wicked schemes. 8Cease from anger and forsake wrath; Do not fret; it leads only to evildoing. 9For evildoers will be cut off, But those who wait for the LORD, they will inherit the land. 10Yet a little while and the wicked man will be no more; And you will look carefully for his place and he will not be there. 11But the humble will inherit the land And will delight themselves in abundant prosperity.
>
> —Psalms 37:3–11

It is imperative that we seek him first and foremost. It is only when that relationship with Jesus transcends the desire for worldly things that one is truly in a position to be able to receive wealth and prosperity. When you reach this point, only then will you see these things in their proper perspective. Many may agree with this because the head knowledge is simple. Self dies hard so it can be much more difficult to get it into the heart. For most, this must be experienced.

> [3]You ask and do not receive, because you ask with wrong motives, so that you may spend it on your pleasures. [4]You adulteresses, do you not know that friendship with the world is hostility toward God? Therefore whoever wishes to be a friend of the world makes himself an enemy of God.
>
> —James 4:3–4

If we don't have our priorities and motives right, Scripture is clear that this is adulterous. No one is perfect and we all fail (Romans 3:23). Don't forget that he created us all. He understands us better than we understand ourselves. Very few people have these priorities in perfect order. Our Lord Jesus has promised to take care of us. This is without question. Of course, if someone does something foolish, they should expect to experience the consequences of it. In all these things, we should press toward that upward call (Philippians 3:14). In so doing, remember what the Apostle Paul wrote in 2 Timothy 2:13: "If we are faithless, He remains faithful, for He cannot deny Himself."

Our Lord will make a way where there seems to be no way! Praise God!

Notes

1. *Trust And Obey*, Text: John H. Sammis (1846–1919), Music: Daniel B. Towner (1850-1919), public domain.

God's Judgment

God's judgment will come upon those who fail to live up to his expectations. We must all keep in mind that our Lord is righteous, just, reasonable, loving, holy, and so on. He is perfect in all his ways. Because he is perfect, the boundaries between all of his attributes do not change as they do with people.

Although there are many places throughout the Bible that discuss the blessings of obedience and the curses of disobedience, the focus here is primarily on Matthew 25. This chapter is important because of its applicability in these last days.

It is made clear in 2 Corinthians 5:10 that this is an individual judgment and that Christians will be judged for both the good and the bad. We are each individually responsible for our actions in this life.

> [26]For if we go on sinning willfully after receiving the knowledge of the truth, there no longer remains a sacrifice for sins, [27]but a terrifying expectation of judgment and THE FURY OF A FIRE WHICH WILL CONSUME THE ADVERSARIES. [28]Anyone who has set aside the Law of Moses dies without mercy on the testimony of two or three witnesses. [29]How much severer punishment do you think he will deserve who has trampled under foot the Son of God, and has regarded as unclean the blood of the covenant by which he was sanctified, and has insulted the Spirit of grace? [30]For we know Him who said, "VENGEANCE IS MINE, I WILL REPAY." And

> again, "THE LORD WILL JUDGE HIS PEOPLE." [31]It is a terrifying thing to fall into the hands of the living God.
>
> —Hebrews 10:26–31

Knowing these things, how much more diligent we should be in our relationship with him! How much more so should we all pray to overcome the sins that so easily beset us!

> [1]Therefore, since we have so great a cloud of witnesses surrounding us, let us also lay aside every encumbrance and the sin which so easily entangles us, and let us run with endurance the race that is set before us, [2]fixing our eyes on Jesus, the author and perfecter of faith, who for the joy set before Him endured the cross, despising the shame, and has sat down at the right hand of the throne of God.
>
> —Hebrews 12:1–2

In Matthew 25:1–30, there are two parables. The first, in verses 1 to 13, is the parable of the ten virgins with the lamps of oil. The second, in verses 14 to 30, is the parable of the talents. Both parables are linked even though they are different stories. The first describes the nature of the judgment and the second describes the conditions that bring about judgment.

In studying these parables, it must be kept in mind that our Lord is not arbitrary in anything he does or says, whether he speaks plainly or in a parable. Revelation on a specific passage is the work of the Holy Spirit and not the subject of one's own interpretation or opinion. There may be any number of revelations from the Holy Spirit based on a given parable and all may have valid application. This is the beauty of his word in that a single parable can have many diverse applications.

Both of these parables present the expectation of a fearful judgment upon those who fail to attend to their relationship with Jesus. Many Christians today don't take their relationship with him or the possibility of such a judgment seriously. Indeed, many church and denominational doctrines fail to appropriately address this issue. Whether you agree with this theology or not is not the issue. Your relationship with Jesus and where it is going is the issue. If your choice is to keep one foot in the world and one foot in the church, then you are treading on thin ice. Are you simply seeking fire insurance or do you want to build your relationship with him and fulfill his commandments?

> [14]"Now, therefore, fear the LORD and serve Him in sincerity and truth; and put away the gods which your fathers served beyond the River and in Egypt, and serve the LORD. [15]"If it is disagreeable in your sight to serve the LORD, choose for yourselves today whom you will serve: whether the gods which your fathers served which were beyond the River, or the gods of the Amorites in whose land you are living; but as for me and my house, we will serve the LORD."
>
> —Joshua 24:14–15

6.1 The Parable of the Ten Virgins

> Then the kingdom of heaven will be comparable to ten virgins, who took their lamps and went out to meet the bridegroom.
>
> —Matthew 25:1

> Five of them were foolish, and five were prudent.
>
> —Matthew 25:2

> For when the foolish took their lamps, they took no oil with them.
>
> —Matthew 25:3

> But the prudent took oil in flasks along with their lamps.
>
> —Matthew 25:4

> Now while the bridegroom was delaying, they all got drowsy and began to sleep.
>
> —Matthew 25:5

> But at midnight there was a shout, "Behold, the bridegroom! Come out to meet him."
>
> —Matthew 25:6

> Then all those virgins rose and trimmed their lamps.
>
> —Matthew 25:7

> The foolish said to the prudent, "Give us some of your oil, for our lamps are going out."
>
> —Matthew 25:8

> But the prudent answered, "No, there will not be enough for us and you too; go instead to the dealers and buy some for yourselves."
>
> —Matthew 25:9

> And while they were going away to make the purchase, the bridegroom came, and those who were ready went in with him to the wedding feast; and the door was shut.
>
> —Matthew 25:10

> Later the other virgins also came, saying, "Lord, lord, open up for us."
>
> —Matthew 25:11

> But he answered, "Truly I say to you, I do not know you."
>
> —Matthew 25:12

> Be on the alert then, for you do not know the day nor the hour.
>
> —Matthew 25:13

Verse 1 establishes who our Lord is speaking about. This is a parable about the kingdom of heaven. It is not talking about the kingdom of darkness, the kingdom of this world, those who are not saved, or the domain of the devil. The kingdom of heaven may be considered the subjects of God's kingdom taken collectively. The kingdom of heaven is the church.

The ten virgins represent Christians. They do not represent any other. In Greek, the word *parthenos* for "virgin" is from the root for "separated." It is evident from many scriptures that we are to be separate from the world.

It is important to note that Jesus stated *twice* who he is speaking about. This fact is important and should leave no doubt in the reader's mind. He is speaking about the church both collectively and to us as individuals. The fact that a subject matter is addressed multiple times in Scripture like this is cause for us to take due notice of it and to treat it with the greatest level of importance.

Each of the virgins had a lamp. The lamp itself represents the physical body, and the oil, representative of the Holy Spirit, is contained within.

Each of these virgins went out to meet the bridegroom. It is clear that they knew and were expecting him to arrive, otherwise there would be no reason to go out to meet him.

Verse 2 tells that five of these ten virgins were wise and five were foolish—that's 50 percent wise and 50 percent foolish. This 50 percent factor is found elsewhere in Scripture (Matthew 24:30–41 and Luke 17:34–36). This indicates that *only* 50 percent of the church will be ready for Jesus's return and, hence, only 50 percent will be taken! Oh that we would pay attention to his word and be ready for his return! Again, understand that God is not arbitrary about anything he says or does.

Verses 3 and 4 tells us that the foolish took their lamps but took no oil with them. The wise took oil in flasks with them. The foolish represent those Christians that, spiritually speaking, live payday to payday. These are people who go to church to just get their "batteries recharged," those who treat church as a social club. They are mediocre Christians. The wise are those who actively pursue the things of God. They are filled with the Holy Spirit.

They are those who are used by God to save the lost, deliver those in bondage, work miracles of healing, signs, and wonders, and so on. The wise are people who are fulfilling the Great Commission. They are reproducing. They are making disciples. Those disciples are then going out and doing the same things.

Verse 5 is where we see that the bridegroom was delayed. The church got drowsy and began to sleep. We know from the letters to the seven churches in Revelation chapter 3 that we live in this age. This is the age of the church of Laodicea. The church, to a great extent, is asleep. The church is not awake and alert to the world events that are fulfilling biblical prophesy right in front of their eyes. Although many Christians see the signs of the time, they do nothing to be ready. The church is not the moving force in society that it once was. Tragically, the church of today is not ready to meet Jesus. They don't even notice the moving of the Holy Spirit to repent of their sins and prepare for his return to take his bride. They hear words spoken that God wants to bring revival but they do nothing except sit around and wait for something to happen.

> But prove yourselves doers of the word, and not merely hearers who delude themselves.
>
> —James 1:22

In verse 6, there is an announcement that the bridegroom (Jesus) is coming and that the church should go out to meet him. This seems to indicate that:

1. Some form of announcement from heaven will be made. It is likely this announcement will come in the form of an event spoken of in other Scriptures.
2. There will only be a very short period of time between the announcement and the arrival of the bridegroom.

In verse 7, here the entire church arises and trims their lamps. The act of trimming is done so a lamp will provide the best light.

From a spiritual standpoint, the act of trimming is an act of repentance and prayer for forgiveness of any remaining sins and for the infilling of the Spirit. Those who are already filled with the Spirit will be fine. Those who are not filled with the Spirit will not be able to complete this task. Again, there will only be a very short period of time to complete this.

The foolish have run out of oil in verses 8 and 9. The reason the wise cannot provide any of their oil is because it will take time. It will take work to minister to the foolish. It will drain them spiritually at a time when they can least afford it. The wise tell the foolish to go out to the dealers to buy some. This "purchasing" is an act that requires them to make payment for something. That payment is our self, our will, our lives. We must die to self and allow Jesus to sit on the throne of our lives. Through this daily surrender, prayer, repentance, asking forgiveness, and ministering to others, we become filled with the Holy Spirit. It is through these activities one's relationship with Jesus is built. All of this takes time and effort and the foolish are out of time.

While the foolish were out working on the process of being filled with the Holy Spirit, the bridegroom arrived in verse 10. Those who were ready went with him. In the words of one commentator[1] those who are ready, are ready "through being clothed with the wedding garment, washed in the blood of Christ, being regenerated and sanctified, and having the oil of grace in their hearts, a spiritual knowledge of Christ, faith in Him, and interest in Him: such are ready for every good work, and to give a reason of their faith and hope, to confess Christ, and suffer for his sake; and are ready for death and eternity, and to meet the bridegroom, and for the marriage of the Lamb, to enter into the new Jerusalem." The foolish were not there. These are those who hold to a form of righteousness but deny its power. They were left behind. The door to heaven and the wedding feast of the Lamb is shut.

Verses 11 through 13 shows that when the foolish arrived, they knocked on the doors of heaven asking to be let in. In verse 12, Jesus issues a most alarming statement. He says, "Truly I say to you, I do not know you." Whether we think Jesus will return for us now or in a thousand years, we do not know. We are therefore instructed to be ready at all times. Knowing the surpassing value of knowing Jesus, why wouldn't any born-again Christian want to know him even better? Those Christians who don't know the love of Christ that surpasses all knowledge, who are not filled up to all the fullness of God, or know the fellowship of his sufferings being conformed to his death, simply don't know him. It is this intimate relationship that Jesus wants with us. It is this relationship that surpasses any human description. It is this relationship that will make the things of this world to be viewed as filth in comparison.

Since it is evident this parable is speaking of the church, what kind of lives ought we be living? What is to become of those who hear the words "Truly I say to you, I do not know you"? Scripture does not say these people are not saved or will lose their salvation. Nevertheless, they will likely pay a terrible price for their mediocre walk with God.

No one can afford to live a mediocre life. It is unacceptable. Jesus died on the cross for us. He paid a terrible price for our sins. We have all eternity before us. In view of these things, what is hindering you from pushing forward? How can we neglect so great a salvation? How can we take this salvation with such a cavalier attitude. Indeed, to do so is sin. It is to spit on the cross on which Jesus died.

If only 50 percent of the church will be considered acceptable to our Lord and make it to the wedding supper of the Lamb, what kind of lives should we be living? What kind of priority should we be placing on our walk with him? Are the worldly things you deal with every day more important to you than your salvation? Your actions speak louder than words!

In Philippians 3, Paul stresses we are to "press" forward. The word *press* is extremely important here. Press means:

1. To urge with force or weight; a word of extensive use, denoting the application of any power, physical or moral, to something that is to be moved or affected.
2. To drive with violence; to hurry; as, to press a horse in motion, or in a race.

And then again, in Philippians 2:12, "So then, my beloved, just as you have always obeyed, not as in my presence only, but now much more in my absence, work out your salvation with fear and trembling."

You have no excuse. God has given us an incredible store of resources today, starting with the Bible. The internet is tremendously valuable as a resource and can provide free materials and software that only a few years ago were only available at significant cost, and likely only found in a pastor's library. The church is without excuse. Today is the day of salvation. Everyone must repent of our sins now. Get your eyes off the things of the world. Focus on your Lord Jesus Christ. The things of this world, the wealth, houses, whatever, are nothing compared to knowing Jesus. Build your relationship with him. When you do this and experience him, nothing else will matter in comparison. You will enter into that promised rest. It is beautiful beyond description. When you accomplish these things:

- It is then that miracles, healing, signs, and wonders will be manifested through you.
- It is then that the world will take notice and seek you to bless you and get what you have.
- It is then that you will store up treasures in heaven that cannot rust or be stolen.
- It is then that your joy will be full.

The spiritual warfare that we all go through now is not an end in itself, it is a means to an end.

There are those who will say, "Well, I don't agree with your theology and this is why…"

My response will be, "Oh, so it's easier for you to argue theology than repent of your sins? Truly you love your sins more than you love God."

There are those who will say, "Well, I get up at four every morning and spend two hours praying and reading the Bible, and I spend three days a week fasting. I do this and that."

My response to you is, "Oh, so you would rather justify yourself than repent of your sins? Truly you love your sins more than you love God."

Some will cite John 10:27–29, which says,

> [27]"My sheep hear My voice, and I know them, and they follow Me; [28]and I give eternal life to them, and they will never perish; and no one will snatch them out of My hand. [29]"My Father, who has given them to Me, is greater than all; and no one is able to snatch them out of the Father's hand.

This is often used as justification for the doctrine of the eternal security of the believer. Without looking any further than just this verse, Jesus stated that no one is able to snatch them out of the Father's hand. He is speaking of someone *other than himself* and that can only be a created being such as an angel, a person, or a demon. Jesus's statement reserves the right for himself to remove someone from his hand by himself and no other.

> He who overcomes will thus be clothed in white garments; and I will not erase his name from the book of life, and I will confess his name before My Father and before His angels.
>
> —Revelation 3:5

Revelation 3:5 makes it clear that Jesus has the authority to erase or not to erase someone's name from the Book of Life. Don't forget what Revelation 3:16 says: "So because you are lukewarm, and neither hot nor cold, I will spit you out of My mouth."

Those who are lukewarm will be rejected by Jesus. Remember, God created us with a free will. This free will never goes away and you still have the right to choose whom you will follow. Scripture is clear that there are people who have turned away (Matthew 13:20–21; Mark 4:5–6; Luke 8:14; Acts 7:39) and "gone back to Egypt."

Why is it easier for you to make an excuse of some form rather than repent of your sins? It is because you love your sins more than you love God. "If you love Me, you will keep My commandments" (John 14:15).

As was said earlier, there is no excuse. All of us have the flesh and the world to deal with so we must be diligent with repentance and seeking forgiveness from our Father in heaven through Jesus Christ our Savior. All of us must be diligent about pressing forward in our walk with Jesus. We are to be a holy people. This is not an option for the Christian. It takes work.

We all have a narrow path to walk. We cannot afford to be distracted to the left or the right. We must keep our eyes focused on our Lord Jesus Christ. If we veer either way, we will be snagged by the things of the world. These things will do nothing but cause us injury and hinder our progress. We are to run the race in order to win the prize. We are not in competition with each other. We are in competition with the flesh and the things of the world—the lust of the flesh, the lust of the eyes, and the boastful pride of life. The race is to overcome these things and to be a righteous and holy people that our Lord will be pleased with. It is those who are running this race, regardless of their present condition, who will cross the finish line and win.

Where do you stand? What are you going to do about it? What is your choice in view of all eternity set before you?

Will you be like those Jesus spoke of in Luke 14:16–24, who made all sorts of excuses and thus failed to enter in?

6.2 The Parable of the Talents

The next section in Matthew 25 is the parable of the talents.

> For it is just like a man about to go on a journey, who called his own slaves, and entrusted his possessions to them.
>
> —Matthew 25:14

> And to one he gave five talents, to another, two, and to another, one, each according to his own ability; and he went on his journey.
>
> —Matthew 25:15

> Immediately the one who had received the five talents went and traded with them, and gained five more talents.
>
> —Matthew 25:16

> In the same manner the one who had received the two talents gained two more.
>
> —Matthew 25:17

> But he who received the one talent went away and dug in the ground, and hid his master's money.
>
> —Matthew 25:18

> Now after a long time the master of those slaves came and settled accounts with them.
>
> —Matthew 25:19

> And the one who had received the five talents came up and brought five more talents, saying, "Master, you entrusted five talents to me; see, I have gained five more talents."
>
> —Matthew 25:20

His master said to him, "Well done, good and faithful slave; you were faithful with a few things, I will put you in charge of many things, enter into the joy of your master."

—Matthew 25:21

The one also who had received the two talents came up and said, "Master, you entrusted to me two talents; see, I have gained two more talents."

—Matthew 25:22

His master said to him, "Well done, good and faithful slave; you were faithful with a few things, I will put you in charge of many things; enter into the joy of your master."

—Matthew 25:23

And the one also who had received the one talent came up and said, "Master, I knew you to be a hard man, reaping where you did not sow, and gathering where you scattered no seed."

—Matthew 25:24

"And I was afraid, and went away and hid your talent in the ground; see, you have what is yours."

—Matthew 25:25

But his master answered and said to him, "You wicked, lazy slave, you knew that I reap where I did not sow, and gather where I scattered no seed."

—Matthew 25:26

"Then you ought to have put my money in the bank, and on my arrival I would have received my money back with interest."

—Matthew 25:27

> "Therefore take away the talent from him, and give it to the one who has the ten talents."
>
> —Matthew 25:28

> "For to everyone who has shall more be given, and he shall have an abundance; but from the one who does not have, even what he does have shall be taken away."
>
> —Matthew 25:29

> "And cast out the worthless slave into the outer darkness; in that place there shall be weeping and gnashing of teeth."
>
> —Matthew 25:30

In this parable, we have three categories of people.

1. A servant who was given five talents and earned five more.
2. A servant who was given two talents and earned two more.
3. A servant who was given one talent and buried it out of fear of his master.

All of these servants were given talents according to their abilities. All of them had equal opportunities to bring increase. All were servants of the same master.

The third servant recognized some important and deep understanding of the nature of God. The devil does not have this understanding nor can he imitate it. This parable is not talking about the unsaved, it is about Christians.

The demise of the third and unfaithful slave is fearful. It is so horrible it may seem that this one never new Jesus as Lord and Savior. But in order to be consistent with other Scriptures, it seems that he did. Or did he not know God? One could also argue that if he truly did know God, then he would have known his true nature rather than seeing him as a "hard man." Clearly, all the perceived characteristics this slave had are contrary to Jesus's true character. There is a dividing line here that only God can determine. We would all do well to steer clear of this precarious situation and be as productive with the gifts God has given us as possible!

How many people in the churches today pretend to know him, pretend to have faith in him, yet do not follow his basic commandments? John 14:15 says, "If you love Me, you will keep My commandments." How many are hiding the gifts God has given? If you are not actively pushing forward, you are in danger of a terrible end.

God's warnings to us don't stop here. Lets look at the letter to the church in Laodicea from Revelation 3:14–22 again. This is often recognized as representing the apostate church of today.

> 14"'To the angel of the church in Laodicea write: The Amen, the faithful and true Witness, the Beginning of the creation of God, says this: 15'I know your deeds, that you are neither cold nor hot; I wish that you were cold or hot. 16'So because you are lukewarm, and neither hot nor cold, I will spit you out of My mouth. 17'Because you say, "I am rich, and have become wealthy, and have need of nothing," and you do not know that you are wretched and miserable and poor and blind and naked, 18I advise you to buy from Me gold refined by fire so that you may become rich, and white garments so that you may clothe yourself, and that the shame of your nakedness will not be revealed; and eye salve to anoint your eyes so that you may see. 19'Those whom I love, I reprove and discipline; therefore be zealous and repent. 20'Behold, I stand at the door and knock; if anyone hears My voice and opens the door, I will come in to him and will dine with him, and he with Me. 21'He who overcomes, I will grant to him to sit down with Me on My throne, as I also overcame and sat down with My Father on His throne. 22'He who has an ear, let him hear what the Spirit says to the churches.'"

The focus here is the lukewarmness of the church. It is sadly apparent that the church of today fits this description all too well.

The thought of being spewed out of the mouth of our Lord and Savior because of the failure to grow is horrible and fearful. It is an act of complete and utter rejection by our Lord. The only reason people fail is because they love their sins more than they love God.

Sin is the worst form of insanity. We can see it outlined in chapter 10 of the book of Hebrews:

> [26]For if we go on sinning willfully after receiving the knowledge of the truth, there no longer remains a sacrifice for sins, [27]but a certain terrifying expectation of judgment, and THE FURY OF A FIRE WHICH WILL CONSUME THE ADVERSARIES. [28]Anyone who has set aside the Law of Moses dies without mercy on the testimony of two or three witnesses. [29]How much severer punishment do you think he will deserve who has trampled under foot the Son of God, and has regarded as unclean the blood of the covenant by which he was sanctified, and has insulted the Spirit of grace? [30]For we know Him who said, "VENGEANCE IS MINE, I WILL REPAY." And again, "THE LORD WILL JUDGE HIS PEOPLE." [31]It is a terrifying thing to fall into the hands of the living God.
>
> —Hebrews 10:26–31

Indeed, we have all sinned willfully. We will all suffer loss on judgment day. Nevertheless, we must look forward and not back. We must all press forward. We must take the Bible seriously. The word of God must become our life-blood. We must live it, eat it, and love it. This book holds the keys to life and death. It is critically important that we put it into practice in our daily lives. Even though we have repeatedly fallen, let us not lose heart but endure to the end.

And then in Hebrews 10:35–38, we learn:

> [35]Therefore, do not throw away your confidence, which has a great reward. [36]For you have need of endurance, so

> that when you have done the will of God, you may receive what was promised. [37]FOR YET IN A VERY LITTLE WHILE, HE WHO IS COMING WILL COME, AND WILL NOT DELAY. [38]BUT MY RIGHTEOUS ONE SHALL LIVE BY FAITH; AND IF HE SHRINKS BACK, MY SOUL HAS NO PLEASURE IN HIM.

The word *confidence* in verse 35 is important. *Webster* defines confidence as "a trusting, or reliance; an assurance of mind or firm belief in the integrity, stability or veracity of another, or in the truth and reality of a fact."

It carries with it a degree of boldness. We are to have a holy confidence and boldness in prayer, free from a servile and bashful spirit. The foundation of our confidence and boldness is faith. Therefore, let us not hesitate in pursuing righteousness, holiness, and victory. Gaining these things is a process, a path, that we must be actively pursuing. This confidence also speaks of the level of relationship with Jesus. It is to be frank, open, bold, with courage. Confidence accompanied with works is the evidence of faith (James 2:26). "However, when the Son of Man comes, will He find faith on the earth?" (Luke 18:8b).

As Paul says in the book of Philippians:

> [13]Brethren, I do not regard myself as having laid hold of it yet; but one thing I do: forgetting what lies behind and reaching forward to what lies ahead, [14]I press on toward the goal for the prize of the upward call of God in Christ Jesus.
>
> —Philippians 3:13–14

It is abundantly clear throughout Scripture that our Lord has given us everything we need to excel and be victorious. In the letter to the church of Laodicea, it is clear we have a way out. We do not need to follow the crowd. Jesus advises us to buy gold refined by fire from him.

What is this gold refined by fire? The gold is the substance of one's relationship with Jesus. The evidence of this is the fruit of the Spirit as described in Galatians 5:22–23:

> [22]But the fruit of the Spirit is love, joy, peace, patience, kindness, goodness, faithfulness, [23]gentleness, self-control; against such things there is no law.

The refining by fire represents the efforts, trails, and tribulations we go through to facilitate our growth discussed in James 1:2–4:

> [2]Consider it all joy, my brethren, when you encounter various trials, [3]knowing that the testing of your faith produces endurance. [4]And let endurance have its perfect result, so that you may be perfect and complete, lacking in nothing.

Where you are is important, but it is not as important as where you are going! Push toward the upward call of God in Christ Jesus!

It is so appropriate that Paul wrote in Ephesians 3:14–21,

> [14]For this reason, I bow my knees before the Father, [15]from whom every family in heaven and on earth derives its name, [16]that He would grant you, according to the riches of His glory, to be strengthened with power through His Spirit in the inner man; [17]so that Christ may dwell in your hearts through faith; and that you, being rooted and grounded in love, [18]may be able to comprehend with all the saints what is the breadth and length and height and depth, [19]and to know the love of Christ which surpasses knowledge, that you may be filled up to all the fullness of God. [20]Now to Him who is able to do exceeding abundantly beyond all that we ask or think, according to the power that works within us, [21]to Him be the glory in the church and in Christ Jesus to all generations forever and ever. Amen.

The door to victory is open wide. There is nothing but your own decisions keeping you from entering in.

> [1]Therefore, since we have so great a cloud of witnesses surrounding us, let us also lay aside every encumbrance and the sin which so easily entangles us, and let us run with endurance the race that is set before us, [2]fixing our eyes on Jesus, the author and perfecter of faith, who for the joy set before Him endured the cross, despising the shame, and has sat down at the right hand of the throne of God.
>
> —Hebrews 12:1–2

Notes

1. John Gill's Exposition of the Entire Bible, public domain, 1748–1763, 1809

Who You Are in Jesus Christ

Before you can be effective in prayer, you need to know more about who you are in Jesus Christ. Most of us have a basic knowledge of this, but we will find out that in most cases, this basic knowledge is insufficient. It is the devil that deceives Christians into believing they are powerless and without authority. Unfortunately, the devil has lulled the church into a false sense of security. He has deceived many that being spiritually lazy is not only acceptable but the right thing to do. This philosophy is usually based on the lie that states that since Jesus did everything, we don't need to do anything but sit back, relax, and wait for Jesus's return. That, coupled with the spirit of entertainment (and others), has led to the result of the church being powerless today.

Other than spiritual laziness which was addressed earlier, much of the present state of the church today is caused by lack of knowledge. If the knowledge of who we are through Jesus Christ, what our responsibilities are, and how to carry out those responsibilities was present in the church today, our society would be much different, and better. Because of this lack of knowledge, the church has largely lost sight of its mission and how to fulfill it.

> Therefore My people go into exile for their lack of knowledge; And their honorable men are famished, And their multitude is parched with thirst.
>
> —Isaiah 5:13

> My people are destroyed for lack of knowledge. Because you have rejected knowledge, I also will reject you from being My priest. Since you have forgotten the law of your God, I also will forget your children.
>
> —Hosea 4:6

It should be clear from the above verses that the consequences of the lack of knowledge are grave. It is everyone's responsibility to gain knowledge. As Christians, we are expected to be a priestly nation. Attaining to the office of a priest requires knowledge of his word and all that goes with it (faith, miracles, etc.). This knowledge does not necessarily need to come from pastors and teachers, although it is their responsibility to provide this teaching. Remember, our Father has provided the Holy Spirit as our helper. It is the Holy Spirit that teaches us in all things. Knowledge is so lacking among people today the only choice (and it is a good one) is to learn to rely on and listen to the Holy Spirit. Even though this is something that we should be doing anyway, the need today is that much more pressing.

> But the Helper, the Holy Spirit, whom the Father will send in My name, **He will teach you all things**, and bring to your **remembrance all that I said to you**.
>
> —John 14:26

> As for you, the anointing which you received from Him abides in you, and you have no need for anyone to teach you; but as **His anointing teaches you about all things**, and is true and is not a lie, and just as it has taught you, you abide in Him.
>
> —1 John 2:27

Most people have the tendency to look to other people for knowledge. Learning how to listen to the Holy Spirit is accomplished largely by building their relationship with the Holy

Spirit through prayer and unfortunately few have endeavored to do this.

This teaching (revelation) from the Holy Spirit will come easier than you think. Be aware that *any* revelation you may think you receive must be filtered through the Bible and the Holy Spirit (2 Corinthians 10:5). The devil is very crafty and makes every attempt to deceive God's people. Learning the voice of the Holy Spirit comes with building your relationship with him, and this comes through prayer. This is a process that goes forward a step at a time. Be diligent to press forward and at the same time allow the Holy Spirit to be your guide, for if you try to get ahead too fast you will likely make many more mistakes. Just as with a child that grows into an adult, growing spiritually is a process. As 1 John 2:27 says, it is imperative that we abide in him. Backsliding is not an option. In time, this will become relatively effortless as you learn to recognize the voice of the Holy Spirit and the lies of the devil.

As an example, I attended a seminar on prophecy several years ago. It was open to anyone who wanted to attend and there were around a hundred people in the audience. The teacher had each of us pick someone we didn't know and prophecy to them. We were then to trade places and repeat it. This caught me off guard. My mind was blank and I felt uncomfortable being put in this situation. Being put on the spot like this and having only the Holy Spirit to trust to provide a word proved to be an amazing experience. Some very positive and interesting words came out of this exercise for the whole group. A key factor to keep in mind is that the Holy Spirit was there as an *active participant* to teach his people how to listen to him.

Let's briefly examine a few of the attributes of what it means to be one of his people. Perhaps the best analogy is to compare this with an earthly kingdom, such as was found in Europe centuries ago. A king was considered the absolute ruler of his domain. All others were subservient to him. The king's children, his princes and princesses, carried the same power and authority as the king since they were part of the royal bloodline. They commanded the same level of authority, power, respect, and honor as their father, the king. Any violation or offense against them had the potential of dire consequences. The children of the king also had responsibilities by virtue of their position. They are to carry out the wishes of the king in the governing of his domain. In so doing, these princes and princesses were expected to uphold their status as royalty through their behavior.

Since the true Christian has been transformed into a new creature, being born of the Spirit, we are now in that incredible and glorious position of being his sons and daughters—princes and princesses of God Almighty. Although through the analogy of a human kingdom we can understand the worldly benefits of this position, it hardly compares to the magnitude of what we have through Jesus Christ. We may never truly understand the depth and breadth of what it means to have this position with Jesus Christ in this life. It is necessary that we don't have this defined in explicit terms in the Bible. The knowledge and understanding (revelation) of this is gained through our relationship with Jesus, and this is what we are to focus on.

> I will give you the keys of the kingdom of heaven; and whatever you bind on earth shall have been bound in heaven, and whatever you loose on earth shall have been loosed in heaven.
>
> —Matthew 16:19

The sheer scope of this verse in Matthew will never be truly understood in this life. This, along with many other Scriptures, can help to shed some light on what this relationship means and the incredible things he has for us. It is far beyond what anyone can dream of. In view of the level of power and authority all Christians have, the devil is nothing more than a bug to be squashed under one's foot. Christians not only have a right to exercise this power and authority, but also a responsibility to use it to advance the church.

In the Gospel of Luke, chapter 10, Jesus sends his disciples out to heal the sick and preach the Gospel. In verse 19, Jesus gives them the authority over Satan. "Behold, I have given you authority to tread on serpents and scorpions, and over **all the power of the enemy**, and nothing will injure you."

The serpents and scorpions are representative of demons. Jesus also gave them all power over the enemy. Since all Christians are his disciples, that power and authority belongs to us as well. Note that he didn't give *some* power over the enemy but *all* power over the enemy. This means that not even Satan can stand against a Christian. All it takes is a little faith.

The position of being his sons and daughters should never be a point of pride. Pride is sin and will only lead to destruction. Remember Jesus, although knowing who he was while on this earth, humbled himself and remained obedient and sinless, even to the point of death (Philippians 2:8). So too we should follow this example of humility and obedience.

By maintaining a humble state of mind, the door to pride is closed.

7.1 A Nation Of Priests

Who you are in Jesus Christ includes a job description, which is we are to be a nation of priests. A priest has a responsibility before God to be righteous and holy so he can faithfully execute the duties of his office. Priestly duties also include civic responsibilities.

> [5]"Now then, if you will indeed obey My voice and keep My covenant, then you shall be My own possession among all the peoples, for all the earth is Mine; [6]and you shall be to Me a kingdom of priests and a holy nation.' These are the words that you shall speak to the sons of Israel.
>
> —Exodus 19:5–6

You also, as living stones, are being built up as a spiritual house for a holy priesthood, to offer up spiritual sacrifices acceptable to God through Jesus Christ.

—1 Peter 2:5

But you are A CHOSEN RACE, A royal PRIESTHOOD, A HOLY NATION, A PEOPLE FOR God's OWN POSSESSION, so that you may proclaim the excellencies of Him who has called you out of darkness into His marvelous light.

—1 Peter 2:9

But you will be called the priests of the LORD; You will be spoken of as ministers of our God. You will eat the wealth of nations, And in their riches you will boast.

—Isaiah 61:6

And He has made us to be a kingdom, priests to His God and Father–to Him be the glory and the dominion forever and ever. Amen.

—Revelation 1:6

But the LORD has taken you and brought you out of the iron furnace, from Egypt, to be a people for His own possession, as today.

—Deuteronomy 4:20

For you are a holy people to the LORD your God; the LORD your God has chosen you to be a people for His own possession out of all the peoples who are on the face of the earth.

—Deuteronomy 7:6

Yet on your fathers did the LORD set His affection to love them, and He chose their descendants after them, even you above all peoples, as it is this day.

—Deuteronomy 10:15

> For you are a holy people to the LORD your God, and the LORD has chosen you to be a people for His own possession out of all the peoples who are on the face of the earth.
>
> —Deuteronomy 14:2

> [11]For the grace of God has appeared, bringing salvation to all men, [12]instructing us to deny ungodliness and worldly desires and to live sensibly, righteously and godly in the present age, [13]looking for the blessed hope and the appearing of the glory of our great God and Savior, Christ Jesus, [14]who gave Himself for us to redeem us from every lawless deed, and to purify for Himself a people for His own possession, zealous for good deeds. [15]These things speak and exhort and reprove with all authority. Let no one disregard you.
>
> —Titus 2:11–15

The office of the priest has requirements. The priest must have a solid knowledge of God's word, which defines all the duties and responsibilities of the priest. The priest must also have a relationship with and be anointed by God. The priest has a honored position in society. The priest has the position of being an intercessor between the people and God. That is, we as priests are intercessors between God and those who do not know Jesus as Lord and Savior. As intercessors, we are to spread the Gospel and pray for their salvation and do as Paul did in 1 Corinthians 2:4–5. The priest is also to act as a moral compass for the community and subsequently the nation. The church is to be the focal point of society. The church is to occupy that power base in society. If the church fails to do this, then the wicked will, and they do so with a great deal of aggression and a militant attitude. In addition, the wicked try to fill this position because they think they have a birthright to it. This, of course, is a lie of the devil.

The book of Leviticus describes the duties and responsibilities of the priest. The many physical activities of the priest can be translated into spiritual activities we should be practicing today, some of which we do by nature without realizing it. How all this translates to us today is a considerable study in and of itself. This points to the dire need for knowledge. Since the church is so lacking in knowledge, it suffers the consequences presented in Isaiah and Hosea:

> Therefore My people go into exile for their lack of knowledge; And their honorable men are famished, And their multitude is parched with thirst.
>
> —Isaiah 5:13

> My people are destroyed for lack of knowledge. Because you have rejected knowledge, I also will reject you from being My priest. Since you have forgotten the law of your God, I also will forget your children.
>
> —Hosea 4:6

Some of this lack of knowledge can be traced back to the cultural divide that occurred in the early days of the church. The cultural divide between the Christian church today and its Jewish roots needs to be repaired.

It is up to the church today to be a repairer of the breach, a restorer of the streets in which to dwell.

> 11"And the Lord will continually guide you, And satisfy
> your desire in scorched places, And give strength to your
> bones; And you will be like a watered garden, And like a
> spring of water whose waters do not fail. 12"Those from
> among you will rebuild the ancient ruins; You will raise
> up the age-old foundations; And you will be called the
> repairer of the breach, The restorer of the streets in which
> to dwell. 13"If because of the sabbath, you turn your foot
> From doing your own pleasure on My holy day, And call
> the sabbath a delight, the holy day of the Lord honorable,
> And honor it, desisting from your own ways, From seeking
> your own pleasure And speaking your own word, 14Then
> you will take delight in the Lord, And I will make you

> ride on the heights of the earth; And I will feed you with the heritage of Jacob your father, For the mouth of the LORD has spoken."
>
> —Isaiah 58:11–14

This passage from Isaiah is a promise with a condition. If we keep the Sabbath and honor it as a holy day, and delight in him, then he will bless us (see also Mark 2:27). It doesn't take much of a leap to see that it is not just the Sabbath but also to keep *all* of his commandments. It starts with the Sabbath since it is the easiest to neglect.

Do you love him or do you view the Sabbath, the festivals and holidays and other teachings of the Old Testament as outdated, cumbersome, and not applicable today? "If you love Me, you will keep My commandments" (John 14:15).

7.2 Children of the King

In the beginning and before Adam and Eve sinned, God gave mankind dominion over the entire planet.

> [26]Then God said, "Let Us make man in Our image, according to Our likeness; and let them rule over the fish of the sea and over the birds of the sky and over the cattle and over all the earth, and over every creeping thing that creeps on the earth." [27]God created man in His own image, in the image of God He created him; male and female He created them. [28]God blessed them; and God said to them, "Be fruitful and multiply, and fill the earth, and subdue it; and rule over the fish of the sea and over the birds of the sky and over every living thing that moves on the earth."
>
> —Genesis 1:26–28

After sin entered the scene, that dominion was passed on to the devil. He retained this until Jesus died on the cross. That dominion has now been passed back to its rightful owners—the children of the King. The problem is, the devil doesn't want to relinquish what he thinks is his. This dominion must be taken from him by force. This is a battle.

> For our struggle is not against flesh and blood, but against the rulers, against the powers, against the world forces of this darkness, against the spiritual forces of wickedness in the heavenly places.
>
> —Ephesians 6:12

An example of this situation is the civil rights movement that started in the early 1960s. Slavery had been abolished at the end of the civil war but the wicked didn't want to lose their power and control over people. It wasn't until nearly one hundred years later that people had enough and demanded their lawful rights and position in society that they were finally allowed to exercise that status.

Similarly, we as Christians need to take back dominion of this world from the wicked. Not that long ago, the church had a solid position of dominion in the community and in the governing affairs of this nation. The primary method regaining this is through repentance and prayer (2 Chronicles 7:14).

It is up to the church to follow his plan to regain it. As children of the King of kings and Lord of lords, we not only have the right, but the responsibility to pursue this. It will never happen through man's methods.

As a reminder:

It will invariably be more difficult and take more work and effort to recover from sin than it would to resist temptation in the first place.

As children of the King, we have all the power and authority through Jesus Christ to make this happen. The sooner this effort begins, the better. The more time that passes before the church rises up, the more difficult it will be to regain the lost ground.

Many Christians hear the words spoken in sermons that they are children of the King, yet do nothing with this position but feel good about themselves. It is time to put God's word into action.

Power of the Spoken Word

We must all be careful of the words that come out of our mouths. Words carry power and a lot more than most realize. Look in particular at Matthew 16:19 below. What it means to have the keys to the kingdom of heaven is a study in and of itself and would likely be a real eye opener for all. We simply have no idea the scope of what it means to be a Christian. Knowing these limits brought about by our own lack of knowledge, how much more careful should we be with the words that come out of our mouths.

> You will also decree a thing, and it will be established for you; And light will shine on your ways.
>
> —Job 22:28

> For by your words you will be justified, and by your words you will be condemned.
>
> —Matthew 12:37

> I will give you the keys of the kingdom of heaven; and whatever you bind on earth shall have been bound in heaven, and whatever you loose on earth shall have been loosed in heaven.
>
> —Matthew 16:19

> Truly I say to you, whatever you bind on earth shall have been bound in heaven; and whatever you loose on earth shall have been loosed in heaven.
>
> —Matthew 18:18

> [20]With the fruit of a man's mouth his stomach will be satisfied; He will be satisfied with the product of his lips. [21]Death and life are in the power of the tongue, And those who love it will eat its fruit.
>
> —Proverbs 18:20–21

> An evil man is ensnared by the transgression of his lips, But the righteous will escape from trouble.
>
> —Proverbs 12:13

> [3]For though we walk in the flesh, we do not war according to the flesh, [4]for the weapons of our warfare are not of the flesh, but divinely powerful for the destruction of fortresses. [5]We are destroying speculations and every lofty thing raised up against the knowledge of God, and we are taking every thought captive to the obedience of Christ.
>
> —2 Corinthians 10:3–5

James chapter 3 also has much to say about the dangers of the tongue.

In addition to these Scriptures, much can be inferred about the level of power and authority we have as Christians through the spoken word. As his sons and daughters, children of the King, a royal priesthood, the power of the spoken word must be taken seriously. All too often and without recognizing the wiles of the devil, people say things that allow the devil to interfere with and oppress us, and gain victory in situations where he would otherwise be a failure. We must allow the Holy Spirit and knowledge of his word to assist in the process of self-discipline.

As an example, I know of a pastor who has an incredible deliverance ministry. The devil came to him one day and said he would destroy this ministry. The pastor's response was that the devil might have the power to do this or that. It is subtle but what happened is by ignorance of what he said, he gave the devil permission to cause problems. As a result, his marriage was destroyed and problems abounded in his church.

The process of disciplining one's self begins with the mind as is indicated in 2 Corinthians 10:5. In order to bring your thought life into the obedience of Christ, everything you receive with your senses or thinking must be filtered through the word and through the Holy Spirit. The effectiveness of this effort, as always, is based on the level of your relationship with Jesus. The more you build that relationship, the more you will be empowered to build this discipline as well as accomplish the many other things you need to do. The apostle Paul wrote in Philippians 4:13:

> I can do all things through Him who strengthens me.

And in Philippians 4:6–8, Paul wrote:

> [6]Be anxious for nothing, but in everything by prayer and supplication with thanksgiving let your requests be made known to God. [7]And the peace of God, which surpasses all comprehension, will guard your hearts and your minds in Christ Jesus. [8]Finally, brethren, whatever is true, whatever is honorable, whatever is right, whatever is pure, whatever is lovely, whatever is of good repute, if there is any excellence and if anything worthy of praise, dwell on these things.

The power of the spoken word when spoken by someone in right standing with God was demonstrated by Jesus himself as well as the apostles. When they spoke, demons were cast out, people were healed, and many signs, wonders, and miracles were manifest.

When you come to the realization of who you are in Christ, build your relationship with him, and put into practice the things written in his word (faith without works is dead), you too will witness the hand of God move in miraculous ways!

An Effective Style of Prayer

This chapter introduces an aggressive style of prayer and explains why it works. To gain an understanding of this, we need to look at some Scriptures:

> We know that God does not hear sinners; but if anyone is God-fearing and does His will, He hears him.
>
> —John 9:31

> [7]Ask, and it will be given to you; seek, and you will find; knock, and it will be opened to you. [8]For everyone who asks receives, and he who seeks finds, and to him who knocks it will be opened.
>
> —Matthew 7:7–8

> Again I say to you, that if two of you agree on earth about anything that they may ask, it shall be done for them by My Father who is in heaven.
>
> —Matthew 18:19

> And all things you ask in prayer, believing, you will receive.
>
> —Matthew 21:22

> Therefore I say to you, all things for which you pray and ask, believe that you have received them, and they will be granted you.
>
> —Mark 11:24

[9]So I say to you, ask, and it will be given to you; seek, and you will find; knock, and it will be opened to you. [10]For everyone who asks, receives; and he who seeks, finds; and to him who knocks, it will be opened.

—Luke 11:9–10

[13]Whatever you ask in My name, that will I do, so that the Father may be glorified in the Son. [14]If you ask Me anything in My name, I will do it. [15]If you love Me, you will keep My commandments.

—John 14:13–15

If you abide in Me, and My words abide in you, ask whatever you wish, and it will be done for you.

—John 15:7

[23]In that day you will not question Me about anything. Truly, truly, I say to you, if you ask the Father for anything in My name, He will give it to you. [24]Until now you have asked for nothing in My name; ask and you will receive, so that your joy may be made full.

—John 16:23–24

And when they had prayed, the place where they had gathered together was shaken, and they were all filled with the Holy Spirit and began to speak the word of God with boldness.

—Acts 4:31

Therefore let us draw near with confidence to the throne of grace, so that we may receive mercy and find grace to help in time of need.

—Hebrews 4:16

Therefore, brethren, since we have confidence to enter the holy place by the blood of Jesus.

—Hebrews 10:19

> [35]Therefore, do not throw away your confidence, which has a great reward. [36]For you have need of endurance, so that when you have done the will of God, you may receive what was promised.
>
> —Hebrews 10:35–36

> In whom we have boldness and confident access through faith in Him.
>
> —Ephesians 3:12

> For through Him we both have our access in one Spirit to the Father.
>
> —Ephesians 2:18

> [4]Such confidence we have through Christ toward God. [5]Not that we are adequate in ourselves to consider anything as coming from ourselves, but our adequacy is from God, [6]who also made us adequate as servants of a new covenant, not of the letter but of the Spirit; for the letter kills, but the Spirit gives life.
>
> —2 Corinthians 3:4–6

In many churches, people are of the opinion that prayer is largely expected to be spontaneous, Spirit-led, and generally of a "Caspar Milquetoast" demeanor. One's spiritual level is often measured by such prayers. Although there is nothing wrong with spontaneous Spirit-led prayers, one's spiritual level should be judged by the effectiveness of their prayers. This "Caspar Milquetoast" style of prayer so common today is not the prayer of a warrior, nor is it the style we should adhere to today. As was stated earlier:

We are to have a holy confidence and boldness in prayer, free from a servile and bashful spirit.

Many of the prayers in the chapters that follow are general enough to be used for multiple subjects. Others specific to a subject can be easily modified to suit many other subjects. Write your own prayers. Not every situation can be addressed in a single book. If you write them down, there is no need to memorize them. Forgetting is too easy. Don't give the devil an opportunity to steal effective prayers the Holy Spirit put in your mind to speak. Writing them down will ensure they don't get lost and forgotten.

Although fairly long, the prayers in the chapter on Finances and Employment are a good model that can be modified to suit a wide range of needs.

Feel free to mix and match prayers to suit your situation.

The devil can and does set up evil networks in the spiritual realm against us. Such networks may be established by witchcraft or be purely demonic, or both (witchcraft is by definition demonic). Curses or demonic activities against us don't have to be done locally. They can be done from virtually anywhere in the world. Regardless, we as Christians have all authority over these things (Luke 10:19).

Don't focus on or be intimidated by the
size of the problem.
Focus on the greatness of your Lord Jesus Christ!

Remember when Jesus walked on the water (Matthew 14:28–31). Peter didn't start sinking until *after* he took his eyes off Jesus and saw the waves and storm around him.

It is common for those in ministry, or any Christian that wants to grow in their relationship with Jesus, to be attacked, often viciously, by demons or by witchcraft. Satanists often infiltrate churches to cause problems of many kinds. We as Christians must be vigilant and close to the Holy Spirit so we are aware of these things and can expose them. Ideally, the church should be so on fire for God and the presence of the Holy Spirit so powerful that none of these people would even be able to enter into a church building. Those who have the gift of spiritual discernment must be allowed to do their job in the church. The church leadership must follow up to deal with the problems.

> Even those I will bring to My holy mountain And make them joyful in My house of prayer. Their burnt offerings and their sacrifices will be acceptable on My altar; **For My house will be called a house of prayer for all the peoples**.
>
> —Isaiah 56:7

Remember, regardless of how one arrives at the point where their prayers are effective and accompanied with miracles, signs, and wonders, it all boils down to this:

It is the power of the spoken word and the faith behind it that gets results.

When you pray:

- Stand up, walk around the room while praying.
- Speak out and command with authority. Do so aggressively and with conviction, confidence, and boldness. If it helps to be loud then be loud.
- Refuse to back down. Pray to win until you win.
- Repeat each of the prayers as many times as needed. A tree doesn't always come down with one swing of the ax.
- You have all power and authority through your Lord Jesus Christ at your disposal—*use it*!

Such physical actions adds a degree of finality to prayer. This is in reality faith! This well-known physiological and psychological principle is widely used, particularly in the military and law enforcement. The physical action builds an association with faith. As time passes, faith grows and the need for the physical action will likely decrease.

Expect results and you will get them. Don't focus on the style as an end in itself, focus on Jesus and realize the goal is to get answers to prayer, to build faith, and build your relationship with Jesus. I say this because I have seen some people view this style as an end in and of itself. When this happens, the prayers become little more than a religious exercise of useless chanting.

As faith increases, you will find that a word spoken softly will have the same results as what previously took much longer, repetitive, and aggressive prayer. If a problem refuses to budge, there is nothing wrong with going back to the more aggressive style to get resolution. Do what needs to be done. Don't let pride get in the way.

There is nothing wrong with being repetitive. Daniel spent three weeks praying without knowing about the spiritual warfare taking place on his behalf. Jesus spent hours praying in the garden before gis crucifixion. During this time, it isn't likely he engaged in a single boring monologue. It is more likely he petitioned the Father over and over concerning what he was facing.

The only thing Jesus said negatively about repetition was against the meaningless repetition done by the Gentiles in Matthew 6:7. In this chapter, he rebuked them for their hypocrisy and vanity. They prayed to exalt themselves before men rather than God. When Jesus spoke against meaningless repetition, it also implies repetition can also be meaningful provided it is used correctly as he outlines in that chapter.

> For God hath not given us the spirit of fear; but of power, and of love, and of a sound mind.
>
> —2 Timothy 1:7, KJV

God has not given us a spirit of fear (or timidity). We are to approach the throne of grace *boldly* (Hebrews 4:16). This boldness has the characteristic of being aggressive. Being aggressive about prayer is a key ingredient. It works! Don't be afraid! I have known a number of people who, with only a little instruction about this style of prayer, were amazed at how soundly their prayers were heard and answered.

In order to have the power spoken of in 2 Timothy 1:7, we must have the love of Christ dwelling in us. Love must be our primary motivation. A sound mind is a mind that is free from sin as sin is the worst form of insanity. A sound mind is the characteristic of one who is righteous and holy. Without the love of Christ and a sound mind, power would be abused. God will give you power as you are able to use it in accordance with his word and will.

> But in all these things we overwhelmingly conquer through Him who loved us.
>
> —Romans 8:37

> But thanks be to God, who gives us the victory through our Lord Jesus Christ.
>
> —1 Corinthians 15:57

Jesus won the war on the cross and it is through him and the example that he provided us that we can experience the same victory. The devil prowls about the earth seeking whom he may devour. Whether we realize it or not, he has caused a significant hindrance in our lives and churches. The devil has lulled the church into a false sense of security and subsequent apathy. The mere fact that we don't see many signs, wonders, and miracles today is ample evidence of this. God is the same yesterday, today, and forever. There is no reason why we can't experience the miracles written in the Bible *today*!

God has called his people to be warriors, not cowards.

> [7]Only be strong and very courageous; be careful to do according to all the law which Moses My servant commanded you; do not turn from it to the right or to the left, so that you may have success wherever you go. [8]This book of the law shall not depart from your mouth, but you shall meditate on it day and night, so that you may be careful to do according to all that is written in it; for

> then you will make your way prosperous, and then you will have success. [9]Have I not commanded you? Be strong and courageous! Do not tremble or be dismayed, for the LORD your God is with you wherever you go.
>
> —Joshua 1:7–9

> But for the cowardly and unbelieving and abominable and murderers and immoral persons and sorcerers and idolaters and all liars, their part will be in the lake that burns with fire and brimstone, which is the second death.
>
> —Revelation 21:8

Like it or not, we are all on the frontlines of battle. If you are warming a pew instead of overcoming the enemy, you are defeated. It is time to get out of that comfort zone of slumber and into the glorious victory of our Lord and Savior Jesus Christ!

Prayer is a very powerful tool. Not only is it profitable for our growth and building our relationship with Jesus, but it is critical for overcoming our enemies. I must stress yet again that building our relationship with Jesus is by far the most profitable of any goal we might have. The fellowship and intimate relationship with the Holy Spirit goes beyond any description by any human language. This relationship must, above all things, be the focal point of our lives. Everything else is secondary and will be addressed in due course.

Prayer is powerful for warfare against the devil because of who we are in Christ, and because there is power in the spoken word. Proverbs 18:21 says,

> Death and life are in the power of the tongue, And those who love it will eat its fruit.

Along with this, discipline is just as important (to whom much is given, much is required). See also James 3:1–12. Job 22:28 says,

> You will also decree a thing, and it will be established for you; And light will shine on your ways.

We must be careful of what we speak. We must be careful not to make negative confessions. It is these negative confessions that give the devil ground to cause problems.

A prayer session should follow the following pattern:

1. Repent of any known sins and ask forgiveness. This is the first step. Many people start with praise and worship, but this should come after repenting because sins need to be dealt with first. Isaiah 59:1–2 says,

    > [1]Behold, the Lord's hand is not so short That it cannot save; Nor is His ear so dull That it cannot hear. [2]But your iniquities have made a separation between you and your God, And your sins have hidden His face from you so that He does not hear.

2. Be specific when asking forgiveness for sins. God knows them anyway but you should speak it out. If you are praying with other people and you don't want to disclose certain personal sins to others, it would be best to deal with them prior to the prayer session.
3. Praise and worship. Sing a few praise songs before prayer. Worship him for God inhabits the praise of his people. Too many churches place praise and worship before repentance. When this is done, praising and worshipping tend to become more of an emotional experience because sin has not been dealt with first. It is only after sin is forgiven and the worshiper cleansed that the Holy Spirit will be able to bring the experience of praise and worship in its fullness.
4. Start the prayer session. The prayers will also deal with sins that pertain to specific situations that may otherwise go unrecognized. After this, any spiritual matters of dealing with the devil will be addressed. This will be followed with addressing subject specific issues.

An important concept to understand is that the act of prayer for the purpose of building your relationship with the Holy Spirit as well as for solving problems and working your faith is an *upward* spiral. The more you do these things, the following happens:

- You will grow closer and more intimate with the Holy Spirit.
- Your faith will grow.
- More and more of your prayers will be answered.
- Your worship will increase in quality.

In the chapters that follow, you may mix and match or write your own prayers. Just about every subject can have multiple causes. Section 16.5 has a variety of these causes that can and should be prayed.

9.1 Fasting

Fasting is an important tool in growth and spiritual warfare. Its purpose is to weaken the desires of the flesh and strengthen the spirit. Prayer and fasting must go together. One of the sins we all must deal with is pride. This is the sin that brought Satan down. Fasting will help with becoming humble before our God. Pride and humility are opposites. Pride is rebellion against God. Humility is an act of our will. Humility is denying one's self and putting Jesus on the throne of their life.

All of this may sound like a lot of work. It isn't. It is simply fulfilling our responsibilities. It is doing what we should have been doing all along but haven't because of ignorance or laziness.

Not everyone can fast. If you can, you will find that it will help you to grow faster than you would otherwise. If you can't fast, don't worry. God is not unreasonable and he will meet you and help you where you are.

> [5]Is it a fast like this which I choose, a day for a man to humble himself? Is it for bowing one's head like a reed And for spreading out sackcloth and ashes as a bed? Will you call this a fast, even an acceptable day to the LORD? [6]Is this not the fast which I choose, To loosen the bonds of wickedness, To undo the bands of the yoke, And to let the oppressed go free And break every yoke? [7]Is it not to divide your bread with the hungry And bring the homeless poor into the house; When you see the naked, to cover him; And not to hide yourself from your own flesh? [8]Then your light will break out like the dawn, And your recovery will speedily spring forth; And your righteousness will go before you; The glory of the LORD will be your rear guard. [9]Then you will call, and the LORD will answer; You will cry, and He will say, "Here I am." If you remove the yoke from your midst, The pointing of the finger and speaking wickedness.
>
> —Isaiah 58:5–9

From the above verses in Isaiah, we see that the purpose of fasting is to:

- humble one's self,
- loosen the bonds of wickedness,
- undo the bands of the yoke, and
- take care of those who are less fortunate.

If you make this a practice, then God will fulfill his part.

- The glory of the Lord will be your rear guard.
- Your righteousness will go before you.
- Your light will break out like the dawn.
- Your prayers will be heard and answered.
- The Lord will continually guide you.

- You will be strengthened.
- You will be like a watered garden, and a spring of water whose waters do not fail.
- You will rebuild the ancient ruins;
- You will raise up the age-old foundations.
- You will be called the repairer of the breach, the restorer of the streets in which to dwell.

It is evident that those who forsake the desires of the flesh and make their highest priority their relationship with Jesus will be blessed greatly. They will be blessed beyond their imagination. Praise be to our Lord Jesus Christ!

In reading the passage from Isaiah, it is evident that it is primarily pride and the sins that fall out of it that need to be repented of and placed in subjection. We are also required to take care of those who are poor and less fortunate.

9.2 The Warrior Mindset

The United States Army has a Warrior Ethos that says:

1. I will always place the mission first.
2. I will never accept defeat.
3. I will never quit.
4. I will never leave a fallen comrade.

Although this was written to be applied to physical warfare, it is just as applicable to the spiritual as it outlines the mental attitude we should have and the subjects we must keep in mind in the face of battle and in every aspect of our Christian lives. I urge you to memorize this. How easy it is to allow our eyes to drift to the things of the world and its distractions!

Let's look at the Warrior Ethos again with some comments added.

1. I will always place the mission first. The mission is for each individual to do their God-ordained part to fulfill the Great Commission. Each of us has a specific function to fill. This is a fact that Paul made clear.
2. I will never accept defeat. Defeat is not an option. We are overwhelming victors through Christ. Fight the good fight. Your own personal victories will increase as you grow. Remember, it is a learning and faith-building process.
3. I will never quit. Run the race to win. It is Christ who strengthens you. You can never succeed with your own strength. This too is a process that must be learned and built as faith increases.
4. I will never leave a fallen comrade. *Never ever* shoot the wounded.

> Brethren, even if anyone is caught in any trespass, you who are spiritual, restore such a one in a spirit of gentleness; each one looking to yourself, so that you too will not be tempted.
>
> —Galatians 6:1

Lift up and help those who have stumbled, knowing full well you are not immune to the attacks of the devil and that you must also deal with the weaknesses of the flesh. Shooting the wounded is a tactic of the devil used to divide and conquer. Be aware of the wiles of the devil. The practice of shooting the wounded is a great evil in the church today and must be repented of.

Every good soldier goes through the process of physical and mental discipline. The apostle Paul makes the need for self discipline clear in 1 Timothy 4:7–8:

> 7But have nothing to do with worldly fables fit only for old women. On the other hand, **discipline yourself for**

> **the purpose of godliness**; [8]for bodily discipline is only of little profit, but godliness is profitable for all things, since it holds promise for the present life and also for the life to come.

Then in more Scriptures, we can see even more exhortations that when put into practice, lead the way to overwhelming victory:

> For God hath not given us the spirit of fear; but of power, and of love, and of a sound mind.
>
> —2 Timothy 1:7, KJV

> Have I not commanded you? Be strong and courageous! Do not tremble or be dismayed, for the LORD your God is with you wherever you go.
>
> —Joshua 1:9

> The LORD is the one who goes ahead of you; He will be with you. He will not fail you or forsake you. Do not fear or be dismayed.
>
> —Deuteronomy 31:8

> No temptation has overtaken you but such as is common to man; and God is faithful, who will not allow you to be tempted beyond what you are able, but with the temptation will provide the way of escape also, so that you will be able to endure it.
>
> —1 Corinthians 10:13

> But thanks be to God, who gives us the victory through our Lord Jesus Christ.
>
> —1 Corinthians 15:57

> For whatever is born of God overcomes the world; and this is the victory that has overcome the world—our faith.
>
> —1 John 5:4

> "These things I have spoken to you, so that in Me you may have peace. In the world you have tribulation, but take courage; I have overcome the world."
>
> —John 16:33

Demons and satanic activities are not to be feared. Fear is of the devil. Faith is of God. Jesus won the victory on the cross and has overcome the world. All we need to do is tap into this victory. The path to that victory is faith. Faith is like our physical muscles. When you want to get in shape you go to a gym and work out. It takes effort, repetition, work, and sometimes some pain. After a while, you become much stronger and more physically fit than before. The same is true with faith. You need to exercise it, use it, and work at it (James 2:17). It will grow over time if you don't give up.

In Ephesians 6:10–17, we read about the tools of warfare.

> 10Finally, be strong in the Lord and in the strength of His
> might. 11Put on the full armor of God, so that you will be
> able to stand firm against the schemes of the devil. 12For
> our struggle is not against flesh and blood, but against the
> rulers, against the powers, against the world forces of this
> darkness, against the spiritual forces of wickedness in the
> heavenly places. 13Therefore, take up the full armor of God,
> so that you will be able to resist in the evil day, and having
> done everything, to stand firm. 14Stand firm therefore,
> HAVING GIRDED YOUR LOINS WITH TRUTH,
> and HAVING PUT ON THE BREASTPLATE OF
> RIGHTEOUSNESS, 15and having shod YOUR FEET
> WITH THE PREPARATION OF THE GOSPEL OF
> PEACE; 16in addition to all, taking up the shield of faith
> with which you will be able to extinguish all the flaming
> arrows of the evil one. 17And take THE HELMET OF
> SALVATION, and the sword of the Spirit, which is the
> word of God.

Paul draws comparisons between the Roman soldier's armor and weapons of warfare and the spiritual weapons we have at our disposal. In verse 13, we are to take up the full armor of God. What is this armor? Armor is a defensive protection from the attacks of the enemy. We gain the full armor from a full and complete knowledge of the Word, along with the maturity that the knowledge and its application to everyday life means, and by applying the blood of Jesus. Gaining this knowledge is critical. As it says in Hosea. 4:6, "My people are destroyed for lack of knowledge. Because you have rejected knowledge, I also will reject you from being My priest. Since you have forgotten the law of your God, I also will forget your children." Clearly, Jesus takes gaining knowledge seriously.

We must also understand our enemy to effectively fight and win. Most of what we need can be learned from life experiences, by being observant, learning from others, listening to the Holy Spirit, and knowing his word. Some people aspire to learn more than necessary by looking into the nature and details of satanism and witchcraft. This has obvious drawbacks and traps, and more often than not will serve only to lure one into this world of darkness and distract them from gaining a victory over the devil. We are to focus on our Lord Jesus Christ!

We are to live in truth and righteousness (v. 14). We are to use faith to extinguish all the flaming missiles the devil throws at us (John 6:29). The helmet of salvation is a particularly powerful statement. We are to keep in mind always who we are in Jesus Christ. We are his sons and daughters. We have a rightful place of royalty in this age as well as the next. In Romans 8:36–37, we find the world sees us as sheep for the slaughter. This is because they hate and despise us. Their minds are darkened by sin. In verse 37, we find we are overwhelming conquerors through Jesus. Since we know this is so, we need to go after the blessings and promises that God has given us and that the devil has stolen because of our lack of knowledge and resolve.

> [18]And I say also unto thee, That thou art Peter, and upon this rock I will build my church; and the gates of hell shall not prevail against it. [19]And I will give unto thee the keys of the kingdom of heaven: and whatsoever thou shalt bind on earth shall be bound in heaven: and whatsoever thou shalt loose on earth shall be loosed in heaven.
>
> —Matthew 16:18–19, KJV

The gates of hell shall not prevail, or overpower, the church. The focal point here is the battle between the devil with his hoards of evil demons and the church. Any soldier on the frontlines of battle who refuses to learn the ways and weapons of warfare and refuses to fight is in danger of being killed. This is true for Christians too.

A case in point concerns Christians in many African countries. I have known and spoken with a number of people from several African countries, and life for Christians there can sometimes be very difficult. In Nigeria, for example, Christians in certain regions are surrounded by Muslims who have made it a practice of entering churches during a service then gunning down as many as they can. In addition, and if this isn't bad enough, witchcraft is socially acceptable, practiced openly, and considered a viable means of getting what one wants. Demonic activities are rampant and often seen openly. Christians must learn to pray aggressively because their lives are in a constant state of danger. Failure to pray and trust in Jesus could be a death sentence, and should someone be killed, ensuring one is in right standing with God is that much more important. Such persecution is on the rise all over the world but almost never reported in the mainstream media.

Persecution against Christians in America is now on the rise. I have known people who see persecution as a measure of their spirituality. This is a lie of the devil. It is a glaring indication of the failure of the church to pray and rise up to its rightful position in society.

The good part is in verse 19 in that the Christian has all power and authority over the enemy. We only need to learn and use it effectively.

The church cannot fight and sleep at the same time.

In Philippians 3:12, Paul makes a very important statement. We are to press forward. To press means we must apply effort (1 Peter 4:18) against a resistance. That resistance takes several forms: the world, spiritual warfare, and sin. The three root sins we all deal with are the lust of the flesh, lust of the eyes, and the boastful pride of life (1 John 2:16). It is from these three root sins (or categories of sin) that all others fall under. There are many verses in Scripture that can be applied to this. In short, we are to diligently apply the word of God in our lives every day. We are to pray fervently (Romans 12:11, James 5:16). We are to be diligent about our growth and relationship with Jesus.

Prayer is a very powerful tool! Not only is it profitable for our growth and building our relationship with Jesus, but it is critical for overcoming our enemies!

We have all authority and power in heaven and earth at our disposal. All we need to do is use it in accordance with God's word. Spiritual warfare is not something to shun or be stressed about. The devil is something to gain victory over.

> Some of us are already warriors in one form or another. Being a warrior means throwing your heart and soul into something you believe in and never looking back. Having a warrior mindset means you won't quit. It encompasses the Spartan philosophy of bringing back your shield or being carried back on it.
>
> Having a warrior mindset means doing whatever it takes to be prepared because warriors don't just survive, they overcome and win. At the end of the day, life is nothing but a mind game; it's important that you play to win. Your life depends on it.

It's not always the biggest and strongest who make it, but those with the most heart; those who keep on going no matter what is thrown at them. It's a lesson you need to remember if you want to become a true warrior.[1]

"When things look bad, and it looks like you're not gonna make it, then you gotta get mean. I mean plumb mad dog mean. Cause if you lose your head and you give up, then you neither live nor win, that's just the way it is."[2]

This quote from *The Outlaw Josey Wales*[3] and the preceding paragraphs by Amaury Murgado[4] outline the mental attitude you need to win. Don't give up. Refuse to allow your problem to survive. Pray through it until the job is done. If you become overwhelmed, get help. There is power in numbers, which we can see in Matthew and in Acts:

> 18"Truly I say to you, whatever you bind on earth shall have been bound in heaven; and whatever you loose on earth shall have been loosed in heaven. 19"Again I say to you, that if two of you agree on earth about anything that they may ask, it shall be done for them by My Father who is in heaven. 20"For where two or three have gathered together in My name, I am there in their midst."
>
> —Matthew 18:18–20

> 5So Peter was kept in the prison, but prayer for him was being made **fervently by the church to God**. 6On the very night when Herod was about to bring him forward, Peter was sleeping between two soldiers, bound with two chains, and guards in front of the door were watching over the prison. 7And behold, an angel of the Lord suddenly appeared and a light shone in the cell; and he struck Peter's side and woke him up, saying, "Get up quickly." And his chains fell off his hands. 8And the angel said to him, "Gird yourself and put on your sandals." And he did so. And he said to him, "Wrap your cloak around you and follow me." 9And he went out and continued to follow, and

> he did not know that what was being done by the angel was real, but thought he was seeing a vision. [10]When they had passed the first and second guard, they came to the iron gate that leads into the city, which opened for them by itself; and they went out and went along one street, and immediately the angel departed from him. [11]When Peter came to himself, he said, "Now I know for sure that the Lord has sent forth His angel and rescued me from the hand of Herod and from all that the Jewish people were expecting."
>
> —Acts 12:5–11

In Matthew 18:18–20 and in Luke 10, Jesus establishes the authority you have. In Acts 12:5–11, you can see this put into action, with miraculous results.

I have heard numerous people, preachers in churches and on television who make statements similar to, "We take authority over the devil," and then do nothing with that authority! If you take that authority, *use it*! Go on the offense, be aggressive about it, don't miss an opportunity to destroy the devil!

It is amazing and sad to see how often people touch on powerful spiritual principles, barely scratch the surface of them, and then do nothing. It is essential to start thinking outside this small box of church cultural and learn to be an overwhelming conqueror!

If you come under a demonic attack then attack back. Of course you may need to take defensive measures as well such as covering yourself or others with the blood of Jesus. Don't stop with just the demons attacking you. Go after their support, replacements, command structure, evil devices (weapons), and evil influences. Evil devices, or machines, have to be manufactured somehow. Go after those facilities and the demons that manufacture them too. Destroy all of them! Clear the field and don't back down until the job is done!

When you maintain this warrior attitude and do these things, you will be amazed at the results. As you become stronger, you will not be afraid and you will win greater and greater battles. Satan himself will not be able to stand against you. You will have the attitude that says, "Okay, Satan, bring it on! The more demons you send my way, the more will be utterly destroyed, and they will never bother me or anyone else again!" By the time you get to this point, it is doubtful the devil would even try such a thing because he knows he will get trashed for it.

Don't forget that Satan and all his demons were once angels in heaven until they rebelled and were thrown out. Many of them were quite intelligent and possessed a considerable amount of knowledge. As we have the resources to manufacture a great many things on this earth, they too possess resources of some degree to manufacture evil machines in the spiritual world. They then use these machines to perpetrate their evil on this earth.

Get in the practice of sending all these demons and all their garbage into the abyss until Judgment Day in Jesus's name. As a child of the King, a royal priesthood, you absolutely do have the power and authority to do this. There is nothing in Scripture that says you can't. Doing this gets these demons off this earth and prevents them from doing any of their evil deeds. They are gone until the Great White Throne Judgment and will never bother you or anyone else again. As radical as this may sound, it works.

If the devil comes to you and says he is going to do this or that, just say, "No you won't!" (Matthew 5:37). Do not get into a conversation with the devil. Just say no! Leave it at that. Remember it is *you* who has all power and authority over the devil, and that it is *your* word that stands. You have the final word, not the devil! Again, do not get into a conversation with the devil! He is far craftier than you think. After all, he has been doing this for many thousands of years. Never *ever* compromise with the devil on anything. Destroy him!

Mercy is a Godly quality. Demons do not and cannot have any Godly quality. They will beg for mercy if it is in their advantage to do so. The only reason they may do this is to get *your permission* to continue with their evil deeds. Don't give it to them. Do not show them any mercy! Destroy them!

Doing such things inevitably falls outside that small box of church cultural most are so familiar with today. Many well-meaning Christians (even pastors) will tell you you can't do this, but they won't be able to provide any solid biblical evidence that you can't. As was said earlier, if you want victory, you must think outside the box and use the resources our Lord has provided. Keep in mind that "thinking outside the box" doesn't mean thinking or doing anything outside the boundaries of his word.

Before I ever attempted to do this, I had read the Bible from cover to cover and spent some time in prayer seeking the guidance of the Holy Spirit. Not getting a negative answer from either, I tried it and it worked. Since then (which was more than thirty-five years ago), I have experienced many victories and have more testimonies than I care to count, many of which are pretty amazing. I have even had demons come to me to tell me I can't do this. My response was simple. I said, "I just did. You go there too until Judgment Day in the name of Jesus." They're gone—end of story!

It is the devil who has deceived the church into thinking we don't have the power, authority, and position through our Lord Jesus that we in reality do have. It is time to learn it and use it. Praise God for all he has given us!

Don't limit God for when you do you limit what
He can do through you.

Much of the experiences the nation of Israel went through from the Exodus through the occupation of the Promised Land are representative of the spiritual walk we as Christians experience today. There are many lessons we can learn from this. Perhaps one of the most notable as it applies to this discussion is that Israel never fully occupied the land God gave them.

> But just as it is written, "THINGS WHICH EYE HAS NOT SEEN AND EAR HAS NOT HEARD, AND which HAVE NOT ENTERED THE HEART OF MAN, ALL THAT GOD HAS PREPARED FOR THOSE WHO LOVE HIM."
>
> —1 Corinthians 2:9

So too today, we have not entered fully into the promised land God has promised us. Don't limit the possibilities of what God can do with you. Just because you don't see it doesn't mean there isn't anything there. It is time to get outside the narrow comfort zone of church culture! It is essential to be open to the Holy Spirit and willing to accept what he has for you. It is essential to "think outside the box" and accept the things God has for you. Keep in mind that this decision and mental attitude does not mean you open yourself to the deceptions of the devil. Although making such a decision is the first step, growing to the point you are able to accept what God has for you and reject the deceptions of the devil takes time. In all of this, your relationship with Jesus must come first.

9.3 The Importance of Persistence

Being persistent is a quality that is essential for getting results. Perhaps the most notable example in Scripture is from Daniel chapter 10. Here, Daniel prayed and fasted for three weeks before seeing the results. During this time, Daniel was unaware of the battle taking place on his behalf. Similarly, we must use persistence when praying.

> 11And we desire that each one of you show the same diligence so as to realize the full assurance of hope until the end, 12so that you will not be sluggish, but imitators of those who through faith and patience inherit the promises.
>
> —Hebrews 6:11–12

[1]I will bless the LORD at all times; His praise shall continually be in my mouth. [2]My soul will make its boast in the LORD; The humble will hear it and rejoice. [3]O magnify the LORD with me, And let us exalt His name together. [4]I sought the LORD, and He answered me, And delivered me from all my fears. [5]They looked to Him and were radiant, And their faces will never be ashamed. [6]This poor man cried, and the LORD heard him And saved him out of all his troubles. [7]The angel of the LORD encamps around those who fear Him, And rescues them. [8]O taste and see that the LORD is good; How blessed is the man who takes refuge in Him! [9]O fear the LORD, you His saints; For to those who fear Him there is no want. [10]The young lions do lack and suffer hunger; But they who seek the LORD shall not be in want of any good thing. [11]Come, you children, listen to me; I will teach you the fear of the LORD. [12]Who is the man who desires life And loves length of days that he may see good? [13]Keep your tongue from evil And your lips from speaking deceit. [14]Depart from evil and do good; Seek peace and pursue it. [15]The eyes of the LORD are toward the righteous And His ears are open to their cry. [16]The face of the LORD is against evildoers, To cut off the memory of them from the earth. [17]The righteous cry, and the LORD hears And delivers them out of all their troubles. [18]The LORD is near to the brokenhearted And saves those who are crushed in spirit. [19]**Many are the afflictions of the righteous, But the LORD delivers him out of them all.** [20]He keeps all his bones, Not one of them is broken. [21]Evil shall slay the wicked, And those who hate the righteous will be condemned. [22]The LORD redeems the soul of His servants, And none of those who take refuge in Him will be condemned.

—Psalm 34

[1]Now He was telling them a parable to show that at all times they ought to pray and not to lose heart, [2]saying, "In a certain city there was a judge who did not fear God and

> did not respect man. [3]"There was a widow in that city, and
> she kept coming to him, saying, 'Give me legal protection
> from my opponent.' [4]"For a while he was unwilling; but
> afterward he said to himself, 'Even though I do not fear
> God nor respect man, [5]yet because this widow bothers me,
> I will give her legal protection, otherwise by continually
> coming she will wear me out.'" [6]And the Lord said, "Hear
> what the unrighteous judge said; [7]now, will not God bring
> about justice for His elect who cry to Him day and night,
> and will He delay long over them? [8]"I tell you that He will
> bring about justice for them quickly. However, when the
> Son of Man comes, will He find faith on the earth?"
>
> —Luke 18:1–8

> Pray without ceasing.
>
> —1 Thessalonians 5:17

We all experience adversity at various times and degrees throughout life. There are many examples throughout scripture of people (Daniel, Joseph, David, and Nehemiah, to name but a few) who persisted while going through adverse circumstances. In every case, God honored their persistence and gave victory. Joshua 1:7–9 and Philippians 4:13 make it clear that it is our Lord who decrees and provides the strength and courage to press forward. It is up to us to tap into this resource. This is done through prayer and building one's relationship with Jesus (James 5:16b, Ephesians 6:10).

> The effective prayer of a righteous man can accomplish much.
>
> —James 5:16b

> Finally, be strong in the Lord and in the strength of His might.
>
> —Ephesians 6:10

> Therefore, take up the full armor of God, so that you will be able to resist in the evil day, and having done everything, to stand firm.
>
> —Ephesians 6:13

> Be on the alert, stand firm in the faith, act like men, be strong.
>
> —1 Corinthians 16:13

Adversity can come to build, refine, and test us. It can also come as a result of demonic activities and attacks. In either case, persistence in prayer and standing on God's word is the key to victory. Remember the warrior ethos discussed previously. Memorize it.

The more you learn to be effective in prayer, the more you should expect the devil to attack. The last thing he wants is a Christian who knows their power, authority, and position through Jesus Christ. He realizes that once Christians gain this knowledge and faith, he is done for because he has no power or authority against them. This won't go on forever. The more you grow, the less the devil will be able to pose a threat.

> [9]So there remains a Sabbath rest for the people of God.
> [10]For the one who has entered His rest has himself also
> rested from his works, as God did from His. [11]Therefore
> let us be diligent to enter that rest, so that no one will fall,
> through following the same example of disobedience.
>
> —Hebrews 4:9–11

Should you decide to go down this path and put the lessons taught in this book into action, you must realize one thing. This is a one-way path. If you persist, victory is certain and it is overwhelming because Jesus has promised this in his word. If you go down this path and then turn back, you place yourself in danger of vicious attacks by the devil. As soon as you show up on his radar, you become a persistent target.

I can tell you in all honesty that if God can do this with me and bring me to the point of writing this book to teach others, he can and will do it with you if you let him. You absolutely cannot rely on your own strength. You must rely on Jesus and the strength and courage he provides. You can do all things through Christ who strengthens you (Philippians 4:13).

> But in all these things we overwhelmingly conquer through Him who loved us.
>
> —Romans 8:37

Webster defines *conquer* as:

> To gain by force; to win; to take possession by violent means; to gain dominion or sovereignty over, as the subduing of the power of an enemy generally implies possession of the person or thing subdued by the conqueror. Thus, a king or an army conquers a country, or a city, which is afterward restored.

This is a military term and it implies a battle. It is a battle that is won through our Lord Jesus Christ and not of our own strength, knowledge, or ability. When we rely on him, use his methods of warfare, the knowledge he provides in his word and by the Holy Spirit, victory is not just certain, it is overwhelming! Praise God for his grace and mercy! Praise God for the victory we have through him!

> Then he said to me, "This is the word of the LORD to Zerubbabel saying, 'Not by might nor by power, but by My Spirit,' says the LORD of hosts.
>
> —Zechariah 4:6

> Finally, be strong in the Lord and in the strength of His might.
>
> —Ephesians 6:10

This battle, although ultimate victory is certain, does not always come with ease or without work. Sometimes battles within the greater war are unfortunately lost. Adversity comes in many forms and each of us must deal with the adversity we face. There are times when the battle becomes overwhelming and we need to ask for help from others. There is nothing wrong with this, but you will find that with time and experience, faith will grow. When faith grows, the victories will be easier and more certain.

> [1]A Psalm of David. Do not fret because of evildoers, Be not envious toward wrongdoers. [2]For they will wither quickly like the grass And fade like the green herb. [3]Trust in the LORD and do good; Dwell in the land and cultivate faithfulness. [4]Delight yourself in the LORD; And He will give you the desires of your heart. [5]Commit your way to the LORD, Trust also in Him, and He will do it. [6]He will bring forth your righteousness as the light And your judgment as the noonday. [7]Rest in the LORD and wait patiently for Him; Do not fret because of him who prospers in his way, Because of the man who carries out wicked schemes. [8]Cease from anger and forsake wrath; Do not fret; it leads only to evildoing. [9]For evildoers will be cut off, But those who wait for the LORD, they will inherit the land. [10]Yet a little while and the wicked man will be no more; And you will look carefully for his place and he will not be there. [11]But the humble will inherit the land And will delight themselves in abundant prosperity. [12]The wicked plots against the righteous And gnashes at him with his teeth. [13]The Lord laughs at him, For He sees his day is coming. [14]The wicked have drawn the sword and bent their bow To cast down the afflicted and the needy, To slay those who are upright in conduct. [15]Their sword will enter their own heart, And their bows will be broken. [16]Better is the little of the righteous Than the abundance of many wicked. [17]For the arms of the wicked will be broken, But the LORD sustains the righteous. [18]The LORD knows the days of the blameless, And their inheritance will be

forever. [19]They will not be ashamed in the time of evil, And in the days of famine they will have abundance. [20]But the wicked will perish; And the enemies of the LORD will be like the glory of the pastures, They vanish—like smoke they vanish away. [21]The wicked borrows and does not pay back, But the righteous is gracious and gives. [22]For those blessed by Him will inherit the land, But those cursed by Him will be cut off. [23]The steps of a man are established by the LORD, And He delights in his way. [24]When he falls, he will not be hurled headlong, Because the LORD is the One who holds his hand. [25]I have been young and now I am old, Yet I have not seen the righteous forsaken Or his descendants begging bread. [26]All day long he is gracious and lends, And his descendants are a blessing. [27]Depart from evil and do good, So you will abide forever. [28]For the LORD loves justice And does not forsake His godly ones; They are preserved forever, But the descendants of the wicked will be cut off. [29]The righteous will inherit the land And dwell in it forever. [30]The mouth of the righteous utters wisdom, And his tongue speaks justice. [31]The law of his God is in his heart; His steps do not slip. [32]The wicked spies upon the righteous And seeks to kill him. [33]The LORD will not leave him in his hand Or let him be condemned when he is judged. [34]Wait for the LORD and keep His way, And He will exalt you to inherit the land; When the wicked are cut off, you will see it. [35]I have seen a wicked, violent man Spreading himself like a luxuriant tree in its native soil. [36]Then he passed away, and lo, he was no more; I sought for him, but he could not be found. [37]Mark the blameless man, and behold the upright; For the man of peace will have a posterity. [38]But transgressors will be altogether destroyed; The posterity of the wicked will be cut off. [39]But the salvation of the righteous is from the LORD; He is their strength in time of trouble. [40]The LORD helps them and delivers them; He delivers them from the wicked and saves them, Because they take refuge in Him.

—Psalms 37

Climbing a mountain takes work and persistence to get to the top. Once there, the glory of the scenery is spectacular. So too when you climb this spiritual mountain and reach the top, the glories you see and experience will be beyond words. The rewards of persistence are far greater than you can imagine!

9.4 Thanksgiving, Praise, Worship, and Rejoicing

The book of Psalms is most notable for offering praise to God. The word *praise* occurs more times in Psalms than in all the other books of the Bible combined. David went through countless trials, tribulations, and life-threatening situations during his life. Rather than caving in to defeat, he always went before God and offered praise, worship, and rejoicing. God blessed him greatly despite his failures. All of us should apply this example David provided regardless of what we may be going through. We should offer up the sacrifice of praise, worship, and rejoicing in the good times and the bad. This will solidify our relationship with him to a degree never dreamed possible. David experienced this and so can we.

> [14]"Offer to God a sacrifice of thanksgiving And pay your vows to the Most High; [15]Call upon Me in the day of trouble; I shall rescue you, and you will honor Me."
>
> —Psalms 50:14–15

> [1]It is good to give thanks to the LORD And to sing praises to Your name, O Most High; [2]To declare Your lovingkindness in the morning And Your faithfulness by night.
>
> —Psalms 92:1–2

> Through Him then, let us continually offer up a sacrifice of praise to God, that is, the fruit of lips that give thanks to His name.
>
> —Hebrews 13:15

I call upon the Lord, who is worthy to be praised, And I am saved from my enemies.

—Psalms 18:3

Sing praise to the Lord, you His godly ones, And give thanks to His holy name.

—Psalms 30:4

Sing for joy in the Lord, O you righteous ones; Praise is becoming to the upright.

—Psalms 33:1

Praise the Lord! For it is good to sing praises to our God; For it is pleasant and praise is becoming.

—Psalms 147:1

Worship the Lord with reverence And rejoice with trembling.

—Psalms 2:11

Come, let us worship and bow down, Let us kneel before the Lord our Maker.

—Psalms 95:6

Therefore I urge you, brethren, by the mercies of God, to present your bodies a living and holy sacrifice, acceptable to God, which is your spiritual service of worship.

—Romans 12:1

If the angels in heaven worship and praise the Lord, how much more should we whom he has redeemed with so great a price!

[9]And when the living creatures give glory and honor and thanks to Him who sits on the throne, to Him who lives forever and ever, [10]the twenty-four elders will fall down before Him who sits on the throne, and will worship

> Him who lives forever and ever, and will cast their crowns
> before the throne, saying, [11]"Worthy are You, our Lord and
> our God, to receive glory and honor and power; for You
> created all things, and because of Your will they existed,
> and were created." [12]saying with a loud voice, "Worthy is
> the Lamb that was slain to receive power and riches and
> wisdom and might and honor and glory and blessing."
> [13]And every created thing which is in heaven and on the
> earth and under the earth and on the sea, and all things
> in them, I heard saying, "To Him who sits on the throne,
> and to the Lamb, be blessing and honor and glory and
> dominion forever and ever." [14]And the four living creatures
> kept saying, "Amen." And the elders fell down and
> worshiped.
>
> —Revelation 5:9–14

Thanksgiving, praise, worship, and rejoicing are essential ingredients for answered prayers. Thanksgiving, praise, worship, and rejoicing will:

1. Give glory and credit where it is due. He is worthy!
2. Acknowledge the lordship of Jesus Christ.
3. Help to build and solidify one's relationship with Jesus.
4. Provide a verbal confession and confirmation that prayers have been heard and answered.
5. Build faith.
6. Based on the power and authority we have through Jesus, provide a seal of finality on your prayers.
7. Move the hand of God in miraculous ways.

These characteristics are most visible throughout the book of Psalms. In many of the Psalms, David starts with a petition and ends it with statements of thanksgiving, praise, and worship for the answers to his prayers. These actions are evidence of faith and confidence that his prayers were heard and answered. We would do well to follow this example!

We all go through various trials. Often these are for the purpose of testing our faith. Some trials are the result of demonic attacks, either directly or indirectly. Others may just be the result of dealing with a sinful world and sinful, wicked people. Some trials are self imposed because of sin. In these, too, you must pick yourself up, repent, ask forgiveness, and go on. In any case, backing up your prayers and spiritual warfare with thanksgiving, praise, and worship will enable you to more easily endure and be victorious.

Don't let the devil steal your joy! Rejoice in the Lord always!

> [4]Rejoice in the Lord always; again I will say, rejoice! [5]Let your gentle spirit be known to all men. The Lord is near. [6]Be anxious for nothing, but in everything by prayer and supplication with thanksgiving let your requests be made known to God. [7]And the peace of God, which surpasses all comprehension, will guard your hearts and your minds in Christ Jesus.
>
> —Philippians 4:4–7

It can be quite difficult to do these things regardless of how beneficial it is understood to be when you are overwhelmed by problems, oppression, and attacks. Despite the emotions we all deal with, it is essential to offer up that praise, worship, thanksgiving, and rejoicing. It is so easy to lose sight of the goal of the upward call of God in Christ Jesus (Philippians 3:14) when the tribulations become overwhelming. It is therefore that much more important to press forward and put his word into practice.

Thanksgiving, praise, worship, and rejoicing in our Lord is medicine for the soul and an avenue for the Holy Spirit to bring victory.

> [2]Consider it all joy, my brethren, when you encounter various trials, [3]knowing that the testing of your faith

> produces endurance. [4]And let endurance have its perfect result, so that you may be perfect and complete, lacking in nothing.
>
> —James 1:2–4

Regardless of the emotions we deal with, and how painful the trials and tribulations are, and how difficult it may be to do so, worship the Lord. Praise him and rejoice in him. This will open the door to his provision. It will open the door for him to bring joy beyond description regardless of the situation you may be going through.

9.5 The Blood of Jesus

Jesus invariably used physical situations, such as analogies or parables, to describe spiritual matters. He did this because the people would not have been able to understand the spiritual nature of the message he was attempting to convey. Analogies are with us to a great extent today as well. The term "blood of Jesus" is and has been used to deal with a myriad of spiritual matters but few ever consider what the blood of Jesus really is.

The blood of Jesus is a spiritual power, or energy, that comes from God. Satan and his demons have no power or means to counter it. It is a tool that God has provided for us to use. As with any tool, it is most effective when used properly. The "blood of Jesus" is primarily defensive in nature. It is normally used for protection against demonic attacks and influences (powers). It can be used to cover or permeate inanimate objects, or living things such as people or animals. It is used to prevent evil powers from gaining an advantage. Sometimes people will attempt to use the blood of Jesus to bring about healing for various ailments but this is not what it is intended for. The Holy Spirit is the one that heals. However, the blood of Jesus can also be used to cleanse or drive out evil powers that cause ailments. In this instance, it should be secondary to just using your authority over any and all evil powers and demons and the things they do. Remember, it is the Holy Spirit that works the miraculous.

9.6 A Note on Prayers Dealing with the Mind

Emotions, or any number or other issues that pertain to one's mental state, may need to be dealt with through any combination of spiritual, psychological, and medical means. Everyone is different and each situation is different, and therefore this must be addressed on an individual basis. If a problem is severe enough it may be necessary to seek professional help. There is no shame in this. The reader should use some common sense and seek professional help if it is necessary and not rely on prayer alone. Keep in mind that acknowledging a problem is half the battle.

Although prayer is certainly a powerful and essential tool (James 5:16), it should not be viewed as the *only* tool.

Notes

1. *Developing a Warrior Mindset*, Amaury Murgado, article from the website www.policemag.com (May 12, 2012).
2. *The Outlaw Josey Wales*, Clint Eastwood as Josey Wales, Warner Bros. (1976).
3. Ibid.
4. *Developing a Warrior Mindset*, Amaury Murgado, article from the website www.policemag.com (May 12, 2012).

Prayers to Start With

The preliminary prayers here start with spiritual warfare to deal with demonic influences, witchcraft, and various types of oppression. It is important to address these first. If they aren't, it will be more difficult to get through any of the other prayer subjects given in this book.

These prayers are effective for defeating satanic networks. One of the prayers addresses evil machines. It is doubtful if many people have even considered the existence of such things, but they do exist. We should not be so naive as to underestimate the resourcefulness of demons or their ability to construct such things. Some of them are quite intelligent, and, having once been angels, no doubt have a considerable amount of knowledge that they now use for evil. There are those in the ministry that will deny such assertions but they do so in ignorance and without any appreciable experience in these spiritual matters.

- Regardless of their perceived capabilities, the Christian has all power and authority over these evil creatures and any of the resources they employ.
- Regardless of what anyone says to you concerning spiritual warfare, it is real. The devil is real and he does possess power. However, the Christian has all power and authority over Satan and all his demons and weapons of warfare.

- Jesus won the victory and through him you can have that overwhelming victory too.

Having said these things, it is important to be aware of your limitations (level of faith). Don't go picking a fight with the devil just because you have come to realize the power and authority you have through Jesus. Let God pick your fights and he will be there with you and he will protect you and teach you. You don't want to get yourself into a situation you are not prepared to deal with.

Again, many in the ministry and throughout Christendom are of the opinion that the devil is a nonentity that we don't need to be concerned about. This very mindset is a demonic deception designed to render Christians ineffective so the devil can go about his evil activities unhindered.

10.1 Scripture Reading

> Just as it is written, "BEHOLD, I LAY IN ZION A STONE OF STUMBLING AND A ROCK OF OFFENSE, AND HE WHO BELIEVES IN HIM WILL NOT BE DISAPPOINTED."
>
> —Romans 9:33

> The God of peace will soon crush Satan under your feet. The grace of our Lord Jesus be with you.
>
> —Romans 16:20

> Do not participate in the unfruitful deeds of darkness, but instead even expose them.
>
> —Ephesians 5:11

> [13]For He rescued us from the domain of darkness, and
> transferred us to the kingdom of His beloved Son, [14]in
> whom we have redemption, the forgiveness of sins. [15]He is
> the image of the invisible God, the firstborn of all creation.
>
> —Colossians 1:13–15

[13]When you were dead in your transgressions and the uncircumcision of your flesh, He made you alive together with Him, having forgiven us all our transgressions, [14]having canceled out the certificate of debt consisting of decrees against us, which was hostile to us; and He has taken it out of the way, having nailed it to the cross. [15]When He had disarmed the rulers and authorities, He made a public display of them, having triumphed over them through Him.

—Colossians 2:13–15

[31]What then shall we say to these things? If God is for us, who is against us? [32]He who did not spare His own Son, but delivered Him over for us all, how will He not also with Him freely give us all things? [33]Who will bring a charge against God's elect? God is the one who justifies; [34]who is the one who condemns? Christ Jesus is He who died, yes, rather who was raised, who is at the right hand of God, who also intercedes for us. [35]Who will separate us from the love of Christ? Will tribulation, or distress, or persecution, or famine, or nakedness, or peril, or sword?

—Romans 8:31–35

Therefore, keep up your courage, men, for I believe God that it will turn out exactly as I have been told.

—Acts 27:25

God brings them out of Egypt, He is for them like the horns of the wild ox.

—Numbers 23:22

[8]"Then it will sweep on into Judah, it will overflow and pass through, It will reach even to the neck; And the spread of its wings will fill the breadth of your land, O Immanuel. [9]"Be broken, O peoples, and be shattered; And give ear, all remote places of the earth. Gird yourselves, yet

> be shattered; Gird yourselves, yet be shattered. [10]"Devise a plan, but it will be thwarted; State a proposal, but it will not stand, For God is with us."
>
> —Isaiah 8:8–10

> [14]For this reason I bow my knees before the Father, [15]from whom every family in heaven and on earth derives its name, [16]that He would grant you, according to the riches of His glory, to be strengthened with power through His Spirit in the inner man, [17]so that Christ may dwell in your hearts through faith; and that you, being rooted and grounded in love, [18]may be able to comprehend with all the saints what is the breadth and length and height and depth, [19]and to know the love of Christ which surpasses knowledge, that you may be filled up to all the fullness of God. [20]Now to Him who is able to do far more abundantly beyond all that we ask or think, according to the power that works within us, [21]to Him be the glory in the church and in Christ Jesus to all generations forever and ever. Amen.
>
> —Ephesians 3:14–21

10.2 Confession

Speak out the following confessions. The Scriptures are provided as a reference for each confession. You may speak out these scriptures too if you wish.

1. The Lord shall anoint me with the oil of joy above my fellows.

   > You have loved righteousness and hated wickedness; Therefore God, Your God, has anointed You With the oil of joy above Your fellows.
   >
   > —Psalms 45:7

2. No weapon formed against me will prosper.

> "No weapon that is formed against you will prosper; And every tongue that accuses you in judgment you will condemn. This is the heritage of the servants of the LORD, And their vindication is from Me," declares the LORD.
>
> —Isaiah 54:17

3. My future is secure in Christ.

> [38]For I am convinced that neither death, nor life, nor angels, nor principalities, nor things present, nor things to come, nor powers, [39]nor height, nor depth, nor any other created thing, will be able to separate us from the love of God, which is in Christ Jesus our Lord.
>
> —Romans 8:38–39

4. I am the head and not the tail.

> [13]The LORD will make you the head and not the tail, and you only will be above, and you will not be underneath, if you listen to the commandments of the LORD your God, which I charge you today, to observe them carefully, [14]and do not turn aside from any of the words which I command you today, to the right or to the left, to go after other gods to serve them.
>
> —Deuteronomy 28:13–14

5. I will trust in my Lord Jesus always for he can never fail.

> [4]I sought the LORD, and He answered me, And delivered me from all my fears. [5]They looked to Him and were radiant, And their faces will never be ashamed. [6]This poor man cried, and the LORD heard him And saved him out of all his troubles. [7]The angel of the LORD encamps around those who fear Him, And rescues them. [8]O taste

and see that the LORD is good; How blessed is the man who takes refuge in Him!

—Psalms 34:4–8

6. There will be no poverty in my life.

> [26]You will have plenty to eat and be satisfied And praise the name of the LORD your God, Who has dealt wondrously with you; Then My people will never be put to shame. [27]Thus you will know that I am in the midst of Israel, And that I am the LORD your God, And there is no other; And My people will never be put to shame.
>
> —Joel 2:26–27

7. I have favor in the eyes of God and man all the days of my life.

> For it is You who blesses the righteous man, O LORD, You surround him with favor as with a shield.
>
> —Psalms 5:12

> [3]Do not let kindness and truth leave you; Bind them around your neck, Write them on the tablet of your heart. [4]So you will find favor and good repute In the sight of God and man.
>
> —Proverbs 3:3–4

8. I shall not labor in vain.

> They will not labor in vain, Or bear children for calamity; For they are the offspring of those blessed by the LORD, And their descendants with them.
>
> —Isaiah 65:23

9. I shall walk in victory and liberty of the Holy Spirit.

> But thanks be to God, who gives us the victory through our Lord Jesus Christ.
>
> —1 Corinthians 15:57

> For whatever is born of God overcomes the world; and this is the victory that has overcome the world—our faith.
>
> —1 John 5:4

10.3 Prayers

1. Father Lord, I ask for forgiveness for all my sins I have committed against you in the name of Jesus. [Name your sins].
2. Father Lord, cause my life, ministry, and prayer life to be extremely dangerous to the kingdom of darkness in the name of Jesus.
3. By the authority I have in Jesus, I stand against every distraction to prayer in the name of Jesus.
4. I cover myself, my family, my job and career, my home, and everything that concerns me with the blood of Jesus in the name of Jesus.
5. I hold the blood of Jesus as a shield against any power established to resist me in the name of Jesus.
6. I stand on the word of God and declare myself unmovable in the name of Jesus.
7. I receive the anointing and power of the Holy Spirit in the name of Jesus.

8. I take the shield of faith and quench every fiery dart of the enemy in the name of Jesus.
9. My destiny is attached to God, therefore I decree that I shall never fail in the name of Jesus.
10. All plans of the devil concerning my life shall not stand in the name of Jesus.
11. No weapon formed against me shall prosper in the name of Jesus.
12. Father Lord, cause your purpose which no power can alter to become operational in my life now in the name of Jesus.
13. Holy Ghost fire,[†] destroy every strongman assigned against me in the name of Jesus.
14. Every generational curse operating in my life, I render you null and void in the name of Jesus.
15. Every cycle causing repeated problems for me, break in the name of Jesus.
16. I destroy every evil device and machine established against me in the name of Jesus.
17. In Jesus's name, I ask you, Father, to help me get my eyes off the world and its cares and on you.
18. In Jesus's name, I ask you, Father, to draw me closer to you so I can know you better.
19. In Jesus's name, I ask you, Father, for revelation into the kind of relationship you want with me.
20. In Jesus's name, I ask you, Father, to move me into this relationship you want with me.

† See 2 Kings chapter one.

21. In Jesus's name, I ask you, Father, to bring me to the point of understanding the unfathomable riches of knowing you.
22. My Father, I give you all the praise, glory, and honor for answering my prayers in the name of Jesus.
23. *I believe and I receive* the answers to all my prayers in the name of Jesus.
24. Thank you, Lord, in Jesus's name.

Morning Prayers

Morning sets the stage for the rest of the day. It is best to set that stage with prayer. Morning is the best time of the day to clear the way for God's blessings to manifest throughout the day. It is the best time to clear the field of demonic powers and to decree blessings, prosperity, health, favor, and so on.

> In the morning, O Lord, You will hear my voice; In the morning I will order my prayer to You and eagerly watch.
>
> —Psalms 5:3

> But as for me, I shall sing of Your strength; Yes, I shall joyfully sing of Your lovingkindness in the morning, For You have been my stronghold And a refuge in the day of my distress.
>
> —Psalms 59:16

> 12Have you ever in your life commanded the morning, And
> caused the dawn to know its place, 13That it might take
> hold of the ends of the earth, And the wicked be shaken out of it?
>
> —Job 38:12–13

One of the most revelational scriptures concerning the morning is found in Job 38:12–13. Let's look at this again from the Amplified Bible:

> [12]Have you commanded the morning since your days began and caused the dawn to know its place, [13]So that [light] may get hold of the corners of the earth and shake the wickedness [of night] out of it?
>
> —Job 38:12–13 (AMP)

It is the nature of wickedness to operate in the night. This is because they operate in sin and are full of spiritual darkness.

> Consider the covenant; For the dark places of the land are full of the habitations of violence.
>
> —Psalms 74:20

Evil doesn't want light to be shed on it ways, either in the spiritual or in the physical.

As Christians, we must take our rightful position and take dominion away from the devil. Remember, he has given us the power and authority to make it happen. The above verses in Job also indicate that we also have authority over this creation. This may be an entirely new concept to some and be hard to swallow, but God's word is true and trustworthy. Don't forget that it is the devil who attempts to deceive you into believing the word of God is not true and that you are very limited in your power and authority.

11.1 Scripture Reading

> [1]He who dwells in the shelter of the Most High Will abide in the shadow of the Almighty. [2]I will say to the LORD, "My refuge and my fortress, My God, in whom I trust! " [3]For it is He who delivers you from the snare of the trapper And from the deadly pestilence. [4]He will cover you with His pinions, And under His wings you may seek refuge; His faithfulness is a shield and bulwark. [5]You will not be afraid of the terror by night, Or of the arrow that flies by day; [6]Of the pestilence that stalks in darkness, Or of the destruction that lays waste at noon. [7]A thousand

may fall at your side And ten thousand at your right hand, But it shall not approach you. [8]You will only look on with your eyes And see the recompense of the wicked. [9]For you have made the LORD, my refuge, Even the Most High, your dwelling place. [10]No evil will befall you, Nor will any plague come near your tent. [11]For He will give His angels charge concerning you, To guard you in all your ways. [12]They will bear you up in their hands, That you do not strike your foot against a stone. [13]You will tread upon the lion and cobra, The young lion and the serpent you will trample down. [14]"Because he has loved Me, therefore I will deliver him; I will set him securely on high, because he has known My name. [15]"He will call upon Me, and I will answer him; I will be with him in trouble; I will rescue him and honor him. [16]"With a long life I will satisfy him And let him see My salvation."

—Psalm 91

11.2 Confession

Speak out the following confessions. The Scriptures are provided as a reference for each confession. You may speak out these scriptures too if you wish.

1. I am seated with Jesus Christ in heavenly places above all principalities and powers of the devil.

    [4]But God, being rich in mercy, because of His great love with which He loved us, [5]even when we were dead in our transgressions, made us alive together with Christ (by grace you have been saved), [6]and raised us up with Him, and seated us with Him in the heavenly places in Christ Jesus, [7]so that in the ages to come He might show the surpassing riches of His grace in kindness toward us in Christ Jesus.

    —Ephesians 2:4–7

> [38]For I am convinced that neither death, nor life, nor angels, nor principalities, nor things present, nor things to come, nor powers, [39]nor height, nor depth, nor any other created thing, will be able to separate us from the love of God, which is in Christ Jesus our Lord.
>
> —Romans 8:38–39

2. I am not the sheep for slaughter the world says I am. I am an overwhelming conqueror through Jesus Christ.

> [36]Just as it is written, "FOR YOUR SAKE WE ARE BEING PUT TO DEATH ALL DAY LONG; WE WERE CONSIDERED AS SHEEP TO BE SLAUGHTERED." [37]But in all these things we overwhelmingly conquer through Him who loved us.
>
> —Romans 8:36–37

3. I am a new creature in Christ and fashioned after Johovah God.

> Then God said, "Let Us make man in Our image, according to Our likeness; and let them rule over the fish of the sea and over the birds of the sky and over the cattle and over all the earth, and over every creeping thing that creeps on the earth."
>
> —Genesis 1:26

> And put on the new self, which in the likeness of God has been created in righteousness and holiness of the truth.
>
> —Ephesians 4:24

4. I am justified by Jesus Christ and made to be the righteousness of God through Jesus Christ.

> Being justified as a gift by His grace through the redemption which is in Christ Jesus.
>
> —Romans 3:24

> He made Him who knew no sin to be sin on our behalf, so that we might become the righteousness of God in Him.
>
> —2 Corinthians 5:21

5. The word of God says I am a royal priesthood, a holy nation.

> [5]"Now then, if you will indeed obey My voice and keep My covenant, then you shall be My own possession among all the peoples, for all the earth is Mine; [6]and you shall be to Me a kingdom of priests and a holy nation.' These are the words that you shall speak to the sons of Israel.
>
> —Exodus 19:5–6

6. I am a Christian and part of the church so the gates of hell cannot prevail against me.

> I also say to you that you are Peter, and upon this rock I will build My church; and the gates of Hades will not overpower it.
>
> —Matthew 16:18

7. I am empowered through the Holy Spirit to heal the sick and cast out demons.

> "These signs will accompany those who have believed: in My name they will cast out demons, they will speak with new tongues.
>
> —Mark 16:17

8. I shall not fear the arrow that flies by day or the pestilence that stalks in darkness.

> [5]You will not be afraid of the terror by night, Or of the arrow that flies by day; [6]Of the pestilence that stalks in darkness, Or of the destruction that lays waste at noon. [7]A thousand may fall at your side And ten thousand at

> your right hand, But it shall not approach you. [8]You will only look on with your eyes And see the recompense of the wicked.
>
> —Psalms 91:5–8

9. I am an overcomer because whoever is born of God overcomes the world.

> [4]For whatever is born of God overcomes the world; and this is the victory that has overcome the world–our faith. [5]Who is the one who overcomes the world, but he who believes that Jesus is the Son of God?
>
> —1 John 5:4–5

10. By faith, I overcome all the schemes of the devil because greater is the Holy Spirit that dwells in me than the devil who is in the world.

> You are from God, little children, and have overcome them; because greater is He who is in you than he who is in the world.
>
> —1 John 4:4

11. No weapon formed against me shall prosper.

> "No weapon that is formed against you will prosper; And every tongue that accuses you in judgment you will condemn. This is the heritage of the servants of the LORD, And their vindication is from Me," declares the LORD.
>
> —Isaiah 54:17

12. I am the head and not the tail.

> The LORD will make you the head and not the tail, and you only will be above, and you will not be underneath, if you listen to the commandments of the LORD your God, which I charge you today, to observe them carefully.
>
> —Deuteronomy 28:13

11.3 Prayers

1. Lord, forgive me for the sins I have committed in the name of Jesus. [List your sins.]
2. I command every evil power operating in the night to be destroyed in the name of Jesus.
3. Oh Lord, establish me in every good work in the name of Jesus.
4. I command this day in the name of Jesus.
5. I decree that today is a day of blessing, favor, honor, and prosperity for me in the name of Jesus.
6. I decree that the devil shall fail at any attempt to cause me to stumble in the name of Jesus.
7. I decree that all the elements will cooperate with me today in Jesus's name.
8. In the name of Jesus, I destroy every evil network established to take dominion over this day.
9. Father Lord, raise me up to walk worthy of and pleasing to you in the name of Jesus.
10. Father Lord, deliver me from every temptation today in the name of Jesus.
11. Oh Lord, give me favor with you and with man today in the name of Jesus.
12. I believe and I receive the answers to my prayers in the name of Jesus.
13. Thank you, Father, for hearing and answering my prayers in Jesus name.

Evening Prayers

Evening is a special time in Scripture. It is a time to offer up the sacrifice of praise and thanksgiving to God. It is also a time to reflect on Jesus, who is the Passover lamb. It is a time to pray for God's protection and provision through the night. Many people forget that it is predominately during the night that the wicked work their evil activities, such as establishing satanic networks and performing witchcraft.

Evening is also a time of cleansing from the activities of the day. There are many references to this in the book of Leviticus. There are many situations and activities addressed that make a person unclean until evening.

It is also in the night that the devil attacks people in their sleep through evil dreams. A dream doesn't necessarily need to be full of demonic images and such. A dream may be fairly benign—until you compare it with what is written in the Bible. The devil can be quite subtle and crafty at planting erroneous and evil thoughts through dreams. This is yet another example of why we must be well versed in Scripture and why the mental discipline to take every thought captive is so important.

12.1 Scripture Reading and Confession

May my prayer be counted as incense before You; The lifting up of my hands as the evening offering.

—Psalms 141:2

For seven days no leaven shall be seen with you in all your territory, and none of the flesh which you sacrifice on the evening of the first day shall remain overnight until morning.

—Deuteronomy 16:4

But at the place where the Lord your God chooses to establish His name, you shall sacrifice the Passover in the evening at sunset, at the time that you came out of Egypt.

—Deuteronomy 16:6

12.2 Prayers

1. In the name of the Lord Jesus Christ, Father God, I give you all the praise and glory and honor and I thank you for seeing me through this day in the name of Jesus.
2. I take authority over all demons of the night, bad dreams, nightmares, sex dreams, and anyone or anything trying to get into my dreams, and I command them to die now in the name of Jesus.
3. Father, send your warrior angels to protect me, my family, and my property as I sleep.
4. I ask you, Father, for a fiery wall of protection around me in Jesus's name.
5. Father God, forgive me for the sins I have committed today in the name of Jesus. [Name them.]

6. I command every agent of the devil in the physical and in the spiritual working evil against my family, myself, and this night to be destroyed in the name of Jesus.
7. I nullify every evil network established against me in the name of Jesus.
8. Father God, cover my family and me with the blood of Jesus tonight in the name of Jesus.
9. Father God, send you angels to stand guard around us tonight in the name of Jesus.
10. I command every plan of evil against my family and me to be sent into confusion and destroyed in the name of Jesus.
11. In the name of the Lord Jesus Christ, I subject my mind and my dreams only to the work of the Holy Spirit.
12. I ask you, Lord, to bind up all powers of darkness and forbid them to work in my dreams or any part of my subconscious while I sleep in Jesus's name.
13. Father God, cleanse my mind of the evil I have witnessed today in the name of Jesus.
14. Father God, cause me to dwell on good in the name of Jesus (Philippians 4:8).

Prayers for Spiritual Growth

It is difficult to grow beyond the level of what exists in most churches today. It is therefore necessary to put forth the effort as an individual to accomplish this task. The Holy Spirit will guide you. You must be willing to face the road ahead as was spoken of in Matt Sorger's prophecy. It isn't an easy road but the rewards are well worth the effort.

If you wish to go down this road, you will need to apply the principles discussed in Chapter 9 in order to be successful. None of this is complex. It is simple. This doesn't mean it is easy though. Sometimes it can be extremely difficult and trying. The last thing the devil wants is a Christian who knows who they are in Jesus Christ and puts that knowledge and faith into practice. Expect attacks. Use the prayers in this book to counter those attacks. Expect to be put through trials and tribulations, as is written in James 1:2–5. Pray your way through them. Ask for wisdom. Learn everything you can along the way.

By all means write your own prayers. Many of the prayers in this book can be used as a model and changed to suit a particular need.

Don't forget that it is impossible to get where you need to be by your own strength. As Paul says in 2 Corinthians 12:9 and in Philippians 4:13:

> And He has said to me, "My grace is sufficient for you, for power is perfected in weakness." Most gladly, therefore, I

> will rather boast about my weaknesses, so that the power of Christ may dwell in me.
>
> —2 Corinthians 12:9

> I can do all things through Him who strengthens me.
>
> —Philippians 4:13

God will provide that strength and courage as he has promised. His power is perfected in our weakness (2 Corinthians 12:9). This gives no room for any of us to boast in our own strength and it gives God all the glory. Read how God spoke to Joshua in Joshua chapter 1. He wasn't telling Joshua to use his own strength but commanding by way of decree for Joshua to be strong and courageous. Of course, Joshua had to work his faith to realize the results we see throughout this book.

13.1 Scripture Reading

> [12]For though by this time you ought to be teachers, you have need again for someone to teach you the elementary principles of the oracles of God, and you have come to need milk and not solid food. [13]For everyone who partakes only of milk is not accustomed to the word of righteousness, for he is an infant. [14]But solid food is for the mature, who because of practice have their senses trained to discern good and evil.
>
> —Hebrews 5:12–14

> So also we, while we were children, were held in bondage under the elemental things of the world.
>
> —Galatians 4:3

> Therefore leaving the elementary teaching about the Christ, let us press on to maturity, not laying again a foundation of repentance from dead works and of faith toward God.
>
> —Hebrews 6:1

1Therefore, putting aside all malice and all deceit and
hypocrisy and envy and all slander, 2like newborn babies,
long for the pure milk of the word, so that by it you
may grow in respect to salvation, 3if you have tasted the
kindness of the Lord.

—1 Peter 2:1–3

2Consider it all joy, my brethren, when you encounter
various trials, 3knowing that the testing of your faith
produces endurance. 4And let endurance have its perfect
result, so that you may be perfect and complete, lacking
in nothing. 5But if any of you lacks wisdom, let him ask
of God, who gives to all generously and without reproach,
and it will be given to him.

—James 1:2–5

8More than that, I count all things to be loss in view of
the surpassing value of knowing Christ Jesus my Lord,
for whom I have suffered the loss of all things, and count
them but rubbish so that I may gain Christ, 9and may
be found in Him, not having a righteousness of my own
derived from the Law, but that which is through faith
in Christ, the righteousness which comes from God on
the basis of faith, 10 that I may know Him and the power
of His resurrection and the fellowship of His sufferings,
being conformed to His death; 11in order that I may attain
to the resurrection from the dead. 12Not that I have already
obtained it or have already become perfect, but I press on
so that I may lay hold of that for which also I was laid
hold of by Christ Jesus. 13Brethren, I do not regard myself
as having laid hold of it yet; but one thing I do: forgetting
what lies behind and reaching forward to what lies ahead,
14I press on toward the goal for the prize of the upward call
of God in Christ Jesus.

—Philippians 3:8–14

13.2 Confession

I am not what the world or the devil says I am. I am a child of God. I am a royal priesthood. As a child of God, I have been given power and authority through Jesus Christ. By faith I overcome all the wiles of the devil. By faith I apply the word of God in my life. By faith I go down the road to spiritual maturity. By faith I overcome the trials and tribulations the Lord uses to instruct me. The Bible says that because I have received Jesus Christ as my Lord and Savior, I have the power and authority to tread upon serpents and scorpions and all the powers of the devil. I will not fail. I will succeed in the name of Jesus. Deuteronomy 31:8 says,

> The LORD is the one who goes ahead of you; He will be with you. He will not fail you or forsake you. Do not fear or be dismayed.

I put my faith and trust in my Lord Jesus to see me through and bring me into his victory. It is through Jesus Christ that I have right standing with God. It is through Jesus that I have access to the throne of grace. God will not withhold any good thing from me.

> [20]Now the God of peace, who brought up from the dead the great Shepherd of the sheep through the blood of the eternal covenant, even Jesus our Lord, [21]equip you in every good thing to do His will, working in us that which is pleasing in His sight, through Jesus Christ, to whom be the glory forever and ever. Amen.
>
> —Hebrews 13:20–21

I am seated with Christ in heavenly places and am empowered to exercise dominion over his creation in accordance with his plan for me. I am the head and not the tail, as is written in Deuteronomy 28:13–14:

> [28]The LORD will make you the head and not the tail, and you only will be above, and you will not be underneath, if you listen to the commandments of the LORD your God, which I charge you today, to observe them carefully, [14]and do not turn aside from any of the words which I command you today, to the right or to the left, to go after other gods to serve them.

I am fashioned after the likeness of God through Jesus Christ. I am redeemed by Jesus's death on the cross. I am the righteousness of God through Jesus Christ. I am who God says I am. I am seated with Christ in heavenly places far above all principalities and powers. I am an overwhelming conqueror in Jesus's name.

13.3 Prayers

1. Father God, forgive me of my sins in the name of Jesus. [Name them.]
2. Father God, cleanse me and make me holy and pure in your sight in the name of Jesus.
3. Father God, show me my hidden sins in the name of Jesus.
4. Lord Jesus, empower me to be honest with myself and with you in the name of Jesus.
5. Father God, reveal to me sin as you see it in the name of Jesus.
6. Lord Jesus, put your strength and courage in me in the name of Jesus.
7. Father God, open my eyes to the areas of my life that need change in the name of Jesus.
8. Father God, give me a warrior mindset in the name of Jesus.

9. Father God, open my eyes to your word in the name of Jesus.
10. O Lord, give me revelation of the breadth, length, depth, and height of the love of Christ in the name of Jesus.
11. O Lord, infuse in me the desire and drive to pursue holiness in the name of Jesus.
12. O Lord, increase and perfect what is lacking in my faith in the name of Jesus.
13. Father God, give me wisdom in the name of Jesus.
14. O Lord, make a way for me where there seems to be no way in the name of Jesus.
15. O Lord, give me the spirit of discipline in the name of Jesus.
16. O Lord, give me revelation into your word in the name of Jesus.
17. Teach me, O Lord, to listen to you in the name of Jesus.
18. Father God, give me wisdom, understanding, and knowledge of your word in the name of Jesus.
19. O Lord, empower me to put your word into practice in every area of my life in the name of Jesus.
20. The devil will not steal my divine destiny from me in the name of Jesus.
21. Every agent of the devil working against my divine destiny, be scattered forever in the name of Jesus.
22. I am the head and not the tail and the devil will not steal this from me in Jesus's name.
23. I command every evil report concerning me to be erased now in the name of Jesus.
24. I command every evil plan established against me to be completely destroyed in the name of Jesus.

25. Every evil yoke upon my life, I break you now in the name of Jesus.
26. My Father, remove all physical and spiritual barrenness from my life today in the name of Jesus.
27. My Father, revoke every generational curse operating in my life today in the name of Jesus.
28. My Father, remove every oppression and fear in my life today in the name of Jesus.
29. My Father, open every closed door of opportunity for me today in the name of Jesus.
30. My Father, break asunder every hindrance to my breakthroughs today in the name of Jesus.
31. Holy Ghost fire, destroy every demon affecting my life today in the name of Jesus.
32. My Father, break asunder every obstacle to my divine destiny today in the name of Jesus.
33. Thank you, Lord, for hearing and answering my prayers in the name of Jesus.
34. I believe and I receive the answers to my prayers in the name of Jesus.

Prayers for Cleansing the Mind

The mind is the focal point for the battle of your soul. The devil is an expert at deception and has been doing this for thousands of years. There are many situations we find ourselves in today that appear on the surface to be normal but in reality are the results of demonic activities that have occurred over a long period of time and with many people. The heretical teachings on the part of some churches and denominations discussed earlier in this book are typical examples. Closer to home, the devil deceives Christians into thinking they have no power or authority. Another erroneous philosophy is that Christians shouldn't be involved in politics. The list goes on and on.

Most people allow these ideas and thoughts to persist out of ignorance. Once enlightened, it becomes apparent how sinister the situation really is and how crafty the devil is. Even then, there may be many ideas or philosophies that people adhere to that are not of God. This is a sign of immaturity on the part of the Christian. We are supposed to know and act better than this.

It is clear from Scripture that things should not be this way. Our minds have become polluted with the world to the point that there is little in the life of a Christian that distinguishes them from those in the world.

It is imperative that we all be honest with ourselves and with Jesus concerning this situation. It is time to repent and make changes to be transformed into the likeness of Jesus Christ. Repentance and cleansing the mind of all this worldly garbage is where this needs to start. It is also imperative to know the Bible because it is truth, and this truth sheds light on darkness.

14.1 Scripture Reading and Confession

Do not be conformed to this world (this age), [*fashioned after and adapted to its external, superficial customs*], but be transformed (changed) by the [*entire*] renewal of your mind [*by its new ideals and its new attitude*], so that you may prove [*for yourselves*] what is the good and acceptable and perfect will of God, even the thing which is good and acceptable and perfect [*in His sight for you*].

—Romans 12:2 (AMP)

[13]Therefore, prepare your minds for action, keep sober in spirit, fix your hope completely on the grace to be brought to you at the revelation of Jesus Christ. [14]As obedient children, do not be conformed to the former lusts which were yours in your ignorance, [15]but like the Holy One who called you, be holy yourselves also in all your behavior; [16]because it is written, "YOU SHALL BE HOLY, FOR I AM HOLY."

—1 Peter 1:13–16

[20]But you did not learn Christ in this way, [21]if indeed you have heard Him and have been taught in Him, just as truth is in Jesus, [22]that, in reference to your former manner of life, you lay aside the old self, which is being corrupted in accordance with the lusts of deceit, [23]and that you be renewed in the spirit of your mind, [24]and put on the new self, which in the likeness of God has been created in righteousness and holiness of the truth.

—Ephesians 4:20–24

[5]He saved us, not on the basis of deeds which we have done in righteousness, but according to His mercy, by the

washing of regeneration and renewing by the Holy Spirit, [6]whom He poured out upon us richly through Jesus Christ our Savior, [7]so that being justified by His grace we would be made heirs according to the hope of eternal life.

—Titus 3:5–7

[8]Finally, brethren, whatever is true, whatever is honorable, whatever is right, whatever is pure, whatever is lovely, whatever is of good repute, if there is any excellence and if anything worthy of praise, dwell on these things. [9]The things you have learned and received and heard and seen in me, practice these things, and the God of peace will be with you.

—Philippians 4:8–9

[24]When the unclean spirit is gone out of a man, he walketh through dry places, seeking rest; and finding none, he saith, I will return unto my house whence I came out. [25]And when he cometh, he findeth it swept and garnished. [26]Then goeth he, and taketh to him seven other spirits more wicked than himself; and they enter in, and dwell there: and the last state of that man is worse than the first.

—Luke 11:24–26

14.2 Prayers

1. Father God, forgive me for allowing worldly influences in my mind in the name of Jesus.
2. Holy Spirit, cleanse me from every demonic pollutant in the name of Jesus.
3. I command every demonic influence on my mind to die in the name of Jesus.
4. Holy Ghost fire, as you came down on the day of Pentecost, come upon me now in the name of Jesus.

5. Father God, empower me to discipline myself to focus on you and your word instead of the world in Jesus's name.
6. I command every unclean thought to get out of my mind now in the name of Jesus.
7. I command every unclean image to get out of my mind now in the name of Jesus.
8. O Lord, transform me into your likeness in the name of Jesus.
9. In Jesus's name, Father God, remind me of your word whenever I entertain evil things in my mind.
10. In Jesus's name, Father God, convict me of my sins.
11. Father God, empower me to think and do what is good and acceptable in your sight in the name of Jesus.
12. Anointing for Godly thinking, come upon my life in the name of Jesus.
13. Every power using my thoughts against me, be nullified in the name of Jesus.
14. Power of God, arise and move me forward in the name of Jesus.
15. Power of God, arise and manifest in my life in the name of Jesus.
16. My destroyed virtues, receive life from God in the name of Jesus.
17. Father God, arise and make a way for me where there seems to be no way in the name of Jesus.
18. Every agent of the devil assigned against me, scatter in the name of Jesus.
19. Father God, cover me from head to toe with the blood of Jesus in the name Jesus.,

20. Holy Ghost fire, destroy every evil power assigned against me in the name of Jesus.
21. No weapon formed against me will prosper in the name of Jesus.
22. In the name of Jesus, I command every evil influence affecting my mind and thought life to be destroyed right now.
23. Thank you, Lord, for hearing and answering my prayers in the name of Jesus.
24. I give you, Lord, all the praise and glory and honor for answering my prayers in Jesus's name.
25. I believe and I receive the answers to my prayers in the name of Jesus.

Prayers for the Home

This chapter covers prayers for cleansing and protection of the home. The world is a filthy place and we often bring dirt into the house, both spiritually and physically. It is easy to see the physical dirt and clean it up. It can be more difficult and problematic with the spiritual because it isn't always as visible. It is therefore necessary to be diligent about spiritual cleansing. As with doing the physical house cleaning on a regular basis, doing the spiritual cleansing on a regular basis is also necessary. Don't wait for a problem to manifest.

Demons and other spiritual filth can be attracted by objects in the home that are ungodly. These may include pictures, statues, religious objects, or any other thing that is not Godly.

Some objects are obvious, such as statues of other religious gods. You may need to go through your home and cleanse it from these things. What you have in your home is your decision and is between you and Jesus. When in doubt, pray. If he says get rid of the thing, then get rid of it. Just be aware of the spiritual consequences given in Scripture (John 14:15).

The following may be done as a family, but if you are not married, you can complete these steps yourself.

The husband is the spiritual head of the family. It is his God-given responsibility to provide that spiritual umbrella over his family. This is done through prayer, Bible reading and education, spiritual protection, etc. Turn off the TV! Women tend to be more sensitive to the world around them than men. Men tend to ignore many of the things their wives are aware of. God put men and women together as husbands and wives. The husband and wife is a team and as such need to listen to each other.

Both husband and wife should go around the house and sanctify and cover items such as furniture, etc., with the blood of Jesus regularly. The fact that you are a Christian doesn't prevent demons from getting in your home to cause problems. Pray over your pets too. Cover them with the blood of Jesus. Don't forget, demons can inhabit animals too (Matthew 8:32, Mark 5:13, Luke 8:33). Although demons don't care specifically about animals, they can and do use them as a vehicle to cause problems with people. I must stress that these are things that should be taken seriously. Both my wife and I have had several experiences where our pets were harassed by demons. And yes, we had to lay hands on them and deliver them when we had not been as diligent as we should have been. Animals tend to be more sensitive to these things than people. Several times we have had our pets alert us to the presence of demons. Getting rid of the demons is a simple matter of using the power and authority you have through Jesus. I must stress that if you endeavor to grow closer to Jesus and start using the power and authority you have through him, expect demons to harass you. This isn't something to be alarmed about or fearful of. The devil and his demons are ones to be defeated and utterly destroyed. You have the power and authority through Jesus, so use it and *don't back down.*

The following are some starting points that should be done by the husband, or yourself, if you are a single parent, every morning. If you are single, you can do this too by laying hands on yourself and praying for God to do the same for you what would otherwise be done for each family member.

- Repent of your sins and ask forgiveness for them. Be specific. Ask God to reveal any sins you may be unaware of.

- Lay hands on your wife and children individually and pray for them.
- Cover yourself and your family corporately. "Father, surround us with the walls of the blood of Jesus and the walls of your angels, and the wall of your shadow in the name of Jesus."
- Cover each family member with the blood of Jesus and decree blessings and prosperity over them. A good starting point is the Aaronic blessing found in Number 6:24–26.

> [24]The LORD bless you, and keep you; [25]The LORD make His face shine on you, And be gracious to you; [26]The LORD lift up His countenance on you, And give you peace.

Keeping your home clean will ensure that it will be a peaceful refuge from the world.

15.1 Scripture Reading and Confession

> [25]The graven images of their gods you are to burn with fire; you shall not covet the silver or the gold that is on them, nor take it for yourselves, or you will be snared by it, for it is an abomination to the LORD your God. [26]You shall not bring an abomination into your house, and like it come under the ban; you shall utterly detest it and you shall utterly abhor it, for it is something banned.
>
> —Deuteronomy 7:25–26

> [11]Israel has sinned, and they have also transgressed My covenant which I commanded them. And they have even taken some of the things under the ban and have both stolen and deceived. Moreover, they have also put them

among their own things. [12]Therefore the sons of Israel cannot stand before their enemies; they turn their backs before their enemies, for they have become accursed. I will not be with you anymore unless you destroy the things under the ban from your midst.

—Joshua 7:11–12

[1]Now it shall be, if you diligently obey the LORD your God, being careful to do all His commandments which I command you today, the LORD your God will set you high above all the nations of the earth. [2]All these blessings will come upon you and overtake you if you obey the LORD your God: [3]Blessed shall you be in the city, and blessed shall you be in the country. [4]Blessed shall be the offspring of your body and the produce of your ground and the offspring of your beasts, the increase of your herd and the young of your flock. [5]Blessed shall be your basket and your kneading bowl. [6]Blessed shall you be when you come in, and blessed shall you be when you go out. [7]The LORD shall cause your enemies who rise up against you to be defeated before you; they will come out against you one way and will flee before you seven ways. [8]The LORD will command the blessing upon you in your barns and in all that you put your hand to, and He will bless you in the land which the LORD your God gives you. [9]The LORD will establish you as a holy people to Himself, as He swore to you, if you keep the commandments of the LORD your God and walk in His ways. [10]So all the peoples of the earth will see that you are called by the name of the LORD, and they will be afraid of you. [11]The LORD will make you abound in prosperity, in the offspring of your body and in the offspring of your beast and in the produce of your ground, in the land which the LORD swore to your fathers to give you. [12]The LORD will open for you His good storehouse, the heavens, to give rain to your land in its season and to bless all the work of your hand; and you shall lend to many nations, but you shall not borrow. [13]The LORD will make you the head

> and not the tail, and you only will be above, and you will not be underneath, if you listen to the commandments of the LORD your God, which I charge you today, to observe them carefully, [14]and do not turn aside from any of the words which I command you today, to the right or to the left, to go after other gods to serve them.
>
> —Deuteronomy 28:1–14

> And now it has pleased You to bless the house of Your servant, that it may continue forever before You; for You, O LORD, have blessed, and it is blessed forever.
>
> —1 Chronicles 17:27

15.2 Prayers

These prayers should be repeated in each room of your home. Lay hands on furniture and other items. Lay hand on the walls too.

1. My Father, forgive me for my sins in the name of Jesus. [Name them.]
2. O Lord, forgive me for my lukewarmness in the name of Jesus.
3. O Lord, forgive me for my laziness in my walk with you in the name of Jesus.
4. O Lord, forgive me for failing to live up to the standards you established in your word in the name of Jesus.
5. Lord, reveal all my unknown sins to me in the name of Jesus.
6. O Lord, cleanse me of all unrighteousness in the name of Jesus.
7. O Lord, remove anything from my life that is contrary to your will in the name of Jesus.

8. Holy Ghost fire, destroy every strongman established over my household in the name of Jesus.
9. I command every demon, its support, its replacements, its command structure, all evil devices and influences established against my home, to be utterly and completely destroyed by the fire of God in the name of Jesus.
10. I cast all of this garbage into the abyss until Judgment Day in the name of Jesus.
11. I cover everything in this room with the blood of Jesus in Jesus's name.
12. I sanctify everything in this room with the blood of Jesus in Jesus's name.
13. I bind every demon and spiritual pollution in this room/object and cast it into the abyss until judgment day in the name of Jesus.
14. I dedicate, surrender, and consecrate this house/room and everything in it to my Lord Jesus Christ in Jesus's name.
15. Father, send your angels to stand guard around this house in Jesus's name.
16. Thank you, Lord, for hearing and answering my prayers in the name of Jesus.
17. I believe and I receive the answers to my prayers in the name of Jesus.

Health

Health problems can have a number of sources. They may be genetic, demonic, diet-related, sin-related, accidents, war- or job-related injuries, and so on. Oftentimes, sins such as unforgiveness and bitterness will be the mechanism by which demons are able to perpetuate an illness, or inhibit the Holy Spirit from healing. It is therefore important that one be honest with themselves and evaluate their situation. The act of harboring unforgiveness and bitterness can and does give the devil a foothold to bring health problems. Oftentimes, one may have forgotten a situation earlier in life that brought about an illness. Being honest with yourself and open to revelation from the Holy Spirit, either directly or through another person, will help greatly in addressing a health problem.

There will be many more miracles if the church will wake from its slumber.

Regardless of the cause, your case is not impossible for God. It is entirely possible that the Holy Spirit may tell you to do some things such as getting exercise and changing your diet and you will be healed this way. You may also experience a healing miracle.

Healing is often a very sensitive subject. Sometimes people don't get healed and sometimes others experience a dramatic healing miracle. I have heard incredible testimonies from people I have personally known, to include people being raised from the dead. I have personally witnessed people's legs grow, heart problems healed. I have experienced healing myself, and laid hands on people and seen them healed. I have also seen people whom I felt well deserving of healing fail to receive it, and good people die from their illnesses leaving a young family behind. There is a lot that goes on beyond what meets the eye than we are aware of. This speaks of the need for revelation from the Holy Spirit. A common case is someone harboring a sin (which can include bitterness and unforgiveness). Only after a revelation to this effect was communicated to the individual did they repent and then receive their healing.

Healing may not be realized for various reasons, which includes some of the following:

- Sin. This may also be generational.
- Demonic activities and the results of witchcraft.
- Lack of faith.
- Evil covenants.
- Generational curses or evil covenants made by ancestors.
- Wrong motives (e.g., tempting God).
- Unforgiveness or bitterness toward someone who has wronged you.

Unforgiveness and bitterness tend to be one of the more prominent hindrances to healing. This sin gives the devil a foothold from which to cause a lot of problems, both physically and mentally.

There have been times when people have been upset at the person who laid hands on them when they did not receive healing. It is Jesus who heals and not the person, and it is likely this attitude that keeps their healing from manifesting. Such an attitude will bring bitterness, and bitterness is a significant deterrence to healing.

Some people who don't get healed beat themselves up for a perceived lack of faith. Don't. You may not know all the reasons. It might be a lack of faith or it may be something else. Because of the unknowns, it is necessary to pray and seek revelation. Regardless of the reason, pursue a closer relationship with Jesus. Some people in this situation did just this before they finally received their healing.

For anyone who needs to be healed, a first step is to make a good, honest evaluation of yourself to see if there is anything in your life that has either caused the problem or will hinder you from receiving your healing. Generational issues are likely to be unknown but can be revealed through prayer and revelation.

Other than the exercise and diet issues above, health problems can manifest as a result of a wide range of issues. Some can be generational curses, some genetic (it doesn't matter if it is genetic or not, God can still heal), some self imposed, some the results of accidents or war injuries, some demonic, and so on.

Read the four Gospels. Jesus healed people without regard to their spiritual level or background or their physical or mental state. He healed all who came to him. Their act of coming to him was an act of faith that was rewarded by them being healed. For cases when those who needed healing were unable to come to him, others either carried them or conveyed a message. In either case, others interceded on their behalf and they were healed. Jesus never asked what church (or synagogue) they went to. He never asked what denomination they belonged to. He didn't pray for a half hour seeking to know whether God wanted a particular individual healed or not. He just healed them all. And so should we!

A key point is that healing is an undeniable miracle, especially for the recipient. It presents the undeniable fact that the Holy Spirit is here and present with us today. Healing is a profound blessing. Sinners see and experience and get saved. God is always glorified through miraculous healing.

16.1 Scriptural Facts About Foods

The majority of illnesses today are a result of poor diet, lack of exercise, and chemical contaminants in our food and water supplies. Diabetes and other problems have reached epidemic levels. It is therefore important for everyone to become educated in these subjects.

> [19]Or do you not know that your body is a temple of the Holy Spirit who is in you, whom you have from God, and that you are not your own? [20]For you have been bought with a price: therefore glorify God in your body.
>
> —1 Corinthians 6:19–20

Obesity has become a serious problem throughout many countries today. Most of the time, it is not due to disease or genetic problems. It is due to poor diet and the lack of exercise. The failure to take care of the temple of the Holy Spirit so much as it is reasonably possible to do so is sin. Obesity has much of its roots in the spirit of laziness.

Leviticus chapter 11 and Deuteronomy chapter 14 outline the foods that we are and are not to eat. Although not many adhere to a "Kosher" diet today, dismissing what God has to say on the subject is disobedience and has its risks. There are reasons why he listed what we should and should not eat. Some of the practical reasons we know of today are that particular animals may be subject to certain nasty parasites. Some species are prone to carry certain diseases. Others we simply don't know. In any case, God knows best. A general (and incomplete) list of clean and unclean meats are listed here. The specific species of animals listed in Scripture are generally what the Israelites had available in their geographic region.

General Categories of Clean Meats

1. Animals that part the hoof and chew the cud.
2. Fish that have scales and fins.
3. Birds that have clean characteristics (e.g., not birds of prey).
4. Insects of the locust family.

General Categories of Unclean Meats

1. Swine.
2. Animals that walk on paws—canine and feline, bears, etc.
3. Equine.
4. Reptiles and amphibians.
5. Birds of prey.
6. Rodents.

You may wish to do further reading and research on this subject. There are a multitude of books available on healthy diets. A little research and common sense will go a long way. In general, our society eats way too much meat in proportion to the quantity of vegetables, nuts, and fruits eaten.

16.2 Give Credit

No matter how your healing is done or who it is done through, it is Jesus, or perhaps more appropriately the Holy Spirit, who does it. Give all glory, praise, and honor to him.

> But when the crowds saw this, they were awestruck, and glorified God, who had given such authority to men.
>
> —Matthew 9:8

> So the crowd marveled as they saw the mute speaking, the crippled restored, and the lame walking, and the blind seeing; and they glorified the God of Israel.
>
> —Matthew 15:31

> And he got up and immediately picked up the pallet and went out in the sight of everyone, so that they were all amazed and were glorifying God, saying, "We have never seen anything like this."
>
> —Mark 2:12

> 25Immediately he got up before them, and picked up what he had been lying on, and went home glorifying
> God. 26They were all struck with astonishment and began glorifying God; and they were filled with fear, saying, "We have seen remarkable things today."
>
> —Luke 5:25-26

> And He laid His hands on her; and immediately she was made erect again and began glorifying God.
>
> —Luke 13:13

> Immediately he regained his sight and began following Him, glorifying God; and when all the people saw it, they gave praise to God.
>
> —Luke 18:43

The same Jesus who worked these miracles of healing, who never changes, who is perfect in all his ways, is here today. He can and does work the same miracles, and more, today. It doesn't matter what it is—a cold, cancer, an amputated limb, or any other issue. It can be healed. Period.

Notice that 1 Peter 2:24 makes it clear that the healing he provides was already done on the cross. This is past tense. It has already been done. All that is needed is to appropriate this healing today.

16.3 Scripture Reading

> And He Himself bore our sins in His body on the cross, so that we might die to sin and live to righteousness; for by His wounds you were healed.
>
> —1 Peter 2:24

Verses of healing from the four Gospels are too numerous to list. Throughout the four gospels we see the demonstration of power and willingness of the Holy Spirit to heal. The book of Acts also documents numerous cases after the Day of Pentecost and throughout the ministries of the apostles.

> But He was pierced through for our transgressions, He was crushed for our iniquities; The chastening for our well-being fell upon Him, And by His scourging we are healed.
>
> —Isaiah 53:5

> And He Himself bore our sins in His body on the cross, so that we might die to sin and live to righteousness; for by His wounds you were healed.
>
> —1 Peter 2:24

> 2Bless the LORD, O my soul, And forget none of His benefits; 3Who pardons all your iniquities, Who heals all your diseases.
>
> —Psalms 103:2–3

16.4 Confession

> And He said, "If you will give earnest heed to the voice of the LORD your God, and do what is right in His sight, and give ear to His commandments, and keep all His statutes, I will put none of the diseases on you which I have put on the Egyptians; for I, the LORD, am your healer."
>
> —Exodus 15:26

O Lord my God, I cried to You for help, and You healed me.

—Psalms 30:2

He sent His word and healed them, And delivered them from their destructions.

—Psalms 107:20

[7]Do not be wise in your own eyes; Fear the Lord and turn away from evil. [8]It will be healing to your body And refreshment to your bones.

—Proverbs 3:7–8

[2]"But for you who fear My name, the sun of righteousness will rise with healing in its wings; and you will go forth and skip about like calves from the stall. [3]"You will tread down the wicked, for they will be ashes under the soles of your feet on the day which I am preparing," says the Lord of hosts.

—Malachi 4:2–3

Jesus said to him, "I will come and heal him."

—Matthew 8:7

[16]When evening came, they brought to Him many who were demon-possessed; and He cast out the spirits with a word, and healed all who were ill. [17]This was to fulfill what was spoken through Isaiah the prophet: "HE HIMSELF TOOK OUR INFIRMITIES AND CARRIED AWAY OUR DISEASES."

—Matthew 8:16–17

But Jesus, aware of this, withdrew from there. Many followed Him, and He healed them all.

—Matthew 12:15

And large crowds came to Him, bringing with them those who were lame, crippled, blind, mute, and many others, and they laid them down at His feet; and He healed them.

—Matthew 15:30

And He said to her, "Daughter, your faith has made you well; go in peace and be healed of your affliction."

—Mark 5:34

[40]While the sun was setting, all those who had any who were sick with various diseases brought them to Him; and laying His hands on each one of them, He was healing them. [41]Demons also were coming out of many, shouting, "You are the Son of God!"

—Luke 4:40–41

[15]Now one of them, when he saw that he had been healed, turned back, glorifying God with a loud voice, [16]and he fell on his face at His feet, giving thanks to Him. And he was a Samaritan.

—Luke 17:15–16

16.5 Prayers

Because of the varied causes of health problems, prayers are categorized. The prayers for healing are general in nature. As was discussed earlier, many of the prayers for healing can be adapted to address any illness. Also, many of the nonhealth-related prayers can and should be used for any other applicable issue.

Ask Forgiveness for Sins

1. Father God, reveal to me any sin I have committed that caused [name the medical issue] in the name of Jesus.
2. My Father, forgive me for committing these sins in the name of Jesus. [Name them.]

3. I forgive [name them] who have sinned against me in the name of Jesus.
4. Thank you, Father, for your grace and forgiveness in the name of Jesus.

Generational Sins

1. My Father, forgive my mother and father for the sins they have passed down to me in the name of Jesus.
2. My Father, forgive my ancestors four generations back for the sins that have propagated down to me in the name of Jesus.
3. I break every evil hold these ancestral sins have on me in the name of Jesus.
4. I proclaim my freedom from all ancestral sins on both my father's and mother's side of my family in the name of Jesus.

Generational Curses

1. The earth is the Lord's and the fullness of it. I am a child of God in the name of Jesus.
2. I nullify any ancestral curse propagated to me in the name of Jesus.
3. I command every ancestral curse spoken against my family line to be nullified in the name of Jesus.
4. I command every curse spoken by my ancestors against my family line to be nullified in the name of Jesus.
5. I destroy the effects of every ancestral curse spoken against me in the name of Jesus.
6. I proclaim my freedom from the effects of every ancestral curse spoken against me in the name of Jesus.

Curses and Witchcraft

1. My Father, cover me from head to toe with the blood of Jesus in Jesus's name.
2. My Father, send your angels to stand guard around me and protect me in the name of Jesus.
3. In Jesus's name, I command every witchcraft curse spoken against me to be nullified now.
4. In Jesus's name, I command every witchcraft altar established against me to be destroyed now.
5. In Jesus's name, I command every witch practicing against me to fall into their own traps now.
6. In Jesus's name, I command every witchcraft network established against me to be destroyed now.
7. In Jesus's name, I command every evil witchcraft device used against me to be destroyed now.

Evil Ancestral Covenants

1. Every evil ancestral covenant affecting my life and health, I nullify you in the name of Jesus.
2. I command every evil ancestral covenant to be erased by the blood of Jesus in the name of Jesus.
3. I decree my freedom from every evil ancestral covenant in the name of Jesus.

Current Evil Covenants

1. Every evil covenant I may have agreed to, willingly or not, be erased by the blood of Jesus in Jesus's name.
2. I decree my freedom from every evil covenant I may have agreed to in the name of Jesus.

Demonic Influences

1. I command every demon causing [name your medical issue] in Jesus's name. Get out now in the name of Jesus.
2. I destroy every demon causing [name your medical issue] in Jesus's name.
3. I command every demonic influence causing [name your medical issue] in Jesus's name. I destroy you in the name of Jesus.
4. I command every demonic device established against me to cause [name your medical issue] in Jesus's name. I destroy you in the name of Jesus.

General Prayers for Healing

1. Thank you, Lord, for your redemption in Jesus's name.
2. Thank you, Lord, for healing me in the name of Jesus.
3. I lose myself from every infirmity in the name of Jesus.
4. My Father, heal every hidden illness in my body in the name of Jesus.
5. Holy Ghost fire, go through my body from head to toe and cleanse me in the name of Jesus.
6. Holy Ghost fire, go through my body from head to toe and heal me in the name of Jesus.
7. Holy Ghost fire, go through my body and restore [name your medical issue] so that it operates as it is supposed to in the name of Jesus.
8. I command my [name your medical issue] to be healed in the name of Jesus.
9. I command my [name the body part] to get in line with the word of God and work properly in the name of Jesus.

10. My Father, cause every desire and expectation of the enemy to be nullified in the name of Jesus.
11. I decree my freedom from [name your medical issue] in the name of Jesus.
12. My Father, destroy every satanic deposit in my body in the name of Jesus.
13. Lord Jesus, perform a creative healing miracle on me now in the name of Jesus.
14. Lord Jesus, I give you all the glory, all the praise, and all the honor for operating in my life today in the name of Jesus.
15. Thank you, Lord, for hearing and answering my prayers in the name of Jesus.
16. I believe and I receive the answers to my prayers in the name of Jesus.

Salvation for Others

When people choose to reject the leading of the Holy Spirit, they fall into the trap of Satan. For most, there is a distinct event where this occurs, usually at an early age. We have all done this. The devil then blinds people so they don't see the truth and deceives them to turn them away from the Gospel.

> [3]And even if our gospel is veiled, it is veiled to those who are perishing, [4]in whose case the god of this world has blinded the minds of the unbelieving so that they might not see the light of the gospel of the glory of Christ, who is the image of God.
>
> —2 Corinthians 4:3–4

> [4]Who desires all men to be saved and to come to the knowledge of the truth. [5]For there is one God, and one mediator also between God and men, the man Christ Jesus, [6]who gave Himself as a ransom for all, the testimony given at the proper time.
>
> —1 Timothy 2:4–6

The only way anyone will come to the truth is through the power of the Holy Spirit. The Holy Spirit will, of course, move on someone when others pray and intercede for them.

Influences from the world and from the devil distract and hide the truth from people. It is therefore essential to intercede on behalf of these people so they will be saved. This point of prayer is essential for the church to accomplish.

17.1 Scripture Reading and Confession

The following are but a few of the many Scriptures throughout the Bible concerning the wonderful grace and salvation we have through our Lord Jesus Christ.

> [16]"For God so loved the world, that He gave His only begotten Son, that whoever believes in Him shall not perish, but have eternal life. [17]"For God did not send the Son into the world to judge the world, but that the world might be saved through Him.
>
> —John 3:16–17

> The Lord is not slow about His promise, as some count slowness, but is patient toward you, not wishing for any to perish but for all to come to repentance.
>
> —2 Peter 3:9

> Jesus said to him, "I am the way, and the truth, and the life; no one comes to the Father but through Me."
>
> —John 14:6

> Surely, thus says the Lord, "Even the captives of the mighty man will be taken away, And the prey of the tyrant will be rescued; For I will contend with the one who contends with you, And I will save your sons.
>
> —Isaiah 49:25

17.2 Prayers

1. My Father, forgive me for committing these sins [name them] in the name of Jesus.

2. I forgive [name them] who have sinned against me in the name of Jesus.
3. I command every stronghold of the devil blinding [name], be torn off now in the name of Jesus.
4. Thank you, Father, that it is not your will that any perish but that all come to the knowledge of the truth in the name of Jesus.
5. My Father, open the eyes of [name] to your love and truth in the name of Jesus.
6. I claim [name] for the kingdom of heaven in the name of Jesus.
7. I decree that every desire of the enemy upon [name] shall fail in the name of Jesus.
8. I break all curses upon [name] hindering them from coming to Jesus in the name of Jesus.
9. I destroy all evil powers of darkness hindering [name] from coming to Jesus in the name of Jesus.
10. Holy Spirit of God, move on [name] now to get them saved in the name of Jesus.
11. I bind the spirit of blindness in [name] in the name of Jesus.
12. I tear down and destroy every wall of rebellion toward God in [name] in the name of Jesus.
13. I tear down and destroy every wall of deception toward God in [name] in the name of Jesus.
14. My Father, cause your mercy and grace to overwhelm [name] in the name of Jesus.
15. Thank you, Father, for your grace and forgiveness in the name of Jesus.

16. Thank you, Lord, for hearing and answering my prayers in the name of Jesus.
17. I believe and I receive the answers to my prayers in the name of Jesus.

Finances and Employment

Lord Jesus has promised to take care of you. This fact is clear in Scripture. During these hard economic times, it is that much more important to stand on his word. It doesn't matter how bad things may appear, He has promised, and he will keep his promises. This fact is emphatic throughout Scripture. It is up to you to place your faith and trust in him. Faith without works is dead so at the same time you need to be active, such as searching for a job, pursuing business deals, etc.

All this sounds good and well but it is not without direct experience with God's provision that I say these things. Over the years, I have experienced miraculous provisions on multiple occasions and had some truly profound experiences concerning God's provision. So much so that I plan to write about these and many other experiences in another book. It is often difficult to get one's eyes off the problem and on the solution—Jesus. Remember what happened to Peter when he walked on the water and took his eyes off Jesus.

18.1 Scripture Reading

> The Lord is the one who goes ahead of you; He will be with you. He will not fail you or forsake you. Do not fear or be dismayed.
>
> —Deuteronomy 31:8

[7]Ask, and it will be given to you; seek, and you will find; knock, and it will be opened to you. [8]For everyone who asks receives, and he who seeks finds, and to him who knocks it will be opened.

—Matthew 7:7–8

You will also decree a thing, and it will be established for you; And light will shine on your ways.

—Job 22:28

I have been young and now I am old, Yet I have not seen the righteous forsaken Or his descendants begging bread.

—Psalms 37:25

For the LORD loves justice And does not forsake His godly ones; They are preserved forever, But the descendants of the wicked will be cut off.

—Psalms 37:28

[25]"For this reason I say to you, do not be worried about your life, as to what you will eat or what you will drink; nor for your body, as to what you will put on. Is not life more than food, and the body more than clothing? [26]"Look at the birds of the air, that they do not sow, nor reap nor gather into barns, and yet your heavenly Father feeds them. Are you not worth much more than they? [27]"And who of you by being worried can add a single hour to his life? [28]"And why are you worried about clothing? Observe how the lilies of the field grow; they do not toil nor do they spin, [29]yet I say to you that not even Solomon in all his glory clothed himself like one of these. [30]"But if God so clothes the grass of the field, which is alive today and tomorrow is thrown into the furnace, will He not much more clothe you? You of little faith! [31]"Do not worry then, saying, 'What will we eat? ' or 'What will we drink? ' or 'What will we wear for clothing? ' [32]"For the Gentiles eagerly seek all these things; for your heavenly Father knows that you

need all these things. [33]"But seek first His kingdom and His righteousness, and all these things will be added to you. [34]"So do not worry about tomorrow; for tomorrow will care for itself. Each day has enough trouble of its own.

—Matthew 6:25–34

Therefore let us draw near with confidence to the throne of grace, so that we may receive mercy and find grace to help in time of need.

—Hebrews 4:16

"Do not fear, for I am with you; Do not anxiously look about you, for I am your God. I will strengthen you, surely I will help you, Surely I will uphold you with My righteous right hand."

—Isaiah 41:10

18.2 Prayer and Confession

1. I confess that you, Lord, are the God of heaven and earth. You are all sufficient. You are the Alpha and Omega; the beginning and the end. You are the mighty God. Jesus Christ is the Son of God. Jesus is my Lord, my Savior, my King, my Redeemer, my provider, and my victory in Jesus's name.
2. Every generational curse of poverty over my family and me, I break you now in the name of Jesus.
3. I decree my freedom from the spirit of poverty in the name of Jesus.
4. I command every spirit of poverty affecting my family and me to be destroyed in the name of Jesus.
5. I command every evil garment placed on me to be destroyed by the fire of God in the name of Jesus.

6. My Father, put on me the garments of favor, honor, prosperity, priesthood, and kingship in the name of Jesus.
7. I decree prosperity for my family and me in the name of Jesus.
8. I command every spirit of distraction and hindrance to prayers to be destroyed right now in Jesus's name.
9. My Father, shield me in Jesus's blood in the name of Jesus.
10. I ask you, Holy Spirit, to move in my life right now and fulfill your promises to me in the name of Jesus.
11. I ask you, Lord, for the strength to press forward in the name of Jesus. I ask you Lord to renew my strength. The word of God says in Isaiah 40:31,

    > Yet those who wait for the Lord Will gain new strength; They will mount up with wings like eagles, They will run and not get tired, They will walk and not become weary.

12. I ask you, Lord, to honor your word that can never fail in the name of Jesus Christ.
13. In the name of Jesus Christ, I come against all obstacles and walls the enemy has created against me. I command those walls to destroyed be destroyed now in the name of Jesus. I command all the agents of the devil in the physical and in the spiritual to be bound in Jesus's name. I command every demon assigned against my progress to be destroyed now in Jesus's name.
14. In Jesus's name, I come against all monitoring spirits that have been keeping track of me. I command them to be destroyed right now. I cast them to the abyss until judgment day in Jesus's name.
15. I cast out the spirit of fear from my life in Jesus's name. I stand in the authority of the word of God. I stand in the

power of God. I command my situation to change for the best right now in Jesus's name. I will never beg. I am a lender and I am not a borrower in Jesus's name. God has blessed me. The word of God says I am blessed and I am a blessing in Jesus's name.

16. In Jesus's name, I cancel every negative word I have said. I command all of them to be erased right now in Jesus's name. From today, I speak positive words for myself. I speak words of faith into my life in Jesus's name. I believe that everything I have spoken according to God's will for me will come to pass now in Jesus's name. I shall live as God has purposed that I live on this earth, in joy, in peace, in prosperity, in favor, in health, in the name of Jesus.
17. In Jesus's name, I cancel any spirit of confusion and indecision in my life. I cancel any spirit of fear and oppression against me. I have a sound mind in Jesus's name. I reject any deceit or disgrace against me and I refuse these things in Jesus's name. Fire of the Holy Spirit, consume any attempts of the devil to cause me to lose focus because I seek a miracle for [jobs/businesses/finances] in Jesus's name.
18. In Jesus's name, I reject and I destroy every spirit of tiredness, laziness, weakness, and defeat concerning this trial I am in right now. Father, I ask that you renew my strength and my mind in Jesus's name. The Bible says in Luke 1:37,

    > For nothing will be impossible with God.

    I believe God's word is true. As it says in Isaiah 55:11,

    > So will My word be which goes forth from My mouth; It will not return to Me empty, Without accomplishing what I desire, And without succeeding in the matter for which I sent it.

My case is not impossible for God in Jesus's name. In the name of Jesus, I ask for grace to trust God afresh in my situation. I ask for faith in God to arise in me. It is written in the word of God in Hebrews 11:6,

> And without faith it is impossible to please Him, for he who comes to God must believe that He is and that He is a rewarder of those who seek Him.

19. In Jesus's name, I destroy all attempts of the devil to cause people to keep disappointing me. I reject disappointments in Jesus's name. I reject empty promises in Jesus's name. In Jesus's name, anything I do now shall be stable and fruitful. I will no longer go on fruitless ventures. I receive progress, promotion, success, and prosperity in the name of Jesus Christ.
20. I command my spirit, soul, and body to be transformed and renewed by the Spirit of God (Romans 12:2). I rise up in confidence and trust God for a miracle in my [job/business/finances] in Jesus's name. In the name of Jesus Christ, I command every plan of the devil to deceive me and to draw back my faith and trust in Jesus to be destroyed in Jesus's name. It is written in the book of Hebrews 10:38,

    > But my righteous one shall live by faith; and if he shrinks back, my soul has no pleasure in him.

    In Jesus's name, I continue believing and standing in faith for my [job/business/finances] to manifest. The Bible says in Hebrews 6:12,

    > So that you will not be sluggish, but imitators of those who through faith and patience inherit the promises.

21. I stand on God's promises to me as a child of God that I should live in abundance. God has spoken in his word that

the Lord is my provider and that I should lack nothing. Right now, I seek God in confidence that he has already heard me and is still hearing my prayers in Jesus's name. The word of God says in Hebrews 10:23,

> Let us hold fast the confession of our hope without wavering, for He who promised is faithful.

The Bible says in Romans 10:11,

> For the scripture says, Whoever believes in him shall not be disappointed.

In Jesus's name.

22. Almighty God shall never fail for he is faithful and has promised to see me through every tribulation. The Bible says he has promised that he will never leave me nor forsake me in Jesus's name. Psalms 34:19 says,

> Many are the afflictions of the righteous, But the LORD delivers him out of them all.

Deuteronomy 31:8 says,

> The LORD is the one who goes ahead of you; He will be with you. He will not fail you or forsake you. Do not fear or be dismayed.

Hebrews 13:5 says,

> I will never desert you, nor will I ever forsake you.

Lord, lift me up in accordance to your word and your will for me in Jesus's name. Deuteronomy 28:13 says,

> The LORD will make you the head and not the tail, and you only will be above, and you will not be underneath, if you listen to the commandments of the LORD your God, which I charge you today, to observe them carefully.

Isaiah 41:10 says,

> Do not fear, for I am with you; Do not anxiously look about you, for I am your God. I will strengthen you, surely I will help you, Surely I will uphold you with My righteous right hand.

Hebrews 4:16 says,

> Therefore let us draw near with confidence to the throne of grace, so that we may receive mercy and find grace to help in time of need.

The word of God says in Psalms 23:1 that,

> The LORD is my shepherd, I shall not want.

Numbers 23:19 says,

> God is not a man, that He should lie, Nor a son of man, that He should repent; Has He said, and will He not do it? Or has He spoken, and will He not make it good?

23. Almighty Father, I ask you to honor your word in my life today as I speak it. I remind you of your promises to me in Jesus's name.
24. My Father, I ask you to manifest my [job/business/finances] for me in the name of Jesus Christ. You are my only helper. Your word says I should not put my trust in man to help me, so today, Lord, I put my trust in you to arise to my help in Jesus's name.
25. In Jesus's name, I ask you Lord for favor in your sight and in the sight of man. I ask you Lord to lead me to the right places, [jobs/businesses/finances] in Jesus's name. I decree that anywhere I go I shall find favor and I will get exactly what I am requesting to be done for me, whether it is a job, contract, a business, or a financial miracle, in Jesus's name. I will never be a loser. I am a winner in Christ.

God has blessed me and I command those blessings to manifest in full now in Jesus's name.

26. I ask you Lord for a good, stable, secure, and prosperous [job/business/finances] in Jesus's name. I will have more than enough in Jesus's name. Father, I receive your blessings in the name of Jesus Christ.

27. In the name of Jesus Christ, I reject every suffering of any kind I am facing because of the lack of a [job/business/finances]. I command every spirit of hardship and difficulty to be bound in Jesus's name. The Bible says in Joel 2:26,

    > You will have plenty to eat and be satisfied And praise the name of the LORD your God, Who has dealt wondrously with you; Then My people will never be put to shame.

    It is written in Isaiah 43:19,

    > Behold, I will do something new, Now it will spring forth; Will you not be aware of it? I will even make a roadway in the wilderness, Rivers in the desert.

28. In Jesus's name Father I believe that you will make a way for me. I ask for the way to be made now and I receive it by faith now in Jesus's name.

29. It is written in the book of 1 Corinthians 10:13,

    > No temptation has overtaken you but such as is common to man; and God is faithful, who will not allow you to be tempted beyond what you are able, but with the temptation will provide the way of escape also, so that you will be able to endure it.

    In Jesus's name, I ask you Lord to provide me with an escape now. I ask you Lord to deliver me from my situation now in the name of Jesus Christ. I hold on tight to my escape. I hold on tight to my deliverance. I will make it in Jesus's name. I have already made it in Jesus's name.

30. I am a child of God. The earth is the Lord's and all it contains (Psalm 24:1, 1 Corinthians 10:26). I command everything God has purposed for my life to come to pass and manifest now for all eyes to see that I truly serve a living God in Jesus's name. I decree [job/business/financial] openings to manifest now in the name of Jesus. I decree more than enough and I decree open heavens for myself in Jesus's name.
31. I command all the doors to progress to open to me now in the name of Jesus Christ. The word of God says in Revelation 3:7,

    > He who is holy, who is true, who has the key of David, who opens and no one will shut, and who shuts and no one opens, says this.

32. I command the doors to financial breakthrough to open in Jesus's name. Psalms 34:10 (KJV) says, "The young lions do lack, and suffer hunger: but they that seek the LORD shall not want any good thing." I will never lack again. I will never suffer again. I will never be ashamed in Jesus's name (Joel 2:26). I command my deliverance from all these things in Jesus's name.
33. Jesus Christ is the answer to all my needs. The word of God says in the book of Philippians 4:19,

    > And my God will supply all your needs according to His riches in glory in Christ Jesus.

34. I confess that my family and I are cared for and provided for in Jesus's name.
35. Thank you, Lord, for your word says in Matthew 7:7–8,

> [7]Ask, and it will be given to you; seek, and you will find; knock, and it will be opened to you. [8]For everyone who asks receives, and he who seeks finds, and to him who knocks it will be opened.

In Jesus's name.

36. God must be glorified in my life. I ask you, Lord, to use me as a testimony to bring glory to your name. I ask that you use me to testify, to encourage, to show your mercy, to show your grace and faithfulness to the people of the world in Jesus's name.
37. Lord, I have asked and I receive your word. I believe and receive the answers to my prayers in the name of Jesus Christ. Lord, thank you for all the answers. Amen.

Family Relations

Family relations include relationships within and outside the immediate family, such as relatives.

God created a hierarchy within the family with the husband as the head of the household followed by the wife and then the children. Of course, God is the head of the husband. The devil will attempt to upset this hierarchy through a variety of means. We need to be aware of these and recognize when attacks come. Each person in the family must be aware of and follow their God-given roles and responsibilities. Each person in the family must understand that they are ultimately accountable to God for everything they say and do. We all make mistakes, and when they occur, they must be dealt with in an appropriate and Godly manner. Each of us has our weaknesses and it is a duty and responsibility to address them and become more Christlike. It is also the duty and responsibility of others to help the one who falls in a positive and edifying manner according to Scripture. Ephesians chapters 5 and 6 outline some of the methods we are to use for situations within and outside the family.

When there is a conflict in the family, particularly between husband and wife, everyone is righteous in their own eyes and humility and wisdom often take a hike. It is imperative no one lose the proper attitude (cool head) and thus give the devil an opportunity to cause disruptions and division.

There is a lot of truth to the saying that a family that prays together stays together. The family should be a team going forward to the common goal of building their individual relationships with Jesus and to fulfill God's plan for their lives. Prayer is the key to maintaining peace and harmony, and to counter and destroy the attacks of the devil. Keep a watch out for the many "divide and conquer" tactics the devil may attempt to employ.

19.1 Scripture Reading and Confession

> [22]Wives, be subject to your own husbands, as to the Lord. [23]For the husband is the head of the wife, as Christ also is the head of the church, He Himself being the Savior of the body. [24]But as the church is subject to Christ, so also the wives ought to be to their husbands in everything. [25]Husbands, love your wives, just as Christ also loved the church and gave Himself up for her, [26]so that He might sanctify her, having cleansed her by the washing of water with the word, [27]that He might present to Himself the church in all her glory, having no spot or wrinkle or any such thing; but that she would be holy and blameless. [28]So husbands ought also to love their own wives as their own bodies. He who loves his own wife loves himself.
>
> —Ephesians 5:22–28

> [1]Children, obey your parents in the Lord, for this is right. [2]HONOR YOUR FATHER AND MOTHER (which is the first commandment with a promise), [3]SO THAT IT MAY BE WELL WITH YOU, AND THAT YOU MAY LIVE LONG ON THE EARTH. [4]Fathers, do not provoke your children to anger, but bring them up in the discipline and instruction of the Lord.
>
> —Ephesians 6:2–4

19.2 Prayers

1. Father God, reveal to me any sin I have committed in the name of Jesus.
2. My Father, forgive me for committing these sins in the name of Jesus. [Name them.]
3. I forgive [name them] who have sinned against me in the name of Jesus.
4. Thank you, Father, for your grace and forgiveness in the name of Jesus.
5. I take authority over and destroy the strongman established over my household in the name of Jesus.
6. I command every demon trying to convince me that these prayers are nonsense to be completely destroyed in the name of Jesus.
7. I command every demon, its support, its replacements, its command structure, all evil devices and influences established against my household to be utterly and completely destroyed by the fire of God in the name of Jesus.
8. I command every spirit of contention and strife in my family to be wiped away by the blood of Jesus in the name of Jesus.
9. I decree favor and blessing on every member of my family [name them] in the name of Jesus.
10. I cover every member of my family [name them] with the blood of Jesus in Jesus's name.
11. I command the devil to keep his hands off [name each family member] in the name of Jesus.

12. I command every evil plan [name it if you are aware of something] established against my family and me to backfire against the enemy in the name of Jesus.
13. I command every spirit of strife in my family to be destroyed by the fire of God in the name of Jesus.
14. I command every spirit of rebellion in my family to be destroyed by the fire of God in the name of Jesus.
15. Every generational family curse [name them if you know of any] on my mother's side of the family, be nullified in the name of Jesus.
16. Every generational family curse [name them if you know of any] on my father's side of the family, be nullified in the name of Jesus.
17. I decree the blessings of the Lord upon my family [name each family member] in the name of Jesus.
18. The husband should lay hands on each member of the family and proclaim the Aaronic blessing from Numbers 6:24–26 as follows:

    > [24]The LORD bless you, and keep you;[25]The LORD make His face shine on you, And be gracious to you;[26]The LORD lift up His countenance on you, And give you peace.

19. I cover [name each family member] with the blood of Jesus in the name of Jesus.
20. My Father, send your angels to stand guard around [name each family member] today in the name of Jesus.
21. My Father, give [name each family member] the strength and courage to stand in righteousness and to refuse sin in the name of Jesus.

22. Lord, I have asked and I receive your word. I believe and receive the answers to my prayers in the name of Jesus Christ. Lord, thank you for all the answers. Amen.

Ungodly Influences

Ungodly influences on an individual and family can come in many forms. Children are particularly vulnerable. I've heard many a parent justify sending their children to ungodly public schools with the thought that such an environment will provide balance and exposure to what they will face in the world when they grow and become more mature. This philosophy has a lot of problems and is contrary to Scripture. First, a child must be trained and raised in a godly manner and with knowledge of God's word. This will provide a good moral foundation so when they are older and more mature they are much more likely to deal with the evils of this world successfully and not become a contributor to the social problems we have today. Being influenced by evil at an early and impressionable age does not provide the proper foundation for them to make qualified decisions.

> Train up a child in the way he should go, Even when he is old he will not depart from it.
>
> —Proverbs 22:6

Similar statements can be made concerning individuals of all ages as well. It is therefore imperative that everyone become well versed in Scripture and devoted to prayer. It is very important to read and study the Bible. Without the moral and spiritual foundation provided by the Bible, we are doomed to failure. This failure is all too evident in society today.

The moral decay of society has made providing our children with a Godly foundation apart from the evils of this world very difficult for many. The lack of money is almost always the most critical issue faced today. It is therefore that much more important to devote an adequate amount of time to family prayer and instruction in the Bible. There is a lot of truth to the saying that a family that prays together stays together.

In addition to the prayers and confessions that follow, repeat the prayers and confessions from Chapter 15.

20.1 Scripture Reading

> 13Enter through the narrow gate; for the gate is wide and the way is broad that leads to destruction, and there are many who enter through it. 14For the gate is small and the way is narrow that leads to life, and there are few who find it.
>
> —Matthew 7:13–14

> But flee from these things, you man of God, and pursue righteousness, godliness, faith, love, perseverance and gentleness.
>
> —1 Timothy 6:11

> 12So then, my beloved, just as you have always obeyed, not as in my presence only, but now much more in my absence, work out your salvation with fear and trembling; 13for it is God who is at work in you, both to will and to work for His good pleasure.
>
> —Philippians 2:12–13

> 5Thorns and snares are in the way of the perverse; He who guards himself will be far from them. 6Train up a child in the way he should go, Even when he is old he will not depart from it.
>
> —Proverbs 22:5–6

20.2 Confession

1. I am not what the world says I am.
2. I am an overwhelming conqueror through Jesus Christ.
3. I am a redeemed child of God.
4. I am a royal priesthood through Jesus.
5. Because of the position I am placed in through my relationship with Jesus, I have all power and authority over the devil and all that he does.
6. I am empowered through Jesus to exercise dominion over the devil and all his activities.
7. No weapon formed against me shall prosper (Isaiah 54:17).
8. By faith I overcome all the tricks and deceptions of the devil.
9. Read Psalms 91:

> [1]He who dwells in the shelter of the Most High Will
> abide in the shadow of the Almighty. [2]I will say to the
> LORD, "My refuge and my fortress, My God, in whom I
> trust! " [3]For it is He who delivers you from the snare of
> the trapper And from the deadly pestilence. [4]He will cover
> you with His pinions, And under His wings you may seek
> refuge; His faithfulness is a shield and bulwark. [5]You will
> not be afraid of the terror by night, Or of the arrow that
> flies by day; [6]Of the pestilence that stalks in darkness, Or
> of the destruction that lays waste at noon. [7]A thousand
> may fall at your side And ten thousand at your right hand,
> But it shall not approach you. [8]You will only look on with
> your eyes And see the recompense of the wicked. [9]For you
> have made the LORD, my refuge, Even the Most High,
> your dwelling place. [10]No evil will befall you, Nor will any
> plague come near your tent. [11]For He will give His angels

charge concerning you, To guard you in all your ways.
[12]They will bear you up in their hands, That you do not
strike your foot against a stone. [13]You will tread upon the
lion and cobra, The young lion and the serpent you will
trample down. [14]"Because he has loved Me, therefore I will
deliver him; I will set him securely on high, because he
has known My name. [15]"He will call upon Me, and I will
answer him; I will be with him in trouble; I will rescue him
and honor him. [16]"With a long life I will satisfy him And
let him see My salvation."

—Psalms 91:1–16

20.3 Prayers

1. My Father, please forgive me for my sins in the name of Jesus. [Name them.]
2. Thank you, Lord, for your mercy and grace in the name of Jesus.
3. My Father, cover myself and [name each family member] with the blood of Jesus in Jesus name.
4. Father God, give myself and [name each family member] the strength and courage to resist the temptation to entertain ungodly influences in the name of Jesus.
5. Every evil plantation in myself, [name each family member], come out and be destroyed not in Jesus's name.
6. I decree that evil influences and peer pressure shall not touch [name each family member] in the name of Jesus.
7. I reject every evil influence over myself and [name each family member] in the name of Jesus.
8. I command every evil influence over [name each family member] to be broken now in the name of Jesus.

9. I command every demon associated with influencing [name each family member] to be completely destroyed in the name of Jesus.
10. I command every demon, evil influence, evil network, demonic replacements, demonic support, demonic command structure, and all evil devices targeting myself and [name each family member] in the name of Jesus.
11. I cast all this garbage into the abyss until Judgment Day in the name of Jesus.
12. I proclaim my freedom from these things in the name of Jesus.
13. I proclaim freedom from these things for [name each family member] in the name of Jesus.
14. I proclaim blessings and godly influences and thoughts over [name each family member] in the name of Jesus.
15. My Father, send your angels to stand guard around [name each family member] day and night in the name of Jesus.
16. Thank you, Lord, for hearing my prayers in the name of Jesus.
17. I believe and I receive the answers to these prayers in the name of Jesus.

Anger

Anger is a natural emotion that we all experience. We can see from Scripture that anger must be kept within certain boundaries. Anger is also a tool used by the devil to cause a myriad of problems, both with an individual and with those around them. There are demons that specialize in anger and if someone has an inherent anger problem, they are more susceptible to these kind of demonic attacks. In any case, it is essential that we all work toward maintaining a healthy mental attitude and keep anger in check.

Anger can also be connected to the spirit of offense, insecurity, or lack of control. Others may include pride, self-righteousness, and others. Some have learned early in life to use anger as a defensive or coping mechanism. As such, it is unhealthy and must be dealt with on several fronts. Even after all the spiritual aspects are dealt with, counseling may be necessary to break the cycle and retrain the mind to use more healthy means of coping with life's difficulties.

21.1 Scripture Reading and Confession

> He who is slow to anger is better than the mighty, And he who rules his spirit, than he who captures a city.
>
> —Proverbs 16:32

> A man's discretion makes him slow to anger, And it is his glory to overlook a transgression.
>
> —Proverbs 19:11

> [26]BE ANGRY, AND yet DO NOT SIN; do not let the sun go down on your anger, [27]and do not give the devil an opportunity.
>
> —Ephesians 4:26–27

> [31]Let all bitterness and wrath and anger and clamor and slander be put away from you, along with all malice. [32]Be kind to one another, tender-hearted, forgiving each other, just as God in Christ also has forgiven you.
>
> —Ephesians 4:31–32

> [19]This you know, my beloved brethren. But everyone must be quick to hear, slow to speak and slow to anger; [20]for the anger of man does not achieve the righteousness of God.
>
> —James 1:19–20

One of the primary sources of anger comes from offenses. John Bevere has an excellent book and DVD series titled *The Bait of Satan* that deals with this subject.[1]

21.2 Prayers

1. My Father, please forgive me for my sins in the name of Jesus. [Name them.]
2. Thank you, Lord, for your mercy and grace in the name of Jesus.
3. Every inherited spirit of anger, die in the name of Jesus.
4. Every generational curse of anger in my life, I nullify and cast you out in the name of Jesus.
5. I command every demon, evil influence, evil network, demonic replacements, demonic support, demonic

command structure, and all evil devices of anger targeting me in the name of Jesus. I bind all of this garbage and cast it into the abyss until Judgment Day in the name of Jesus.

6. I proclaim my freedom from these things in the name of Jesus.
7. My Father, put your strength in me to resist anger in the name of Jesus.
8. My Father, anoint me with the spirit of self discipline in the name of Jesus.
9. My Father, heal my mind from the ravages of anger in the name of Jesus.
10. My Father, fill me with the Holy Spirit and with your peace in the name of Jesus.
11. My Father, anoint me with the oil of gladness in the name of Jesus.
12. My Father, give me wisdom in all things in the name of Jesus.
13. I decree my freedom from unnatural anger in the name of Jesus.
14. My Father, I give you all the praise, glory, and honor for answering my prayers in the name of Jesus.
15. Thank you, Lord, for your mercies and grace in the name of Jesus.
16. I believe and receive the answers to my prayers in the name of Jesus.

Notes

1. John Bevere, *The Bait of Satan*. Charisma Media, Messenger International, http://messengerinternational.org. 2004.

Anxiety, Fear, and Worry

Anxiety, fear, and worry can be the result of lack of faith, or they may be demonic in origin. In any case, prayer is key. We all have our strengths and weaknesses. It would be nice if faith built strong in one area would easily transfer to another area. Unfortunately, our minds don't always work in such a reasonable and logical manner. Our Lord has provided many Scriptures that address these issues, too many to list here. Perhaps one of the more notable passages is found in the Sermon on the Mount in Matthew chapter 6.

22.1 Scripture Reading and Confession

> 25“For this reason I say to you, do not be worried about your life, as to what you will eat or what you will drink; nor for your body, as to what you will put on. Is not life more than food, and the body more than clothing? 26“Look at the birds of the air, that they do not sow, nor reap nor gather into barns, and yet your heavenly Father feeds them. Are you not worth much more than they? 27“And who of you by being worried can add a single hour to his life? 28“And why are you worried about clothing? Observe how the lilies of the field grow; they do not toil nor do they spin, 29yet I say to you that not even Solomon in all his glory clothed himself like one of these. 30“But if God so clothes the grass of the field, which is alive today and tomorrow

is thrown into the furnace, will He not much more clothe you? You of little faith! [31]"Do not worry then, saying, 'What will we eat? ' or 'What will we drink? ' or 'What will we wear for clothing? ' [32]"For the Gentiles eagerly seek all these things; for your heavenly Father knows that you need all these things. [33]"But seek first His kingdom and His righteousness, and all these things will be added to you. [34]"So do not worry about tomorrow; for tomorrow will care for itself. Each day has enough trouble of its own.

—Matthew 6:25–34

[6]Be anxious for nothing, but in everything by prayer and supplication with thanksgiving let your requests be made known to God. [7]And the peace of God, which surpasses all comprehension, will guard your hearts and your minds in Christ Jesus.

—Philippians 4:6–7

[1]A Psalm of David. The Lord is my light and my salvation; Whom shall I fear? The Lord is the defense of my life; Whom shall I dread? [2]When evildoers came upon me to devour my flesh, My adversaries and my enemies, they stumbled and fell. [3]Though a host encamp against me, My heart will not fear; Though war arise against me, In spite of this I shall be confident.

—Psalms 27:1–3

[1]For the choir director. A Psalm of the sons of Korah, set to Alamoth. A Song. God is our refuge and strength, A very present help in trouble. [2]Therefore we will not fear, though the earth should change And though the mountains slip into the heart of the sea; [3]Though its waters roar and foam, Though the mountains quake at its swelling pride. Selah.

—Psalms 46:1–3

The fear of man brings a snare, But he who trusts in the LORD will be exalted.

—Proverbs 29:25

[25]Do not be afraid of sudden fear Nor of the onslaught of the wicked when it comes; [26]For the LORD will be your confidence And will keep your foot from being caught.

—Proverbs 3:25–26

Therefore let us draw near with confidence to the throne of grace, so that we may receive mercy and find grace to help in time of need.

—Hebrews 4:16

[31]What then shall we say to these things? If God is for us, who is against us? [32]He who did not spare His own Son, but delivered Him over for us all, how will He not also with Him freely give us all things? [33]Who will bring a charge against God's elect? God is the one who justifies; [34]who is the one who condemns? Christ Jesus is He who died, yes, rather who was raised, who is at the right hand of God, who also intercedes for us. [35]Who will separate us from the love of Christ? Will tribulation, or distress, or persecution, or famine, or nakedness, or peril, or sword? [36]Just as it is written, "FOR YOUR SAKE WE ARE BEING PUT TO DEATH ALL DAY LONG; WE WERE CONSIDERED AS SHEEP TO BE SLAUGHTERED." [37] But in all these things we overwhelmingly conquer through Him who loved us. [38]For I am convinced that neither death, nor life, nor angels, nor principalities, nor things present, nor things to come, nor powers, [39]nor height, nor depth, nor any other created thing, will be able to separate us from the love of God, which is in Christ Jesus our Lord.

—Roman 8:31–39

"No weapon that is formed against you will prosper; And every tongue that accuses you in judgment you will condemn. This is the heritage of the servants of the Lord, And their vindication is from Me," declares the Lord.

—Isaiah 54:17

[5]Trust in the Lord with all your heart And do not lean on your own understanding. [6]In all your ways acknowledge Him, And He will make your paths straight. [7]Do not be wise in your own eyes; Fear the Lord and turn away from evil. [8]It will be healing to your body And refreshment to your bones.

—Proverbs 3:5–8

For God hath not given us the spirit of fear; but of power, and of love, and of a sound mind.

—2 Timothy 1:7 (KJV)

There is no fear in love; but perfect love casteth out fear: because fear hath torment. He that feareth is not made perfect in love.

—1 John 4:18

22.2 Prayers

1. My Father, please forgive me for my sins in the name of Jesus. [Name them.]
2. Thank you, Lord, for your forgiveness, mercy, and grace in the name of Jesus.
3. I am a child of God, therefore, fear, anxiety, and worry have no place in me. Get out now in the name of Jesus.
4. My enemies shall stumble and fall in the name of Jesus.
5. I stand upon the word of God and refuse to move off it no matter what I'm going through in the name of Jesus.
6. Every spirit of fear, anxiety, and worry, I take authority over you in the name of Jesus. I cast all of these demons, their

evil devices and influences, their support, replacements, and command structure into the abyss until Judgment Day in the name of Jesus.

7. I decree my freedom from these things in the name of Jesus.
8. My Heavenly Father shall set me securely above my enemies in the name of Jesus.
9. I put my faith and trust in Jesus in the name of Jesus.
10. No weapon formed against me shall prosper in the name of Jesus.
11. I am a child of God. I have the mind of Christ. I reject and cast out every imagination and thing that has exalted itself above the word of God in my life in the name of Jesus.
12. I refuse to live in fear, anxiety, and worry in the name of Jesus.
13. My enemies shall live in fear and dread in the name of Jesus.
14. I shall not be in bondage of fear because the Lord is my shepherd in the name of Jesus.
15. God has not given me a spirit of fear. He has given power, love, and a sound mind in the name of Jesus.
16. All my enemies shall fall into their own traps in the name of Jesus.
17. My Father, I give you all the praise, glory, and honor for answering my prayers in the name of Jesus.
18. Thank you, Lord, for your mercies and grace in the name of Jesus.
19. I believe and receive the answers to my prayers in the name of Jesus.

Depression and Suicide

Depression can be caused by a wide range of factors. Suicide is most often the result of depression or the inability to cope with a situation.

Wikipedia has a good discussion on the subject of suicide.[1]

The scope of the problem throughout the world today is shocking. Some excerpts from this discussion are as follows:

> An estimated 1 million people worldwide take their lives by suicide every year. It is estimated that global annual suicide fatalities could rise to 1.5 million by 2020. Worldwide, suicide ranks among the three leading causes of death among those aged 15–44 years. Suicide attempts are up to 20 times more frequent than completed suicides.
>
> Incidence of suicide in a society depends on a range of factors. Clinical depression is an especially common cause. Substance abuse, severe physical disease or infirmity are also recognized causes. The countries of the Eastern Europe and East Asia have the highest suicide rate in the world. The region with the lowest suicide rate is Latin America. Gender difference plays a significant role: among all age groups in most of the world, females tend to show higher rates of reported nonfatal suicidal behavior, males have a much higher rate of completed suicide.

Depression and suicide are clearly major social problems in most places around the world today. To an extent, hopelessness can lead to depression which can lead to suicide.

Ron Hutchcraft[2] has a good article on his website concerning suicide:

> Wednesday, August 17, 2005
>
> No matter how big you expect the Grand Canyon to be, it's bigger. And when our family has had the privilege to visit there, we've all been impressed with this awesome, divine masterpiece. One big problem there though has been our boys, because they think they're part mountain goat. Of course, mountain goats cannot read the signs that tell you to stay behind the fences. Apparently, our boys can't read them either. They always had this irresistible urge to venture out as far as possible on those rocks that overlook the canyon. Of course, one false step, and it's all over—actually, you're all over. All our lectures about going too far for safety's sake made a lot more sense the morning after we had stopped at one particular overlook. The morning paper reported that on the same afternoon we had been there, two young men went to that same overlook and one never came back. He ended up dead at the bottom of the canyon. The reason? He got too close to the edge.
>
> I'm Ron Hutchcraft and I want to have A Word With You today about "Too Close to the Edge."
>
> God has a word today for someone who's hurting, who's depressed and may be getting too close to the edge. There may be this voice inside you, or someone you know, that's saying, "You know, life just hurts too much. Maybe I should just check out once and for all." You're looking over the edge of the abyss called suicide.
>
> You need to know where that voice is coming from. Our word for today from the Word of God is John 10:10. "The thief comes only to steal and kill and destroy; I have come that they may have life, and have it to the full." Two voices: one is the life-taker—the devil, who wants to destroy you. The other is the life-giver—Jesus, who thought you were worth dying for. Any thoughts of ending

your life are from Satan himself. And you cannot let him take you over the edge and rob you of all the tomorrows God has planned for you.

That edge of the cliff called suicide can only be a consideration if you don't realize how tragically expensive suicide is. First, it's the ultimate act of defiance toward the God who made you. In Psalm 139:13 and 16, it says, "You created my inmost being; You knit me together in my mother's womb...All the days ordained for me were written in your book before one of them came to be." Only the One who gave you your life has the right to end it. And He's the One you meet the moment your life is over. You don't want to go into eternity defying the God you are about to meet.

Suicide is also the ultimate act of selfishness toward the people who love you. They'll never recover from the awful agony of this decision. Don't do this to them. And suicide is the ultimate waste of the life Jesus gave His life for. He didn't die on that cross just to have you throw away the life He gave everything for. One last thing—suicide is the ultimate surrender to the devil who hates you.

It may be that you have gotten too close to the edge recently, and you've been thinking about suicide as an answer. But, believe me, living is always better. Jesus said, "I have come that you might have life." Right now, pour out all that pain and all that struggle at the feet of this One who loves you most. He said, "I was sent to bind up the brokenhearted." And then talk to someone today about your struggle—a pastor or counselor who's probably walked through this with other people. Whatever the risks of reaching out, they're not nearly as expensive as giving up.

The Lord wants you to live—to have all your tomorrows. That's why He sent you this message of life today. Get away from the edge, and don't ever go near it again! In God's own words from His book, "Choose life!"

Life is almost never easy. People get close to the edge when they fail to put their faith, hope, trust, and eyes on Jesus. Remember Peter when he walked on the water:

> [28]Peter said to Him, "Lord, if it is You, command me to come to You on the water." [29]And He said, "Come! " And Peter got out of the boat, and walked on the water and came toward Jesus. [30]But seeing the wind, he became frightened, and beginning to sink, he cried out, "Lord, save me! " [31]Immediately Jesus stretched out His hand and took hold of him, and said to him, "You of little faith, why did you doubt?"
>
> —Matthew 14:28–31

In every situation we find ourselves through life, regardless of how long, hard, or painful it seems to be, it is essential that we stay focused on our Lord Jesus Christ. This is the only way. We must put our faith and trust in him. No one can be a "Lone Ranger" Christian. If you are in a state of depression and have considered or even tried suicide, it is essential to seek help. Of those societies cited in the Wikipedia article above, one of the detractors of depression and suicide is social cohesion. That is to say that people communicate with each other and seek each other out for help.

King David is a good example of someone who had to deal with numerous unpleasant and life-threatening situations throughout his life. Yet we read of the attitude and approach he used throughout the book of Psalms. The focus of his life and solution to all his problems was God. The praise, thanksgiving, and worship he offered up was medicine for his soul and, as always, God not only delivered him but filled him with joy. It may not be easy to sing praises to God and to worship him when it feels like the world dumped on your face. It is nonetheless a pattern of behavior that must be built through discipline.

Someone who is struggling with these issues is a target of the devil since he wants to steal, kill, and destroy your life. Depression and suicide are often exacerbated by or are the direct result of demonic activities. It is essential to deal with the spiritual side of this as well as the physical (counseling, medical help, etc. as needed).

23.1 Scripture Reading and Confession

I shall not die, but live, and declare the works of the LORD.

—Psalms 118:17 (KJV)

Thou hast loved righteousness, and hated iniquity; therefore God, even thy God, hath anointed thee with the oil of gladness above thy fellows.

—Hebrews 1:9 (KJV)

[7]Answer me quickly, O LORD, my spirit fails; Do not hide
Your face from me, Or I will become like those who go
down to the pit. [8]Let me hear Your lovingkindness in the
morning; For I trust in You; Teach me the way in which I
should walk; For to You I lift up my soul.

—Psalms 143:7–8

[18]The Spirit of the Lord is upon me, because he hath
anointed me to preach the gospel to the poor; he hath
sent me to heal the brokenhearted, to preach deliverance
to the captives, and recovering of sight to the blind, to set
at liberty them that are bruised, [19]To preach the acceptable
year of the Lord.

—Luke 4:18–19 (KJV)

[22]But the fruit of the Spirit is love, joy, peace, patience,
kindness, goodness, faithfulness, [23]gentleness, self-control;
against such things there is no law.

—Galatians 5:22–23

> Rejoice in the Lord always; again I will say, rejoice!
>
> —Philippians 4:4

> [16]Rejoice always; [17]pray without ceasing; [18]in everything give thanks; for this is God's will for you in Christ Jesus.
>
> —1 Thessalonians 5:16–18

> The thief comes only to steal and kill and destroy; I came that they may have life, and have it abundantly.
>
> —John 10:10

23.2 Prayers

1. My Father, please forgive me for my sins in the name of Jesus. [Name them.]
2. O Lord, forgive me for not putting my faith, hope, and trust in you in the name of Jesus.
3. Thank you, Lord, for your forgiveness, mercy, and grace in the name of Jesus.
4. Every spirit of death and destruction in my life, die in the name of Jesus.
5. I refuse to accept a satanic destiny in the name of Jesus.
6. I nullify every curse against my life in the name of Jesus.
7. Every evil chain on my destiny, I break you in the name of Jesus.
8. Every spirit of depression and suicide, I take command over you in the name of Jesus.
9. I cast all of these demons, their evil devices and influences, their support, replacements, and command structure into the abyss until Judgment Day in the name of Jesus.
10. I decree my freedom from these things in the name of Jesus.

11. My Father, fill me with your love in the name of Jesus.
12. My Father, fill me with all the fruit of your Spirit in the name of Jesus.
13. My Father, cover me with the blood of Jesus in Jesus's name.
14. My Father, cause all my enemies to fall into their own traps in the name of Jesus.
15. I command any evil domination and control over my life to be destroyed now in the name of Jesus.
16. I nullify every conscious and unconscious covenant made against my divine destiny in the name of Jesus.
17. I command every evil power hindering my blessings from finding me to be destroyed now in the name of Jesus.
18. O Lord, revive and increase my prayer life in the name of Jesus.
19. O Lord, infuse me with your strength and courage in the name of Jesus.
20. O Lord, deliver me from my situation in the name of Jesus.
21. My Father, cause me to prosper to your glory in the name of Jesus.
22. My Father, put the gift of praise and worship in my mouth in the name of Jesus.
23. My Father, put your faith, hope, and love in my heart and mind in the name of Jesus.
24. My Father, raise me up to be an overwhelming conqueror in the name of Jesus.
25. My Father, I give you all the praise, glory, and honor for answering my prayers in the name of Jesus.
26. Thank you, Lord, for your mercies and grace in the name of Jesus.

27. I believe and receive the answers to my prayers in the name of Jesus.

Notes

1. Wikipedia article, *Epidemiology of suicide*, http://en.wikipedia.org/wiki/Epidemiology_of_suicide, 2014.
2. *Too Close to the Edge*, Ron Hutchcraft Ministries, http://www.hutchcraft.com, http://www.hutchcraft.com/a-word-with-you/your-hindrances/too-close-to-the-edge-4853, (August 17, 2005).

Failure at the Edge of Breakthroughs

There are times when people are on the edge of receiving blessing from God, such as a job, business, greater level of relationship with him, finances, and so on. At a critical point, the blessing is stolen. These things are caused by evil powers. They do not attempt to hinder one from going down the path to receive a blessing but at the last moment, steal it from them. That last moment is wherc these demons operate. This has the effect of bringing distrust in God, frustration, anger, and hopelessness. The goal is to bring defeat to God's people.

Often the greatest battles we face are at the edge of breakthroughs. Jesus experienced the same. We can see in Matthew 4:1–11 that the devil attempted to derail Jesus's ministry at the point it was about to take off.

We can see this same evil spirit in operation in many places throughout Scripture. To name a few, Israel was on the verge of entering the promised land but was prevented from doing so because the devil convinced them they couldn't when they should have placed their trust in God. Saul was prevented from retaining his wealth and position because of disobedience. In the parable of the ten virgins with the lamps of oil, 50 percent of them failed to go with the bridegroom because of their failure.

The so-called Murphy's Law we've become so accustomed to is more often than not the activity of demonic forces. This evil persists because most people are unaware of what is actually going on behind the scenes. It is far more prevalent in the world than most realize. It is important to understand the schemes of the devil so we can overcome and destroy them.

24.1 Scripture Reading and Confession

> [1]There is an evil which I have seen under the sun and it is prevalent among men— [2]a man to whom God has given riches and wealth and honor so that his soul lacks nothing of all that he desires; yet God has not empowered him to eat from them, for a foreigner enjoys them. This is vanity and a severe affliction.
>
> —Ecclesiastes 6:1–2

> For a wide door for effective service has opened to me, and there are many adversaries.
>
> —1 Corinthians 16:9

> [23]So rejoice, O sons of Zion, And be glad in the Lord your God; For He has given you the early rain for your vindication. And He has poured down for you the rain, The early and latter rain as before. [24]The threshing floors will be full of grain, And the vats will overflow with the new wine and oil. [25]Then I will make up to you for the years That the swarming locust has eaten, The creeping locust, the stripping locust and the gnawing locust, My great army which I sent among you. [26]You will have plenty to eat and be satisfied And praise the name of the Lord your God, Who has dealt wondrously with you; Then My people will never be put to shame.
>
> —Joel 2:23–26

24.2 Prayers

1. My Father, forgive me for my sins in the name of Jesus. [Name them.]
2. O Lord, forgive me for my lukewarmness in the name of Jesus.
3. Thank you, Lord, for your forgiveness, mercy, and grace in the name of Jesus.
4. Every evil power attacking me at the edge of my breakthroughs, die in the name of Jesus.
5. Every generational spirit and curse causing failure at the edge of my breakthrough, I destroy you now in the name of Jesus.
6. I shall not die, my problem shall die in the name of Jesus.
7. Every satanic plan against my life be nullified in the name of Jesus.
8. I bind and cast out every spirit of bad luck in the name of Jesus.
9. I command every spirit of bad luck to be completely destroyed in the name of Jesus.
10. My blessings shall not be stolen from me in the name of Jesus.
11. Every spirit of disobedience operating in my life I destroy you now in the name of Jesus.
12. Every spirit of backwardness operating in my life I destroy you now in the name of Jesus.
13. Every spirit operating to cause failure at the edge of breakthroughs, I take command over you in the name of Jesus.

14. I cast all of these demons, their evil devices and influences, their support, replacements, and command structure into the abyss until Judgment Day in the name of Jesus.
15. I decree my freedom from these things in the name of Jesus.
16. My Father, cause me to prosper to your glory in the name of Jesus.
17. I command all my stolen blessings to be returned to me sevenfold over in the name of Jesus.
18. My Father, put the gift of praise and worship in my mouth in the name of Jesus.
19. My Father, put your faith, hope, and love in my heart and mind in the name of Jesus.
20. My Father, raise me up to be an overwhelming conqueror in the name of Jesus.
21. My Father, I give you all the praise, glory, and honor for answering my prayers in the name of Jesus.
22. Thank you, Lord, for your mercies and grace in the name of Jesus.
23. I believe and receive the answers to my prayers in the name of Jesus.

Deliverance from Generational Problems

Many problems and personal issues are the result of the sins of one's forefathers as many as four generations back. The Christian is in the unique situation as a new creature in Christ (2 Corinthians 5:17) and redeemed from the curse of the law (Galatians 3:13–14). It is said in 2 Timothy 4:18 that the Lord will rescue us from *every* evil deed. Paul wrote this in thc present tense. In order to avoid taking this verse out of context, other Scriptures must be examined, Galatians 3:13 in particular, and all of the Bible in general.

Nowhere in Scripture is the forgiveness of sins tied to time. Since Christ redeemed us from the curse of the Law and he rescued us from every evil deed, we no longer need to be in bondage of the sins or curses of our ancestors. All that needs to be done is to use the authority through Jesus to break these bonds and be free. Praise God!

25.1 Scripture Reading

> [6]Then the LORD passed by in front of him and proclaimed,
> "The LORD, the LORD God, compassionate and gracious,
> slow to anger, and abounding in lovingkindness and truth;
> [7]who keeps lovingkindness for thousands, who forgives
> iniquity, transgression and sin; yet He will by no means
> leave the guilty unpunished, visiting the iniquity of fathers

on the children and on the grandchildren to the third and fourth generations."

—Exodus 34:6–7

[13]Christ redeemed us from the curse of the Law, having become a curse for us—for it is written, "CURSED IS EVERYONE WHO HANGS ON A TREE"— [14]in order that in Christ Jesus the blessing of Abraham might come to the Gentiles, so that we would receive the promise of the Spirit through faith.

—Galatians 3:13–14

Therefore if anyone is in Christ, he is a new creature; the old things passed away; behold, new things have come.

—2 Corinthians 5:17

The Lord will rescue me from every evil deed, and will bring me safely to His heavenly kingdom; to Him be the glory forever and ever. Amen.

—2 Timothy 4:18

25.2 Confession

Speak out the following confessions. The Scriptures are provided as a reference for each confession. You may speak out these scriptures too if you wish.

1. The Lord shall anoint me with the oil of joy above my fellows.

    You have loved righteousness and hated wickedness; Therefore God, Your God, has anointed You With the oil of joy above Your fellows.

    —Psalms 45:7

2. My future is secure in Christ. He did not create me for nothing. I can never be thrown away or downgraded.

   > [38]For I am convinced that neither death, nor life, nor angels, nor principalities, nor things present, nor things to come, nor powers, [39]nor height, nor depth, nor any other created thing, will be able to separate us from the love of God, which is in Christ Jesus our Lord.
   >
   > —Romans 8:38–39

3. I am the head and not the tail.

   > [13]The LORD will make you the head and not the tail, and you only will be above, and you will not be underneath, if you listen to the commandments of the LORD your God, which I charge you today, to observe them carefully, [14]and do not turn aside from any of the words which I command you today, to the right or to the left, to go after other gods to serve them.
   >
   > —Deuteronomy 28:13–14

4. I will trust in my Lord Jesus always for he can never fail.

   > [4]I sought the LORD, and He answered me, And delivered me from all my fears. [5]They looked to Him and were radiant, And their faces will never be ashamed. [6]This poor man cried, and the LORD heard him And saved him out of all his troubles. [7]The angel of the LORD encamps around those who fear Him, And rescues them. [8]O taste and see that the LORD is good; How blessed is the man who takes refuge in Him!
   >
   > —Psalms 34:4–8

5. There will be no poverty of body, soul, or spirit in my life.

   > [26]You will have plenty to eat and be satisfied And praise the name of the LORD your God, Who has dealt wondrously with you; Then My people will never be put

> to shame. [27]Thus you will know that I am in the midst of Israel, And that I am the LORD your God, And there is no other; And My people will never be put to shame.
>
> —Joel 2:26–27

6. I have favor in the eyes of God and man all the days of my life.

> For it is You who blesses the righteous man, O LORD, You surround him with favor as with a shield.
>
> —Psalms 5:12

> [3]Do not let kindness and truth leave you; Bind them around your neck, Write them on the tablet of your heart. [4]So you will find favor and good repute In the sight of God and man.
>
> —Proverbs 3:3–4

7. I shall not labor in vain.

> They will not labor in vain, Or bear children for calamity; For they are the offspring of those blessed by the LORD, And their descendants with them.
>
> —Isaiah 65:23

8. I shall walk in victory and liberty of the Holy Spirit.

> But thanks be to God, who gives us the victory through our Lord Jesus Christ.
>
> —1 Corinthians 15:57

> For whatever is born of God overcomes the world; and this is the victory that has overcome the world—our faith.
>
> —1 John 5:4

25.3 Prayers

Ask Forgiveness for Sins

1. Father God, reveal to me any sin I have committed that caused [name the problem] in the name of Jesus.
2. My Father, forgive me for committing these sins [name them] in the name of Jesus.
3. I forgive [name them] who have sinned against me in the name of Jesus.
4. Thank you, Father, for your grace and forgiveness in the name of Jesus.

Generational Sins

1. My Father, forgive my mother and father for the sins they have passed down to me in the name of Jesus.
2. Confess the sins of your ancestors, especially those of evil powers if you know what they are.
3. My Father, forgive my ancestors four generations back for the sins that have propagated down to me in the name of Jesus.
4. I break every evil hold these ancestral sins have on me in the name of Jesus.
5. I proclaim my freedom from all ancestral sins on both my father's and mother's side of my family in the name of Jesus.

Generational Curses

1. The earth is the Lord's and the fullness of it. I am a child of God in the name of Jesus.

2. I nullify any ancestral curse propagated to me in the name of Jesus.
3. I command every ancestral curse spoken against my family line to be nullified in the name of Jesus.
4. I command every curse spoken by my ancestors against my family line to be nullified in the name of Jesus.
5. I destroy the effects of every ancestral curse spoken against me in the name of Jesus.
6. I proclaim my freedom from the effects of every ancestral curse spoken against me in the name of Jesus.

Curses and Witchcraft

1. My Father, cover me with the blood of Jesus in Jesus's name.
2. My Father, send your angels to stand guard around me and protect me in the name of Jesus.
3. I command every witchcraft curse spoken against me to be nullified in the name of Jesus.
4. I command every witchcraft altar established against me to be destroyed in the name of Jesus.
5. I command every witch practicing against me to fall into their own traps in the name of Jesus.
6. I command every witchcraft network established against me to be destroyed in the name of Jesus.
7. I command every evil witchcraft device used against me to be destroyed in the name of Jesus.

Evil Ancestral Covenants

1. Every evil ancestral covenant affecting my life and health, I nullify you in the name of Jesus.
2. I command every evil ancestral covenant to be erased by the blood of Jesus in the name of Jesus.

3. I decree my freedom from every evil ancestral covenant in the name of Jesus.

Current Evil Covenants

1. Every evil covenant I may have agreed to, willingly or not, be erased by the blood of Jesus in Jesus's name.
2. I decree my freedom from every evil covenant I may have agreed to in the name of Jesus.

Demonic Influences

1. I command every demon causing [name the issue] in Jesus's name. Get out now in the name of Jesus.
2. I destroy every demon causing [name the issue] in Jesus's name.
3. I command every demonic influence causing [name your medical issue] in Jesus's name. I destroy you in the name of Jesus.
4. I command every demonic device established against me to cause [name your medical issue] in Jesus's name. I destroy you in the name of Jesus.

Power to Excel and Prosper

In the beginning and before Adam and Eve sinned, God gave mankind dominion over the entire planet. After sin entered the scene, that dominion was passed on to the devil. He retained this until Jesus died on the cross. That dominion has now been passed back to its rightful owners—those who know Jesus Christ as Lord and Savior. The problem is, the devil doesn't want to relinquish what he thinks is his. This dominion must be taken from him by force (Matthew 11:12). An example of this situation is the civil rights movement of the early 1960s. Slavery had been abolished at the end of the civil war but the wicked didn't want to lose their power and control over people. It wasn't until nearly one hundred years later that people had enough and demanded their legal rights and position in society that they were finally allowed to exercise that status.

Similarly, we as Christians need to take back dominion of this world from the wicked. Not that long ago, the church had a solid position of dominion in the community and in the governing affairs of this nation. Unfortunately, it will take more work to take back that which was lost than it would have to keep it in the first place.

We have a God-ordained right to excel and prosper. This has nothing to do with the prosperity doctrines found in many churches today. Many have fallen into the trap of humanism and perhaps without realizing it have viewed God as a means to gain wealth. This is sin.

The goal must never be of selfish motivation. Whatever he gives us should be used for his glory. We are to be good stewards of all he has given us, no matter how much or how little it may be.

Scripture makes it clear that prosperity is a conditional promise. If we are obedient to his word then he will bless us.

In view of the battle set before us, there are many cases when the devil has used spiritual means in an effort to prevent Christians from enjoying the position they rightfully own. A spirit of poverty, spirit of failure at the edge of success, and filthy spiritual garments that cause people to view someone with disfavor are examples of some of these.

26.1 Scripture Reading and Confession

> [1]Now it shall be, if you diligently obey the LORD your God, being careful to do all His commandments which I command you today, the LORD your God will set you high above all the nations of the earth. [2]All these blessings will come upon you and overtake you if you obey the LORD your God: [3]Blessed shall you be in the city, and blessed shall you be in the country. [4]Blessed shall be the offspring of your body and the produce of your ground and the offspring of your beasts, the increase of your herd and the young of your flock. [5]Blessed shall be your basket and your kneading bowl. [6]Blessed shall you be when you come in, and blessed shall you be when you go out. [7]The LORD shall cause your enemies who rise up against you to be defeated before you; they will come out against you one way and will flee before you seven ways. [8]The LORD will command the blessing upon you in your barns and in all that you put your hand to, and He will bless you in the land which the LORD your God gives you. [9]The LORD will establish you as a holy people to Himself, as He swore to you, if you keep the commandments of the LORD your God and walk in His ways. [10]So all the peoples of the earth will see that you

are called by the name of the LORD, and they will be afraid of you. [11]The LORD will make you abound in prosperity, in the offspring of your body and in the offspring of your beast and in the produce of your ground, in the land which the LORD swore to your fathers to give you. [12]The LORD will open for you His good storehouse, the heavens, to give rain to your land in its season and to bless all the work of your hand; and you shall lend to many nations, but you shall not borrow. [13]The LORD will make you the head and not the tail, and you only will be above, and you will not be underneath, if you listen to the commandments of the LORD your God, which I charge you today, to observe them carefully, [14]and do not turn aside from any of the words which I command you today, to the right or to the left, to go after other gods to serve them.

—Deuteronomy 28:1–14

[3]You ask and do not receive, because you ask with wrong motives, so that you may spend it on your pleasures. [4]You adulteresses, do you not know that friendship with the world is hostility toward God? Therefore whoever wishes to be a friend of the world makes himself an enemy of God. [5]Or do you think that the Scripture speaks to no purpose: "He jealously desires the Spirit which He has made to dwell in us"?

—James 4:3–5

26.2 Prayers

1. My Father, forgive me for my sins in the name of Jesus. [Name them.]
2. O Lord, forgive me for my lukewarmness in the name of Jesus.
3. O Lord, forgive me for my laziness in my walk with you in the name of Jesus.

4. O Lord, forgive me for failing to live up to the standards you established in your word in the name of Jesus.
5. O Lord, cleanse me of all unrighteousness in the name of Jesus.
6. O Lord, remove anything from my life that is contrary to your will in the name of Jesus.
7. Every garment of disfavor placed on me, be destroyed by the fire of God in the name of Jesus.
8. Thank you, Lord, for your forgiveness, mercy, and grace in the name of Jesus.
9. My Father, give me an anointing of prosperity in the name of Jesus.
10. My Father, give me an anointing of favor in the name of Jesus.
11. I command every spirit of poverty over me to die in the name of Jesus.
12. I release myself from the bondage of poverty in the name of Jesus.
13. O Lord, give me an anointing of excellence after the order of Daniel in the name of Jesus.
14. I am blessed in the name of Jesus.
15. I am prosperous in the name of Jesus.
16. I have favor from God and man in the name of Jesus.
17. My Father, I give you all the praise, glory, and honor for answering my prayers in the name of Jesus.
18. Thank you, Lord, for your mercies and grace in the name of Jesus.
19. I believe and receive the answers to my prayers in the name of Jesus.

Sexual Sins

Sexual sins include pornography, fornication, adultery, homosexuality, and many other perversions.

In these end times and with those who are pro-homosexual becoming increasingly militant, it is important to address this particular issue from the viewpoint of what Scripture has to say.

> [26]For this reason God gave them over to degrading passions; for their women exchanged the natural function for that which is unnatural, [27]and in the same way also the men abandoned the natural function of the woman and burned in their desire toward one another, men with men committing indecent acts and receiving in their own persons the due penalty of their error. [28]And just as they did not see fit to acknowledge God any longer, God gave them over to a depraved mind, to do those things which are not proper, [29]being filled with all unrighteousness, wickedness, greed, evil; full of envy, murder, strife, deceit, malice; they are gossips, [30]slanderers, haters of God, insolent, arrogant, boastful, inventors of evil, disobedient to parents, [31]without understanding, untrustworthy, unloving, unmerciful; [32]and although they know the ordinance of God, that those who practice such things are worthy of death, they not only do the same, but also give hearty approval to those who practice them.
>
> —Romans 1:26–32

> You shall not lie with a male as one lies with a female; it is an abomination.
>
> —Leviticus 18:22

> If there is a man who lies with a male as those who lie with a woman, both of them have committed a detestable act; they shall surely be put to death. Their bloodguiltiness is upon them.
>
> —Leviticus 20:13

> [9]Or do you not know that the unrighteous will not inherit the kingdom of God? Do not be deceived; neither fornicators, nor idolaters, nor adulterers, nor effeminate, nor homosexuals, [10]nor thieves, nor the covetous, nor drunkards, nor revilers, nor swindlers, will inherit the kingdom of God.
>
> —1 Corinthians 6:9–10

> But for the cowardly and unbelieving and abominable and murderers and immoral persons and sorcerers and idolaters and all liars, their part will be in the lake that burns with fire and brimstone, which is the second death.
>
> —Revelation 21:8

It doesn't matter whether anyone on this planet agrees with these Scriptures or not. God said it and that settles it. His judgments are absolute and final. No amount of argument, rationalization, manipulation, justification, taking Scripture out of context, or self-righteous posturing will in any way change this. To reiterate a statement made earlier:

> *If you reject the truth, you will by definition embrace a lie. In the end truth will become an offense and object of hatred to you.*

Realize that Scripture is for mankind's benefit—not God's. Because he loves us, he established boundaries of behavior for our benefit and provided the way of salvation. These were done to help us to avoid falling into sin and eventually damnation, and to point us to the way of salvation.

It is important to note that God is neither male nor female. He is spirit and he created male and female for the purpose of procreation and continuance of the species. God created a hierarchy in which the man is the head of the household and Jesus Christ is the head of everything. Because of this hierarchical order, God is referred to in the masculine sense.

I am not your judge and I do not judge you for your decisions. It is not my place to do so. It is God who will judge you. All of us without exception will stand before him on Judgment Day and give an account of what we have done in this life. What you choose to do with this is your own personal choice and you will either suffer or enjoy the consequences of it.

> [11]For it is written, "AS I LIVE, SAYS THE LORD, EVERY KNEE SHALL BOW TO ME, AND EVERY TONGUE SHALL GIVE PRAISE TO GOD." [12]So then each one of us will give an account of himself to God.
>
> —Romans 14:11–12

> [9]For this reason also, God highly exalted Him, and bestowed on Him the name which is above every name, [10]so that at the name of Jesus EVERY KNEE WILL BOW, of those who are in heaven and on earth and under the earth, [11]and that every tongue will confess that Jesus Christ is Lord, to the glory of God the Father.
>
> —Philippians 2:9–11

Sexual sins are varied and those that are perverted are always the result of demonic influences. The devil perverts our natural instincts and sexual desires that God gave us which are to be enjoyed between a man and a woman within marriage. Sexual sins can be quite difficult to overcome. Overcoming it requires prayer for discipline as well as defeating these demonic influences and activities. Before using the prayers in this section, it would be good to use the prayers in the chapter, "Prayers for Cleansing the Mind." It would be helpful to use both together on a regular basis.

Sinful patterns, sexual in particular, are often established at an early age, usually around puberty, or perhaps even earlier.[†] Such patterns of behavior become ingrained because of the physiological effects that take place in the brain. In other words, the brain becomes physically "wired" to a pattern of thought and behavior. Even after all has been said and done through prayer to deal with the spiritual, the problem or tendency may still persist. This requires a physical healing that only our Lord Jesus Christ can provide. This is no different than any other type of physical healing and can be prayed for just as easily as any other problem. Don't look at the size of the problem. Look at the greatness of our Lord Jesus Christ.

27.1 Scripture Reading and Confession

> For sin shall not be master over you, for you are not under law but under grace.
>
> —Romans 6:14

> [25]Surely, thus says the LORD, "Even the captives of the mighty man will be taken away, And the prey of the tyrant will be rescued; For I will contend with the one who contends with you, And I will save your sons. [26]I will feed your oppressors with their own flesh, And they will become drunk with their own blood as with sweet wine; And all flesh will know that I, the LORD, am your Savior And your Redeemer, the Mighty One of Jacob."
>
> —Isaiah 49:25–26

‡ It is estimated that around 30% of all traffic on the Internet worldwide pertains to pornographic materials!

1Then the Lord spoke to Moses, saying, 2“Speak to the sons of Israel and say to them, 'I am the Lord your God. 3You shall not do what is done in the land of Egypt where you lived, nor are you to do what is done in the land of Canaan where I am bringing you; you shall not walk in their statutes. 4You are to perform My judgments and keep My statutes, to live in accord with them; I am the Lord your God. 5So you shall keep My statutes and My judgments, by which a man may live if he does them; I am the Lord. 6None of you shall approach any blood relative of his to uncover nakedness; I am the Lord. 7You shall not uncover the nakedness of your father, that is, the nakedness of your mother. She is your mother; you are not to uncover her nakedness. 8You shall not uncover the nakedness of your father's wife; it is your father's nakedness. 9The nakedness of your sister, either your father's daughter or your mother's daughter, whether born at home or born outside, their nakedness you shall not uncover. 10The nakedness of your son's daughter or your daughter's daughter, their nakedness you shall not uncover; for their nakedness is yours. 11The nakedness of your father's wife's daughter, born to your father, she is your sister, you shall not uncover her nakedness. 12You shall not uncover the nakedness of your father's sister; she is your father's blood relative. 13You shall not uncover the nakedness of your mother's sister, for she is your mother's blood relative. 14You shall not uncover the nakedness of your father's brother; you shall not approach his wife, she is your aunt. 15You shall not uncover the nakedness of your daughter-in-law; she is your son's wife, you shall not uncover her nakedness. 16You shall not uncover the nakedness of your brother's wife; it is your brother's nakedness. 17You shall not uncover the nakedness of a woman and of her daughter, nor shall you take her son's daughter or her daughter's daughter, to uncover her nakedness; they are blood relatives. It is lewdness. 18You shall not marry a woman in addition to her sister as a rival while she is alive, to uncover her nakedness. 19Also you shall not approach a woman to uncover her nakedness during her menstrual impurity. [20]You shall not have intercourse with your neighbor's wife, to be defiled with her. [21]You shall not give any of your offspring to offer them to Molech, nor shall you profane the name of your God; I am the LORD. [22]You shall not lie with a male as one lies with a female; it is an abomination. [23]Also you shall not have intercourse with any animal to be defiled with it, nor shall any woman stand before an animal to mate with it; it is a perversion. [24]Do not defile yourselves by any of these things; for by all these the nations which I am casting out before you have become defiled. [25]For the land has become defiled, therefore I have brought its punishment upon it, so the land has spewed out its inhabitants. [26]But as for you, you are to keep My statutes and My judgments and shall not do any of these abominations, neither the native, nor the alien who sojourns among you [27](for the men of the land who have been before you have done all these abominations, and the land has become defiled); [28]so that the land will not spew you out, should you defile it, as it has spewed out the nation which has been before you. [29]For whoever does any of these abominations, those persons who do so shall be cut off from among their people. [30]Thus you are to keep My charge, that you do not practice any of the abominable customs which have been practiced before you, so as not to defile yourselves with them; I am the LORD your God.'"

—Leviticus 18

27.2 Prayers

1. My Father, forgive me for my sins in the name of Jesus. [Name them.]
2. O Lord, forgive me for failing to live up to the standards you established in your word in the name of Jesus.

3. O Lord, cleanse me of all unrighteousness in the name of Jesus.
4. O Lord, remove anything from my life that is contrary to your will in the name of Jesus.
5. I break every chain of sexual perversion in my life in the name of Jesus.
6. I break every ancestral curse of sexual perversion over my life in the name of Jesus.
7. I nullify the effects of any ancestral sin of sexual perversion in my life in the name of Jesus.
8. I break the spirit of lust over me in the name of Jesus.
9. I cast out every thought, image, and dream of sexual perversion in the name of Jesus.
10. O Lord, cover my mind with the blood of Jesus in Jesus's name.
11. I take authority over every demon of sexual perversion, their evil devices and influences, their support, replacements, and command structure in the name of Jesus.
12. I cast all of this filth into the abyss until Judgment Day in the name of Jesus.
13. Every contamination brought into my life through dreams, be wiped away by the fire of the Holy Spirit in the name of Jesus.
14. Holy Spirit, purge me of any food eaten in a dream in the name of Jesus.
15. I command destruction on all powers of darkness in my life in the name of Jesus.
16. I decree my freedom and deliverance from sexual perversions in the name of Jesus.

17. Holy Spirit, take control of my eyes and my thoughts in the name of Jesus.
18. My Father, fill me with the Holy Spirit and plug all the holes in my life the enemy has used to attack me in the name of Jesus.
19. My Father, I give you all the praise, glory, and honor for answering my prayers in the name of Jesus.
20. Thank you, Lord, for your mercies and grace in the name of Jesus.
21. I believe and receive the answers to my prayers in the name of Jesus.

Finding the Right Spouse

You may just be searching for the right God-ordained spouse. Or you may have been searching and been through multiple relationships, none of which you found suitable. God has a divine destiny for you. If the devil realizes that part of this destiny involves meeting the right spouse, he may attempt to ruin this by diverting you from the correct spouse or by hindering you from getting the right spouse.

In generations past, parents were generally more involved in the lives of their children. This included providing biblical counsel and practical help with finding the right spouse. Times have changed a lot since then, and not for the better. Whether back in those days or today, with or without family involvement, you need to go to your Heavenly Father in prayer. He is the one who will provide the proper spouse.

It is important to put your faith and trust in God, especially in this age when the divorce rate is so high. Even if you think you have found the right person for you, it is wise to get marriage counseling before getting married.

28.1 Scripture Reading and Confession

> [20]The man gave names to all the cattle, and to the birds of
> the sky, and to every beast of the field, but for Adam there
> was not found a helper suitable for him. [21]So the LORD

> God caused a deep sleep to fall upon the man, and he slept; then He took one of his ribs and closed up the flesh at that place. [22]The LORD God fashioned into a woman the rib which He had taken from the man, and brought her to the man. [23]The man said, "This is now bone of my bones, And flesh of my flesh; She shall be called Woman, Because she was taken out of Man." [24]For this reason a man shall leave his father and his mother, and be joined to his wife; and they shall become one flesh.
>
> —Genesis 2:20–24

28.2 Prayers

1. My Father, forgive me for my sins in the name of Jesus. [Name them.]
2. O Lord, forgive me for failing to live up to the standards you established in your Word in the name of Jesus.
3. O Lord, cleanse me of all unrighteousness in the name of Jesus.
4. O Lord, remove anything from my life that is contrary to your will in the name of Jesus.
5. I destroy all powers of darkness preventing me from finding the right spouse in the name of Jesus.
6. I destroy every generational antimarriage curse spoken over me in the name of Jesus.
7. My Father, give me your wisdom in the name of Jesus.
8. I command every garment of disfavor on me to be burned by the fire of God in the name of Jesus.
9. My Father, put upon me the garments of favor and excellence in the name of Jesus.
10. O Lord, guide me to the right spouse in the name of Jesus.

11. I command all evil prospects to disappear now in the name of Jesus.
12. My Father, open my eyes to the one you have for me in the name of Jesus.
13. My Father, I give you all the praise, glory, and honor for answering my prayers in the name of Jesus.
14. Thank you, Lord, for your mercies and grace in the name of Jesus.
15. I believe and receive the answers to my prayers in the name of Jesus.

Prayers against Marriage Destroyers

As was mentioned in the previous chapter, the devil is doing all he can to destroy marriages and families. This destruction has long-ranging effects on the family, children in particular. We all must be vigilant with protecting ourselves and our families from the destruction the devil wants to bring on us.

When there is a conflict between husband and wife, everyone is righteous in their own eyes and humility and wisdom often take a hike. It is imperative neither lose the proper Godly attitude and thus give the devil an opportunity to cause disruptions and division. Humility, Godly wisdom, and the willingness to listen and communicate in a disciplined manner are essential for all parties.

As Song of Solomon 2:15 says, it is essential that the problems all marriages face are dealt with while they are little, and before they become larger issues. The devil uses the age-old tactic of divide and conquer. It is important to recognize this and to combat it in prayer. You can take two people, no matter how well-matched, and there will be differences of opinion and disagreements. The devil attempts to use these, no matter how innocuous they may seem, to cause division between husband and wife. It may be that these differences may never disappear.

It is therefore necessary to address them in prayer and set them aside if need be. An example of this is that my wife and I don't always agree on home decor. I understand that the home is often an extension of who the woman is and the job and career are often an extension of who the man is. I've learned to leave the home decor issue alone and let her have what she wants. Such minor things are not worth fussing over. The marriage relationship is vastly more important. If the issues you are dealing with are of a nature where there is no clear way of resolution then seeking counseling may be necessary.

You have the authority and power through Jesus Christ to deal with all the spiritual matters. Scripture makes it clear that agreement by multiple people on an issue will carry more weight.

29.1 Scripture Reading and Confession

> Catch the foxes for us, The little foxes that are ruining the vineyards, While our vineyards are in blossom.
>
> —Song of Solomon 2:15

> Marriage is to be held in honor among all, and the marriage bed is to be undefiled; for fornicators and adulterers God will judge.
>
> —Hebrews 13:4

> [4]And He answered and said, "Have you not read that He who created them from the beginning MADE THEM MALE AND FEMALE, [5]and said, 'FOR THIS REASON A MAN SHALL LEAVE HIS FATHER AND MOTHER AND BE JOINED TO HIS WIFE, AND THE TWO SHALL BECOME ONE FLESH'? [6]"So they are no longer two, but one flesh. What therefore God has joined together, let no man separate."
>
> —Matthew 19:4–6

> "Truly I say to you, whatever you bind on earth shall have been bound in heaven; and whatever you loose on earth shall have been loosed in heaven. [19]Again I say to you, that if two of you agree on earth about anything that they may ask, it shall be done for them by My Father who is in

heaven. [20]For where two or three have gathered together in My name, I am there in their midst."

—Matthew 18:18–20

[8]Be of sober spirit, be on the alert. Your adversary, the devil, prowls around like a roaring lion, seeking someone to devour. [9]But resist him, firm in your faith, knowing that the same experiences of suffering are being accomplished by your brethren who are in the world.

—1 Peter 5:8–9

[1]For the choir director. A Psalm of David. A Song. Let God arise, let His enemies be scattered, And let those who hate Him flee before Him. [2]As smoke is driven away, so drive them away; As wax melts before the fire, So let the wicked perish before God. [3]But let the righteous be glad; let them exult before God; Yes, let them rejoice with gladness.

—Psalms 68:1–3

[25]Then the Almighty will be your gold And choice silver to you. [26]For then you will delight in the Almighty And lift up your face to God. [27]You will pray to Him, and He will hear you; And you will pay your vows. [28]You will also decree a thing, and it will be established for you; And light will shine on your ways.

—Job 22:25–28

The thief comes only to steal and kill and destroy; I came that they may have life, and have it abundantly.

—John 10:10

29.2 Prayers

1. My Father, forgive me for my sins in the name of Jesus. [Name them.]

2. O Lord, forgive me for failing to live up to the standards you established in your word in the name of Jesus.
3. O Lord, forgive me if the choice of my spouse was wrong from the beginning in the name of Jesus.
4. My Father, forgive me for any evil things [name them] I have done to bring troubles into my marriage in the name of Jesus.
5. O Lord, cleanse me of all unrighteousness in the name of Jesus.
6. O Lord, remove anything from my life that is contrary to your will in the name of Jesus.
7. I destroy every vagabond spirit working in my wife's/husband's life in the name of Jesus.
8. I decree my marriage to be off limits to all evil powers in the name of Jesus.
9. I command every agent of the devil working in the life of my wife/husband to be destroyed in the name of Jesus.
10. I command every satanic plan established against my household to be destroyed completely in the name of Jesus.
11. I command every spirit of adultery operating in my wife/husband to be destroyed in the name of Jesus.
12. I destroy every spirit of contention and conflict operating in my marriage to die now in the name of Jesus.
13. I command every spirit of misunderstanding between my wife/husband and me to be destroyed now in the name of Jesus.
14. I command every thought, plan, or desire for divorce in my household to be destroyed now in the name of Jesus.
15. My Father, cover my marriage with the blood of Jesus in Jesus name.

16. Every curse spoken over my marriage, I break you now in the name of Jesus.
17. Every generational curse or sin that has cause problems in my marriage, I break you now in the name of Jesus.
18. My Father, replace every curse spoken over my marriage with blessings in the name of Jesus.
19. I take command of every demon of marriage destruction, their replacements, support, evil devices and influences, plans, and command structure in the name of Jesus.
20. I cast all of this garbage into the abyss until Judgment Day in the name of Jesus.
21. I decree my marriage to be free of all the wiles of the devil in the name of Jesus.
22. My Father, cause your peace to reign in my marriage in the name of Jesus.
23. My Father, bring your divine healing to my marriage in the name of Jesus.
24. My Father, I give you all the praise, glory, and honor for answering my prayers in the name of Jesus.
25. Thank you, Lord, for your mercies and grace in the name of Jesus.
26. I believe and receive the answers to my prayers in the name of Jesus.

Final Thoughts

I wrote this book with the expectation that it would be read by people from a wide range of backgrounds and experiences. Many are so deeply entrenched in church or denominational doctrines that thinking or looking outside that box is difficult or deemed unnecessary. It is for these reasons that I addressed the traditions of man in Chapter 5 as well as address the subject throughout the book. It is essential to look past the traditions of man regardless of how truthful they may seem or how comfortable they may be and focus on Jesus and his word. His word is truth and not necessarily man's interpretation of it. Learn to rely on the Holy Spirit to teach you all things. This takes prayer and steps of faith. The result is that in time you will experience what the apostle Paul wrote in the third chapter of Philippians.

Scripture is quite clear that we will all stand before the judgment seat of Christ. You will stand before that judgment seat and your Creator and Judge will speak the words, "What have you done with my Son?" What will you say? What will the cares and material things of this life matter then? Clearly we all need to set our relationship with Jesus as the highest priority. We all have worldly responsibilities to attend to, and they can certainly be overwhelming at times. It is therefore all the more important to apply discipline to make the time for building your relationship with Jesus. We are to be doing what he commanded us to do in this life. Jesus will be returning soon. Regardless of the signs of the times, no one knows exactly when.

> [44]For this reason you also must be ready; for the Son of Man is coming at an hour when you do not think He will. [45]Who then is the faithful and sensible slave whom his master put in charge of his household to give them their food at the proper time? [46]Blessed is that slave whom his master finds so doing when he comes. [47]Truly I say to you that he will put him in charge of all his possessions.
>
> —Matthew 24:44–47

> "Come now, and let us reason together," Says the Lord, "Though your sins are as scarlet, They will be as white as snow; Though they are red like crimson, They will be like wool. [19]"If you consent and obey, You will eat the best of the land; [20]"But if you refuse and rebel, You will be devoured by the sword." Truly, the mouth of the Lord has spoken.
>
> —Isaiah 1:18–20

The apostle Paul wrote in 1 Corinthians 13:13:

> But now faith, hope, love, abide these three; but the greatest of these is love.

Faith, hope, and love are foundational characteristics upon which your relationship with Jesus is built and the Great Commission is fulfilled. It is essential that the church, individually and corporately, pursue these things.

The apostle Peter sums it up well in 2 Peter 1:2–11:

> [2]Grace and peace be multiplied to you in the knowledge of God and of Jesus our Lord; [3]seeing that His divine power has granted to us everything pertaining to life and godliness, through the true knowledge of Him who called us by His own glory and excellence. [4]For by these He has granted to us His precious and magnificent promises, so that by them you may become partakers of the divine nature, having escaped the corruption that is in the world by lust. [5]Now for this very reason also, applying all diligence, in your faith supply moral excellence, and in

> your moral excellence, knowledge, [6]and in your knowledge, self-control, and in your self-control, perseverance, and in your perseverance, godliness, [7]and in your godliness, brotherly kindness, and in your brotherly kindness, love. [8]For if these qualities are yours and are increasing, they render you neither useless nor unfruitful in the true knowledge of our Lord Jesus Christ. [9]For he who lacks these qualities is blind or short-sighted, having forgotten his purification from his former sins. [10]Therefore, brethren, be all the more diligent to make certain about His calling and choosing you; for as long as you practice these things, you will never stumble; [11]for in this way the entrance into the eternal kingdom of our Lord and Savior Jesus Christ will be abundantly supplied to you.

We see in the book of Joshua a picture of the spiritual walk we have with Jesus. When Israel entered into the promised land, they had many battles to engage in and win. As long as they were obedient to God, the victories were overwhelming. It wasn't until the land had been conquered that God gave them peace and rest. And so it is with us, but the battles we deal with are more often of a spiritual nature and the land we need to conquer is the level of relationship we have with Jesus. It is through this relationship we gain the power and authority to do his will in this world.

> [1]Therefore, let us fear if, while a promise remains of entering His rest, any one of you may seem to have come short of it. [2]For indeed we have had good news preached to us, just as they also; but the word they heard did not profit them, because it was not united by faith in those who heard. [3]For we who have believed enter that rest, just as He has said, "AS I SWORE IN MY WRATH, THEY SHALL NOT ENTER MY REST," although His works were finished from the foundation of the world. [4]For He has said somewhere concerning the seventh day: "AND GOD RESTED ON THE SEVENTH DAY FROM ALL HIS WORKS"; [5]and again in this passage, "THEY

> SHALL NOT ENTER MY REST." [6]Therefore, since it remains for some to enter it, and those who formerly had good news preached to them failed to enter because of disobedience, [7]He again fixes a certain day, "Today," saying through David after so long a time just as has been said before, "TODAY IF YOU HEAR HIS VOICE, DO NOT HARDEN YOUR HEARTS." [8]For if Joshua had given them rest, He would not have spoken of another day after that. [9]So there remains a Sabbath rest for the people of God. [10]For the one who has entered His rest has himself also rested from his works, as God did from His. [11]Therefore let us be diligent to enter that rest, so that no one will fall, through following the same example of disobedience. [12]For the word of God is living and active and sharper than any two-edged sword, and piercing as far as the division of soul and spirit, of both joints and marrow, and able to judge the thoughts and intentions of the heart. [13]And there is no creature hidden from His sight, but all things are open and laid bare to the eyes of Him with whom we have to do. [14]Therefore, since we have a great high priest who has passed through the heavens, Jesus the Son of God, let us hold fast our confession. [15]For we do not have a high priest who cannot sympathize with our weaknesses, but One who has been tempted in all things as we are, yet without sin. [16]Therefore let us draw near with confidence to the throne of grace, so that we may receive mercy and find grace to help in time of need.
>
> —Hebrews 4:1–16

And finally, it is good to pronounce the Aaronic blessing over you, the reader:

> [24]The LORD bless you, and keep you; [25]The LORD make His face shine on you, And be gracious to you; [26]The LORD lift up His countenance on you, And give you peace.
>
> —Numbers 6:24–26